PASSIONATE RIVALS

Acclaim for Radclyffe's Fiction

"*Dangerous Waters* is a bumpy ride through a devastating time with powerful events and resolute characters. Radclyffe gives us the strong, dedicated women we love to read in a story that keeps us turning pages until the end."—*Lambda Literary Review*

"Radclyffe's *Dangerous Waters* has the feel of a tense television drama, as the narrative interchanges between hurricane trackers and first responders. Sawyer and Dara butt heads in the beginning as each moves for some level of control during the storm's approach, and the interference of a lovely television reporter adds an engaging love triangle threat to the sexual tension brewing between them."—*RT Book Reviews*

"*Love After Hours*, the fourth in Radclyffe's Rivers Community series, evokes the sense of a continuing drama as Gina and Carrie's slow-burning romance intertwines with details of other Rivers residents. They become part of a greater picture where friends and family support each other in personal and recreational endeavors. Vivid settings and characters draw in the reader…"—*RT Book Reviews*

Secret Hearts "delivers exactly what it says on the tin: poignant story, sweet romance, great characters, chemistry and hot sex scenes. Radclyffe knows how to pen a good lesbian romance."—*LezReviewBooks Blog*

Wild Shores "will hook you early. Radclyffe weaves a chance encounter into all-out steamy romance. These strong, dynamic women have great conversations, and fantastic chemistry."—*The Romantic Reader Blog*

In **2016 RWA/OCC Book Buyers Best award winner for suspense and mystery with romantic elements** *Price of Honor* "Radclyffe is master of the action-thriller series…The old familiar characters are there, but enough new blood is introduced to give it a fresh feel and open new avenues for intrigue."—*Curve Magazine*

In *Prescription for Love* "Radclyffe populates her small town with colorful characters, among the most memorable being Flann's little sister, Margie, and Abby's 15-year-old trans son, Blake...This romantic drama has plenty of heart and soul."—*Publishers Weekly*

2013 RWA/New England Bean Pot award winner for contemporary romance *Crossroads* "will draw the reader in and make her heart ache, willing the two main characters to find love and a life together. It's a story that lingers long after coming to 'the end.'"—*Lambda Literary*

In **2012 RWA/FTHRW Lories and RWA HODRW Aspen Gold award winner** *Firestorm* "Radclyffe brings another hot lesbian romance for her readers."—*The Lesbrary*

Foreword Review Book of the Year finalist and IPPY silver medalist *Trauma Alert* "is hard to put down and it will sizzle in the reader's hands. The characters are hot, the sex scenes explicit and explosive, and the book is moved along by an interesting plot with well drawn secondary characters. The real star of this show is the attraction between the two characters, both of whom resist and then fall head over heels." —*Lambda Literary Reviews*

Lambda Literary Award Finalist *Best Lesbian Romance 2010* features "stories [that] are diverse in tone, style, and subject, making for more variety than in many, similar anthologies...well written, each containing a satisfying, surprising twist. Best Lesbian Romance series editor Radclyffe has assembled a respectable crop of 17 authors for this year's offering."—*Curve Magazine*

2010 Prism award winner and ForeWord Review Book of the Year Award finalist *Secrets in the Stone* is "so powerfully [written] that the worlds of these three women shimmer between reality and dreams...A strong, must read novel that will linger in the minds of readers long after the last page is turned."—*Just About Write*

Applause for L.L. Raand's Midnight Hunters Series

The Midnight Hunt
RWA 2012 VCRW Laurel Wreath winner *Blood Hunt*
Night Hunt
The Lone Hunt

"Raand has built a complex world inhabited by werewolves, vampires, and other paranormal beings…Raand has given her readers a complex plot filled with wonderful characters as well as insight into the hierarchy of Sylvan's pack and vampire clans. There are many plot twists and turns, as well as erotic sex scenes in this riveting novel that keep the pages flying until its satisfying conclusion."—*Just About Write*

"Once again, I am amazed at the storytelling ability of L.L. Raand aka Radclyffe. In *Blood Hunt*, she mixes high levels of sheer eroticism that will leave you squirming in your seat with an impeccable multi-character storyline all streaming together to form one great read."
—*Queer Magazine Online*

"*The Midnight Hunt* has a gripping story to tell, and while there are also some truly erotic sex scenes, the story always takes precedence. This is a great read which is not easily put down nor easily forgotten."—*Just About Write*

"Are you sick of the same old hetero vampire / werewolf story plastered in every bookstore and at every movie theater? Well, I've got the cure to your werewolf fever. *The Midnight Hunt* is first in, what I hope is, a long-running series of fantasy erotica for L.L. Raand (aka Radclyffe)."—*Queer Magazine Online*

"Any reader familiar with Radclyffe's writing will recognize the author's style within *The Midnight Hunt*, yet at the same time it is most definitely a new direction. The author delivers an excellent story here, one that is engrossing from the very beginning. Raand has pieced together an intricate world, and provided just enough details for the reader to become enmeshed in the new world. The action moves quickly throughout the book and it's hard to put down."—*Three Dollar Bill Reviews*

By Radclyﬀe

Romances

Innocent Hearts

Promising Hearts

Love's Melody Lost

Love's Tender Warriors

Tomorrow's Promise

Love's Masquerade

shadowland

Passion's Bright Fury

Fated Love

Turn Back Time

When Dreams Tremble

The Lonely Hearts Club

Night Call

Secrets in the Stone

Desire by Starlight

Crossroads

Homestead

The Color of Love

Secret Hearts

Passionate Rivals

The Provincetown Tales

Safe Harbor

Beyond the Breakwater

Distant Shores, Silent Thunder

Storms of Change

Winds of Fortune

Returning Tides

Sheltering Dunes

Honor Series

Above All, Honor

Honor Bound

Love & Honor

Honor Guards

Honor Reclaimed

Honor Under Siege

Word of Honor

Code of Honor

Price of Honor

Justice Series

A Matter of Trust (prequel)

Shield of Justice

In Pursuit of Justice

Justice in the Shadows

Justice Served

Justice for All

Rivers Community Romances

Against Doctor's Orders

Prescription for Love

Love on Call

Love After Hours

Visit us at www.boldstrokesbooks.com

PASSIONATE RIVALS

by

RADCLY*f*FE

2018

Credits
Editors: Ruth Sternglantz and Stacia Seaman
Production Design: Stacia Seaman
Cover Design by Sheri (hindsightgraphics@gmail.com)

Acknowledgments

Revisiting a series after a few years is challenging and a bit like coming home (or maybe coming home after an absence is always a challenge). Time changes memories and life moves on and so must our fiction, as much as we want the characters and their stories to continue exactly as we remember them. What I've decided to do with the stories of Quinn and Honor and friends begun distantly in *Passion's Bright Fury* (timewise) and then written in full in *Fated Love, Night Call,* and *Crossroads* is to begin a new series arc set in their world with a new cast of characters who can interact with the already established ones. My plan is to write a new series based on Quinn and Honor's universe (and yes, they will be here), but this could also be a starting point for readers who haven't read the first books. New characters mean new life for everyone (including me). I hope you enjoy this next generation and the role our earlier characters play in these new stories.

Many thanks go to senior editor Sandy Lowe for her guidance and support of the BSB authors (me included) and her excellent publishing expertise in support of BSB's operations, editor Ruth Sternglantz for giving these stories such care and attention, editor Stacia Seaman for never failing to find the bits and pieces that need fixing, and my first readers Paula and Eva for taking time out of their busy lives to send invaluable feedback.

And as always, thanks to Lee for everything. *Amo te.*

Radclyffe 2018

To Lee, always

Chapter One

Philadelphia Medical Center Hospital, Germantown
4:45 a.m.

Emmett kissed the smooth skin behind Zoey's ear and murmured, "Rise and shine, princess."

Zoey dragged the sheet over her face and groaned. "Leave me alone."

"This is your personalized wake-up call."

"Go wake up someone else." Zoey curled into a ball. "Sadie was on last night. Find her."

Chuckling, Emmett slid her hand under the rumpled sheet and over the naked course of Zoey's abdomen, pressing close against her back as she cupped Zoey's breast. "Sadie isn't speaking to me."

"That's because you broke her heart."

Emmett didn't bother defending herself—Zoey knew her better than anyone, even Hank, *especially* Hank, considering he was her little brother. Her sex life was off-limits. Zoey knew she never pretended to be looking for anything other than casual. Anyone in her situation looking for more than that was kidding themselves. Every resident she knew who'd been married or even seriously hooked up had failed to make it work. Divorce, breakups, and broken hearts were the order of the day. Not for her. The only thing she wanted was a full OR schedule and a warm, willing woman with whom to burn off the adrenaline at the end of the day. "Not my fault Sadie read more into—"

"Shut up. Shut up, shut up, shut up!"

"We've got half an hour to shower and change before morning report. Plenty of time, and you'll feel better. Nothing like a satisfy—"

"Not interested." Zoey buried her face in the pillow. "I've only been asleep an hour. I'm dead below the neck."

"I don't think so." Emmett rubbed her cheek against Zoey's shoulder and nudged away the long strands of tousled blond waves. She kissed Zoey's neck, played her fingertips over Zoey's hardening nipple. Zoey's butt tensed against the curve of Emmett's hips. "Mmm. See? Somebody's awake."

Zoey clutched her pillow more firmly over her face. "I hate you."

Suppressing a laugh, Emmett turned Zoey onto her back, pulled the pillow away, and kissed her. "No, you don't."

Zoey peered at her through slitted lids, her deep blue eyes bleary in the faint light coming in through the small frosted window in the on-call room door. "Did you really sleep all night?"

"Nope. I finished removing a ruptured spleen about two thirty." She kissed her again. "Plenty of time to sleep after that."

"It's five fucking a.m.," Zoey said. "I am so sick of never getting enough sleep."

Emmett grinned. "Like I said, I can help with that."

"Do you ever think of anything besides sex?"

"Sure I do. I think about gunshot wounds and motorcycle accidents and broken bones and closed head injuries and—"

"All right, all right, I'm awake." Zoey glared, the sheet bunched in her fist at chest level. "Just because you can work around the clock, super-stud trauma-surgeon-in-the-making, some of us actually require sleep. Also unlike you, my first thought upon awakening is not getting laid."

"How about your second thought, then?" Emmett moved lower on the narrow single bed, taking the sheet with her. She shifted slowly, kissing her way between Zoey's curvaceous breasts and down the center of her sleek abdomen until she rested between her thighs, her cheek pillowed on Zoey's abdomen. When she glanced up, she caught the softening of desire tugging at Zoey's full lips. "You just lie there and I'll see what I can do to start your day off right."

"Shut up," Zoey said breathlessly as she threaded her fingers through Emmett's hair and urged her a little lower. "You've got about two minutes. Mmm. That's nice. Remember the special meeting with Maguire this morning at seven?"

"Yeah, yeah," Emmett murmured, tracing the satiny smooth skin at the apex of Zoey's inner thigh with the tip of her tongue. "Probably just some more administrative rules we're all going to ignore anyhow."

Zoey caught her breath as Emmett's mouth moved over her.

Her hips bucked and she gasped. "Maybe they'll…announce…chief resident this morning."

Emmett didn't move her mouth, at least not to talk. She closed her eyes, one hand on Zoey's abdomen, and immersed herself in Zoey's body—the tension in her hips, the tremor in her limbs, the soft murmurs and surprised cries of excitement. Zoey came quickly, the way she always did, hard and with abandon. Emmett loved that about her, how free she was, how demanding she was of pleasure, and what a pleasure it was to satisfy her. People always bragged about having friends with benefits, but she doubted most of them really knew how good it could be. Zoey'd been her best friend since Emmett had been assigned as a second year to mentor the newbie during those first tumultuous months. They'd clicked right away—bright, vivacious, sorority girl Zoey and dark, intense Emmett from the coal mining town of Bethlehem, PA. The rich girl and the bad girl. By the end of the year they were sharing a run-down Victorian on the wrong side of the tracks a quick walk from the hospital. And sharing a bed when one or the other wasn't in the hospital or with someone else.

They'd known right away they were destined to be friends, first and foremost. The sex was just a natural extension of their connection—effortless and free and without conditions. Zoey tended to keep her lovers around until the heat cooled, and somehow she usually managed to keep them as friends when it was over. Emmett was different. She kept things simple from the start—a few nights, maybe even a few weeks, but never long enough to create problems when she moved on. And she always did. She had more important things to focus on. Like getting every drop of experience she possibly could so she'd come out on top. The top was where she wanted to be—in charge, in control, untouchable.

Emmett raised herself on an elbow when Zoey, muttering, "Enough already," pushed her none too gently away.

"Sure?" Emmett teased.

"You know you killed me." Zoey lifted her head, squinting at Emmett. "Bet you five bucks the hospital meeting's about next year."

"Nah. There's no way Maguire is going to make an early announcement. You know the tradition. The program director announces the chief resident the last week of the fourth year."

"So maybe they're early this year." Zoey snorted. "Like everyone doesn't know who it's going to be anyhow. It's been yours since the first year."

Emmett sat up on the side of the bed, searching for her scrub shirt in the tangle of covers. She was a surgeon, and surgeons were superstitious to a one. She never took anything for granted, never counted on anything until she had it firmly in her grasp. The minute you got comfortable, life kicked you in the teeth. The lesson had nearly broken her in the learning, but learn she had. The only people she counted on were Zoey and Hank. And the only success she believed in was a successful surgery. "You never know how it's going to go. Maguire isn't the only one making the decision. Look at who they picked last year."

"Okay." Zoey grinned. "Amy Baker is an airhead. But come on, Maguire loves you. You're practically her clone. You want trauma, you've got great hands, and you're fearless. Just like her. Hell, you even look like her." Zoey made swoony eyes and pressed her hands to her breast. Her really, really beautiful breast. "Dark and broody and intense. Yummy. All you're missing is your very own Honor Blake."

"As if." Emmett laughed, thinking about the trauma chief's wife. The simmering arousal in her belly flared a little before she quickly doused it with a mental bucket of ice water. Jeez. Maguire's wife, for crap's sake. Okay, so maybe she harbored a *slight* crush on the beautiful, brilliant Honor Blake like half the hospital, but she wasn't about to admit to it. "Maguire doesn't play favorites."

"Doesn't mean it's not you." Zoey ran her fingers down Emmett's spine, her touch familiar and as natural as the sense of rightness Emmett experienced every time she walked into the OR. "Maguire wouldn't be playing favorites where you're concerned. You're the best, and everyone knows it." Zoey kissed Emmett's back between her shoulder blades and threaded both arms around her waist, resting her cheek against Emmett's shoulder. "Give me thirty seconds and—"

Emmett's pager beeped and she pulled it off the chair next to the bed. "It's Hank. He's in the cafeteria for rounds."

"Your brother has impeccable timing," Zoey said.

"Come on—let's grab a shower. Hank can wait a few minutes." Emmett twisted around and kissed Zoey. "I'm good. Maybe I'll see you at home tonight, and we can pick this up then."

"If Anderson doesn't have me here checking post-ops until midnight again." Zoey shook her head. "I really think he hates me."

"Anderson hates all residents. He doesn't play favorites either."

Zoey laughed as Emmett stood and pulled on her scrub pants.

"If we hurry, we can finish rounds before the meeting," Emmett said. "I'm scheduled for an ex lap at eight, and I want to review the labs again before the patient goes down."

"Of course you do, you shark," Zoey said.

"I prefer to think of it as being prepared."

Zoey made gagging noises as she dressed.

Smiling, Emmett filled her pockets with her phone, pen, and wallet, then clipped her ID to her pocket and her pager to her waistband. "Can't wait to see what you're like next year when you're in the race for chief, Ms. Perky I-Love-My-Job-and-All-the-World-Is-Beautiful."

"I'll be a perky shark." Zoey opened the door and almost walked into Sadie Matthews, who stood with her hand raised to knock. "Oh, hey, Sadie. What's up?"

Sadie looked past Zoey to Emmett and glared. "Not a thing."

Sighing inwardly, Emmett followed them down the hall. Great start to the day. Eight o'clock and the first case couldn't come soon enough.

❖

Franklin Health Center Hospital, Northeast Philadelphia
5:45 a.m.

Sydney Stevens double-checked her locker, sliding her hand along the top shelf into both far back corners where she couldn't see, then running her fingertip along the seams to make sure nothing had dropped into the shallow channel between the metal shelf and the side walls of the tall, narrow gray cubby. Anyone watching her would probably think she was being paranoid, but she knew better. In junior high, she'd lost a gold ring with a tiny row of diamonds her mother had given her on her thirteenth birthday. The ring had been her grandmother's, and she'd been so excited to be the oldest of her sisters and the first one to get a special family gift. When she'd discovered it missing, she didn't tell anyone she'd lost it, and the guilt and grief plagued her every day for months. The day she'd found it stuck in the back corner of her locker while searching for loose change, the relief had made her dizzy. The light-headed, heart-pounding sensation came back to her now just thinking about it.

Who knew what she might have lost in this locker. She'd lived out of this locker for four years. This locker was more central to her life than the room in an apartment she shared with two other people. This

locker was the place where she kept her most important possessions—
her white coat, her extra scrubs, her stethoscope and *Merck Manual*,
her shower supplies and secret stash of candy for emergencies.
Locker number 74. Her locker validated her place in the hospital and
symbolized a marker on her road to success. Cleaning it out felt a little
like death—and a lot like failure.

She wasn't supposed to be leaving yet. None of them were. Her
job wasn't finished, her goal unachieved. Her moorings had been cut,
and she was at sea without a life jacket. All around her other surgical
residents mimicked her motions. The atmosphere was funereal, their
expressions reflecting the confusion and helplessness and fear they all
shared. No one spoke. What was there to say? They had no choice in
what had happened to them less then twenty-four hours before or what
would happen to them in the next days and weeks. Some of them she
probably would never see again. Over half had been her interns and
junior residents, her students and colleagues and competitors. Closer
than her sibling had ever been. Her family, this family, was fracturing—
again. By eight a.m. they'd all be gone, and while their absence would
be felt for a while, the relentless forward momentum of hospital life
would soon outpace their memories. Medical students and PAs would
step in to fill the empty spaces at Franklin Hospital, and eventually no
one would remember what it'd been like before. Before what felt like
the end of one life and the beginning of another she hadn't planned. She
thought she'd never be at this crossroads again—displaced, buffeted by
forces she hadn't expected and couldn't change, and unsure of the way
forward. But here she was, with her life veering off path into a future
she couldn't see.

"You ready?" Jerry Katz said, straddling the narrow bench that
ran in front of the wall of lockers, his possessions in a backpack slung
over his shoulder. He still wore green Franklin Hospital scrubs with the
faded initials *FHC* on the pocket.

"Yes, just about. Where's Dani?" Syd said.

Four years ago, the three of them had arrived at FHC along with
six others on the first of July for the start of their surgical internship.
She hadn't known anyone and had grabbed the nearest empty seat in
the small auditorium next to an African American guy in a faded Eagles
jersey and the build of a serious jock. He looked familiar, and a minute
later she'd made the connection.

"Aren't you the Eagles running back—or something?"

Jerry had smiled ruefully, his dark eyes gazing at something only he could see. "Past tense—wide receiver. Retired. I put my surgical training on hold for a while, but now…well, my blown knee sent the message it's time."

"Sorry, I didn't realize—" Feeling awkward, she'd broken off.

"That I was a doc and not just a hot body?"

She'd laughed. "Sorry, not much of a sports fan."

"You're forgiven, seeing how it's our first day and all." He'd laughed too and the awkwardness had disappeared.

The chief of surgery had walked in and everyone stopped like they were playing a game of statue—frozen in midmotion, barely breathing.

His voice rang out, emotionless and merciless. "Look to your right and look to your left. Remember their faces, because by the end of this year one of them will be gone. In five years, there's a fifty percent chance both will be."

Syd stared at Jerry, whose jaw tightened as his gaze met hers. She'd turned to her left and the seat was empty—until Dani Chan dropped into it, a grin on her face and defiance in her eyes.

"What did I miss?" Dani asked, looking from Syd to Jerry.

Syd smiled. "Not much. Just that most of us won't make it through the program."

"Yeah? Heard that before. You guys buying it?"

"No," Syd said, her fear turning to resolution. She wouldn't be beaten. She'd already lost too much time.

"Hell no," Jerry said.

"Me neither." Small, lithe, and perpetually on the verge of being engulfed in a whirlwind of energy and emotion, Dani made up the last of their triumvirate. The Three Musketeers—roommates, cheering squad, and inseparable friends. And putting a lie to the chief's projections, they were three of the five in their residency year to make it all the way to the end. Or they would have been, after their fifth and final year of training. The year they'd all been chasing after and that had been right around the corner.

"D's waiting for us in the lobby." Jerry looked around and winced as the locker room, usually filled with chatter and clanging metal doors, slowly emptied. "It's really happening, isn't it?"

"I think so."

He shook his head, his expression vacillating between angry and resigned. "I can't believe they didn't tell us before this."

Syd laughed mirthlessly. "Not as if we'd have any say in it."

"It's our careers on the line," he said.

"I know." Syd suppressed her anger. Jerry was right, but no point tilting at windmills. This battle was lost. They had a long day to get through, and she needed all her energy to face it.

"At least we have jobs, for now," he muttered.

"Yes." She closed her locker carefully, making sure the latch caught, as if something of value still remained inside. Behind her, a few stragglers slammed theirs and walked out. She zipped her duffel and turned her back on number 74.

Another chapter in her life, ending not as she had planned it, not as she had imagined it, but with a cold, lost feeling in the pit of her stomach. A feeling she had to bury along with the others.

Syd squared her shoulders. "Let's go, then."

❖

"I can take Jack to daycare this morning," Honor said as she slid toast in front of Arly, another slice in front of Quinn, and finally grabbed her own coffee off the counter.

Quinn corralled a slice of toast with one hand and directed Jack's spoon back toward his oatmeal and not his left eye. His eye-hand coordination was exceptional for a two-and-a-half-year-old—he took after his mother, after all—but he had his own brand of exuberance that sometimes derailed his efforts.

"I've got time before the department meeting," Quinn said between bites. "As long as he doesn't need a bath first."

"Then you'd better watch that spoon."

"On it."

Honor snagged the last piece of toast and sipped her coffee. "How do you think it's going to go?"

Quinn shook her head. "It'll be bumpy for a while. Surgeons aren't known for sharing cases."

Honor sighed. "You can't blame them."

"No. But the agreements are in place, and we'll all have to make the best of it." She glanced at Arly, who was absorbed in something on her iPad. "Why are you up so early?"

"No reason."

"You ready for tonight?"

"Yep," Arly said without looking up.

Quinn shot Honor a silent query, and she shrugged. At almost thirteen, Arly might just be displaying the inevitable teen disinterest in sharing feelings with her parents, but Arly had never been typical and today was not an ordinary day.

Quinn said, "You comfortable with the seventh form?"

"Yup."

"I've cleared my schedule," Quinn said, "and I can be home by six. We can run through it—"

Arly set her iPad down and studied Quinn, her dark brown eyes so like Honor's Quinn was surprised every time. Calm, thoughtful, and so damn strong. Arly grinned, and then she was thirteen again—a little cocky, a little amused.

"What?" Quinn said.

"You're nervous," Arly said.

"No, I'm not."

Arly smirked. "Yes, you are."

"Arly test," Jack proclaimed.

Honor laughed and managed to save his shirt from a helping of oatmeal as he waved his spoon in the air.

"Yes, she is taking a test," Honor said, "and she's going to do great. And so is Quinn."

"Yay," Jack said with another flourish of his spoon.

"I'm not nervous," Quinn said. "I just thought—"

"I know," Arly said with a wise expression. "You're worried I'll feel bad if I don't pass tonight. But I won't feel bad."

"Okay." Quinn sat back. Maybe she was a little nervous. She just wished she could save Arly from disappointment, keep her from ever being hurt. An impossible task, but she couldn't help it. She could hide it, though, in fairness to Arly. "If you change your mind, let me know."

Arly nodded. "Here's what I think. If I don't pass, it's because I'm not ready. But I am."

"You're right. You are."

"Besides, you'll be there, right?"

"Sure."

Honor hugged Arly and kissed the top of her head. "We'll both be there."

"Okay then." Arly went back to her iPad, the issue clearly settled.

Quinn sighed. Time to get to the hospital and deliver the news that would put all her residents to the test they had no idea was coming. But if they wanted to be surgeons, they'd have to get used to that.

CHAPTER TWO

Northeast Philadelphia, 5:50 a.m.

"So how do you think they decided the split?" Dani leaned on the horn as she threaded her ancient Volkswagen Bug through Broad Street traffic, heading south into the heart of Philadelphia and the expressway west. "Come on, buddy, the light's yellow! You don't stop on a yellow!"

"Us, you mean?" Jerry braced one arm on the dash to avoid face-planting into the windshield.

"Well, yeah, duh," Dani said.

"Maybe they drew straws," Syd said. "Do you think you could ease up on the stop-and-go a little bit? I'm about to dislocate something back here."

"Bite me," Dani said.

"Right. No thanks." Syd'd taken one for the team and let Jerry have the front seat where at least his knees didn't quite reach to his chin. She was almost as tall as him, although with his build he looked taller than six feet, and she had to scrunch sideways in the minuscule cramped rear seat. Every few seconds the Bug went from sixty to zero, and she was almost thrown onto the floor. At least it wasn't winter. Somehow Dani never seemed to notice the little red car had no heat. Maybe compared to Buffalo, nothing the Philadelphia winters threw at her registered.

"Could be a lottery," Jerry said, "or some other kind of random draw."

"Like names in a hat," Syd said. The idea was absurd, but so was heading off to a new hospital with less than twenty-four hours' notice. So was being essentially homeless from one day to the next. "This..."

"Sucks?" Dani snarled.

"Yes." Syd sighed. "Does it matter at this point, how they decided between the three other programs in the city?"

Dani made a snorting sound. "It might. It can't be a coincidence the three of us are together."

"True," Jerry said. "We've always been—you know—top of the pile. Right?…I mean, I'm just saying…"

Syd knew it. At this point in their training, everyone had a pretty good idea how they ranked, and false modesty was not a surgeon's trait. After four years together, everyone recognized each other's strengths and weaknesses. Everyone knew how the pack had sorted itself out. True to the chief's predictions, a quarter of the interns in their group had switched to other specialties before the first year was over. Pathology and anesthesia were two of the most popular choices when a surgical intern decided surgery wasn't really for them—that the hours and the stress and the punishing training weren't what they'd signed up for. At least in anesthesia they were still working in the OR, frequently in the heat of emergencies, but unlike in surgery, at the end of the day they could go home and not think about the patients any longer. They wouldn't be on call every second or third night for five years and a few more of fellowship training and wouldn't be called in from home at all hours for the rest of their lives. They could manage families and take vacation and maybe even stay married for more than a few years. Pathology was a little more removed from surgery, but the challenge of ferreting out the nature of disease and helping to make decisions about treatment remained. And the lifestyle was one of the best in medicine considering the patients were either already dead or at least missing organs on someone else's watch.

Half were gone by the end of the second year, either by choice or because they hadn't made the cut. Their ranks diminished even further over the next two years through natural selection, and the five who remained were the alphas of their year. The Three Musketeers were the top dogs. Exactly which of them—Syd, Jerry, or Dani—was at the pinnacle was still a question, though. They each had their special skills.

Dani was the brainiac, her memory like a steel trap. When attendings asked for the potential causes of a patient's symptoms on rounds, her list was always the longest. Most of the time that kind of encyclopedic knowledge wasn't critical, but every now and then, some patient would present with strange, exotic symptoms and Dani would be the one to nail it. Her cool intellect was balanced by her hot temper, both of which would suit her well in oncologic surgery, where the battle with cancer required a fire in the blood. Jerry was fearless and quick to act, the kind of decisive personality you'd want to have in the midst of a chaotic scene, unflappable and seemingly impenetrable to the possibility of failure. Of course he was trauma all the way, even though he knew he'd be disadvantaged in the race for a fellowship, coming from a program that didn't have a level one trauma rating.

Syd knew her strengths—and she could barely take credit for them. She was blessed with good hands, the one thing that couldn't be taught. She had more operating experience than anyone in her year and probably more than some fifth years, because she'd been able to do from the onset what more senior residents couldn't. She had a feel for the instruments, for the tissue, for the rhythm of the blade and scissors and needles passing through flesh. She was fast and she was good, the perfect combination for a surgeon. She planned on being a pediatric surgeon, and when every single organ that she'd be operating on was a tenth or even a hundredth of the size of the adult counterpart, good hands were an absolute essential.

She also refused to admit defeat. She didn't believe in giving up, not until everything she could think of had been tried, and maybe some things she'd never tried before. That kind of fortitude was key when dealing with the nearly hopeless cases that premature infants and sick newborns and kids with chronic diseases presented. She had the other essential skill too—the hardest skill to acquire. She knew when to stop. She'd learned that lesson a long time ago.

"You think we've got any chance at this place?" Jerry said, the undercurrent of anger vibrating in his voice.

"Oh, sure," Dani said dismissively. "They're going to just let us walk right in like we've been there the whole time. Good luck with that."

"We'll just have to prove ourselves," Syd said quietly.

"Yeah? How?" Dani leaned on the horn again, the Bug's nose an inch from the ass end of a cement mixer. "Frickin' hell, we're going to be late at this point. Terrific."

Jerry said, "Told you to take the back route over to Germantown Ave."

"Bite me," Dani snapped.

"Down, Tiger. Save it for the competition." Jerry had coined Dani's nickname the first day they'd all claimed lockers and excitedly changed into their green scrubs, as if the ritual would really make them doctors and not scared rookies right out of med school. Dani had a huge tiger on her shoulder that she later explained was a symbol of her birth year. She might have been third generation, but her family still kept its Chinese roots alive.

"Besides," Dani said, ignoring him, "it's going to be worse for Syd than the rest of us."

"True," Jerry said before Syd could protest, "since everybody knows Syd was set to be chief."

"We don't know that," Syd said.

Sure, she wanted it, hoped for it, but who would be named chief resident in their last year was far from certain. The chief's spot was bestowed on the one resident each year whom the staff felt had progressed to the point where they could treat patients with minimal supervision and operate independently. The chief resident determined which of the other residents scrubbed where, had the first choice of cases, and almost always had their pick of fellowships or staff positions at the end of the final year. Along with the perks came the pressures of attending responsibilities, but every resident craved the time when they could reign in their own OR. Syd had had a good shot—maybe the best shot—to be chief, but now…in a new place where no one knew her, coming from a program without a high-powered reputation, there was no chance that was going to happen. She'd be lucky if she could get a fellowship at all.

She'd be lucky, they'd all be lucky, if they made it through the next year with much of anything to show for all their efforts.

"Turn right on Spring Street," Syd said suddenly.

"What?" Dani said. "Why."

"Trust me. Just do it. You can cut around Vine Street, which is going to be a parking lot, and take River Drive in to Mt. Airy that way."

Dani pulled into the bus lane and careened around the corner. "Fuck—we are so going to be late."

"No, we're not," Syd said, the cold calm she always felt when facing an emergency settling in her stomach. She'd faced much worse than this before. Much worse.

Ten minutes later the Bug hurtled down a wide tree-lined avenue toward the medical center. With a little luck…

"What the hell," Dani said. "There's no fricking parking around here."

"There's a sign at the next corner that says *Visitor Parking*," Jerry said.

"Probably a mile away." Dani pulled into the ER lot, swerved into a fire lane, and slammed on the brakes.

"They'll ticket you if you leave it here," Syd said.

"Like I care." Dani pushed her door open. "Come on. We still have to find the place."

Dani and Jerry jumped out, and Syd followed on the run. They were in this together, after all.

❖

PMC Hospital
6:15 a.m.

"It's about time," Hank groused when Emmett, Zoey, and Sadie arrived.

Emmett settled at the round table in the center of the cafeteria with her team and regarded her younger brother impassively. "Did you finish making rounds?"

"I saw everyone in the unit," Hank said. "Sadie has the floors."

Emmett gave him a look, and he cringed. "You know that."

"Yes, Hank. I know that." As the senior on trauma, Emmett was in charge of the residents assigned to the service, and she knew exactly who was responsible for which patients. She'd waited all year for this month, when she'd get the chance to have more responsibility, when she'd be directly reporting to the trauma attendings, just like a trauma fellow, and when she'd have a chance to show she had what it took to be chief resident in July. With no chief resident on the trauma unit this month, she had the chance to perform as if she was one. She assigned her team to their daily assignments, oversaw all the floor work, and scrubbed on the cases that the trauma fellows didn't scoop up first. There was a limit to her power, but she wasn't complaining.

Zoey, a year behind her, was her second in command. Sadie, a second year, had advanced to the point where she was ready to start doing some of the complicated cases with supervision, but still caught her share of scut work. Hank, a fourth year medical student, got the majority of scut and, if he managed to keep things running smoothly and worked quickly, he'd have time to stand at the far end of the OR table where he could see and maybe hold a retractor. A med student's life was one of service.

Emmett took a big bite of her chocolate glazed doughnut, brought up her patient list on her tablet, and pointed at him. "Run it."

Hank reviewed the most recent blood work, X-ray findings, fluid balance, pending labs or procedures, and game plan for the day of each of the eleven patients in the trauma intensive care unit, while Emmett and the others updated their information. If an attending or one of the fellows called them for a status report, any of them could answer.

When he finished, Emmett said, "Fairfax's chest tube should be ready to come out. He's been twenty-four hours with no air leak. As soon as you see this morning's portable X-ray, if the lung is up and there's no sign of air leak in the Pleur-evac, get the tube out and send him to step-down."

"Can I pull the tube?" Hank said.

"You can help Sadie. Make sure you get a film three hours after the tube is out and then get him out of there. It's Friday, which means a full house by morning."

"Right."

"Sadie," Emmett said. "You finish on the floors?"

"Of course," Sadie said curtly, not making eye contact. Her wide, usually sensual mouth was pressed into a hard line.

Inwardly, Emmett sighed. Okay, so she'd made a mistake going home with Sadie a few weeks ago. She'd just come off thirty-six hours on call and a bunch of them had been unwinding at the Catfish, a bar a few blocks away from the hospital. She'd had a beer or two, but she clearly remembered Sadie had been the one to put out the first signals, and they'd ended up in bed. Once should've been the end of it, but once had turned into three times before she realized Sadie was going out of her way to catch her alone when they were on call, and the signs of getting serious had all been there. Sadie was looking for something a lot more long-term than Emmett. As soon as she clued to that, she'd shut things down, and now Sadie was pissed. Bad read on her part, but they still had to work together and the work was what mattered.

"Okay, Sadie, let's hear it."

Sadie reeled off a stripped-down version of all the information Hank had provided on the stable patients who had been moved to regular care floors. Many were ready to go home.

"I'll confirm the list of discharges for you," Emmett said when Sadie finished, "and you can take care of that first thing this morning."

Sadie stiffened. "I thought I was doing the triple tubes with Dr. Maguire."

"Zoey will cover that. I need you free to cover trauma admitting while the two of us are in the OR."

"Great," Sadie muttered.

"Hank, Sadie, get started on wound checks and dressing changes." Emmett finished her coffee and rose. She wanted to eyeball the patient she was operating on that morning herself, just to be sure everything was in order. "And don't forget the meeting this morning. It's mandatory."

Wordlessly, Sadie scraped back her chair and charged away, Hank hustling along in her wake.

"Nice work, hotshot," Zoey said. "You know what they say about not crapping where you—"

"Yeah, I know." Emmett tossed her cup in the trash. "I screwed up, but she'll get over it."

"Yeah, and in the meantime, the rest of us have to put up with her mood."

"I said I screwed that one up."

"Maybe if you screwed a little less—"

Emmett's trauma beeper went off and Zoey's followed. "Speaking of crap."

"Hey," Zoey gasped as they ran, "better than sitting through a boring staff meeting about some new HIPAA regulation or other bullshit."

"True." Emmett skidded around the corner to the ER, ran smack into a wall, and fell on her ass. The wall fell on top of her. A really nice smelling wall with unfortunately sharp elbows, one of which landed in her solar plexus.

Someone cried, "Oh, hey, I'm sorry," but Emmett was too busy trying to suck air into her aching lungs to answer.

CHAPTER THREE

H ey," Syd said again. She pushed herself up on one arm and, feeling like a human pretzel, tried to disentangle her legs from the person on the floor. Her right knee throbbed and the palm of her left hand stung—probably scraped—but she was basically in one piece. The person she'd run into had cushioned her fall. She couldn't even remember seeing anyone in her path before she crashed. "I'm really sorry. Are you okay?"

The face a few inches away from hers twisted into a grimace and cobalt blue eyes widened, the pupils dilating in pain…or maybe anger. Beneath her, firm breasts pressed into hers and the erratic, desperate thud of a heartbeat pounded against her chest. Features swam into focus and Syd's breath caught. It couldn't be…but it was. Some faces were impossible to forget. Some moments were impossible to forget, even when you told yourself you had. And at the moment, all that mattered was the panic etched across the handsome face. Syd finally got her legs free and shifted to one knee to give the woman beneath her some space to breathe. Only she wasn't breathing—her diaphragm was paralyzed from the blow to her solar plexus. She must feel like she was suffocating. "Don't try to breathe. Your body will know what to do. Just relax. Don't fight it, relax."

Emmett thrashed in full fight-or-flight mode. The absence of air, the tightness in her chest, and the rush of blood thundering in her ears triggered every primitive survival instinct she had. Her brain screamed to lash out but she couldn't move. She couldn't…breathe.

"Look at me," Syd said, cupping Emmett's chin. "Look at me. You're all right. Wait. Don't fight."

Something about the soothing voice, the cool firm fingers on her jaw, cut through Emmett's panic. She latched on to the coral green eyes that were all she could see and struggled to make sense of the calming sounds. Words took shape. *Relax. Don't try so hard.* Foreign words. *Relax. Don't fight. Wait.* Anathema to everything she was. She gripped the wrist close to her face, held on to the firm, unyielding arm. Held on to the strange refuge offered by the steady, sure gaze. A stream of air flowed into her chest. Filled her.

"Okay," Emmett gasped. "I…am…okay."

Syd eased back and let go of Emmett's chin, placing her palm instead on a flat, hard midsection. No sign of pain registered in Emmett's face, but she'd taken a pretty good hit. She'd be sore later. "Are you hurt?"

Emmett took a deep breath. Breathing had never felt so good. "No." She held up a hand. "Give me a minute." She turned her head, found Zoey among the people standing around her and staring. "Answer the alert. I'll be…right there."

Zoey leaned down. "You sure? Nothing's broken?"

"I'm good. Go."

Zoey sprinted off, and Emmett pushed herself to a sitting position. "Sorry about that."

She squinted at the other faces peering at her, settled on the blonde who'd floored her. The sculpted face, the shoulder-length golden hair, the piercing, amazing, unforgettable eyes snapped into sharp view. Emmett almost gasped again. She knew her. Some women you never forgot, even when there was no reason to remember them and every reason not to want to. She knew Syd recognized her too. Under her scrutiny, Syd's lips parted soundlessly and her cheeks flushed. She looked older and more tired, but then, didn't they all.

"Syd, we gotta go," a guy she didn't recognize said. "We're gonna be late and we—"

"In a minute, Jerry," Syd said.

Emmett took in the big guy who was trying hard not to look amused and the impatient, smaller woman with jet-black hair pulled back into a careless, short ponytail, and wary brown eyes. Actually, suspicious, sharp eyes.

Dismissing them, Emmett turned back to Sydney. "Syd? What the hell?"

"Emmett," Syd said flatly and climbed to her feet. She hadn't expected the past to follow her here, but then, didn't it always. "Are you sure you're not hurt?"

Emmett shook her head, rubbed her midsection, and smothered a wince. She was going to have a bruise the size of California. "I'm okay. Sorry about that. What are you do—"

"My fault," Syd said quietly, aware of Jerry and Dani right behind her. She could practically feel their probing gazes on the back of her head. "Uh, we were looking for the Strom conference room... auditorium, rather. Is that around here?"

"A minute's walk." Emmett rose, tucked in her scrub shirt, and pulled together her shreds of cool. Knocked on her ass, by Sydney Stevens of all people. Four years disappeared in a millisecond and she was sitting back in that conference room with twenty other nervous med students, waiting for the interview that might determine her future. And then this blonde in scrubs had flown in, announcing she was there to take them all on a tour of the hospital. She'd tried to hide her annoyance, but she'd clearly wanted to be somewhere else. Like the OR.

She looked a little like that right now, like she wanted to be somewhere else. Emmett shook the memories away. "Take this hall all the way to the end, turn left, and you'll see a sign by a set of double doors about halfway down the next hall."

"Thanks." Syd backpedaled. "Well...sorry again."

"Don't mention it." Emmett frowned. All three of the visitors looked jumpy. Weird. "Look, I've got to get to the trauma unit, or I'd show you—"

"No!" Syd grabbed her friends and shuffled them all back another few steps. "We're good. Go."

"Right. Okay. Well—"

Syd and her friends disappeared around the corner, and Emmett wondered if she'd imagined the whole thing. The unexpected appearance of a woman she'd never expected to see again but, unlike so many other women in her life, had been unable to forget occupied her mind for an instant until she remembered who she was and where she was going. She hustled down the hall, slapped the wall button for the automatic doors, and sprinted through into the trauma admitting area.

Treatment tables illuminated by overhead lights lined one side of the long room. Everything needed for resuscitation and emergent surgical intervention—oxygen lines, EKG machines and defibrillators, portable ultrasounds, instrument packs, and ventilators—flanked the stainless steel beds with their flat black vinyl mattresses. Pale blue curtains that could be pulled around the beds to isolate the patients when necessary hung from tracks in the ceiling. Those were almost never closed since the patients who ended up in trauma receiving rather than the regular ER were rarely aware of their surroundings and usually didn't stay long. Most were fast-tracked to the OR, if they survived long enough.

Only a few beds were occupied right now. A surgical resident sutured multiple lacerations on a guy with a cervical collar in one bay, an ortho resident immobilized an open tib-fib fracture in the bed next to that, and a trio of interns surrounded a third patient, busily drawing bloods, inserting catheters, and dressing what looked like superficial burns. In the midst of scanning the patients, Emmett caught a glimpse of bright sunshine and a swath of clear blue sky through the automatic doors leading into trauma receiving from the parking lot outside. The disconnect caught her by surprise. It was morning. Springtime. She hadn't been out of the hospital since before dawn the day before. She'd forgotten there was a world out there.

And she was off her game. First ambushed by Sydney and memories from so long ago they belonged in a museum, and now getting seduced by thoughts of running in the brisk morning air with warm spring sunshine slowly lulling her mind and muscles into contented relaxation. Enough. She was a surgeon and she had work to do.

Honor Blake, Zoey, and two ER residents clustered around bed one at the far end of the trauma bay. Emmett hurried over. "What have we got?"

"How's your ass?" Zoey muttered. "Nice reflexes, by the way."

Emmett shot her a look.

"Morning, Dr. McCabe." Honor straightened and raised a brow. "Dr. Cohen said you'd had a bit of an accident. Everything okay?"

"Nothing serious, Chief," Emmett said, catching Zoey's grin out of the corner of her eye. She'd have to kill her later for trying to steal this case out from under her. "Just…got held up."

"Oh. Good." Honor nodded toward the patient. "Bicyclist versus car. Alert in the field, obvious extremity fractures, and head trauma with facial injuries."

Emmett pulled on gloves and moved to the head of the table. A young guy who looked about twenty was strapped to a backboard, his cervical spine immobilized in a stiff collar, a temporary splint on his right lower extremity, and an impressive laceration extending from his eyebrow into his right temporal hairline. He was breathing on his own, a good sign. Vital signs displayed on the monitor beside the bed, all in normal range. He was awake but appeared sedated. His pupils were equal and normally reactive. Brain was okay. She listened to his chest, confirmed he had good breath sounds on both sides, and quickly palpated his abdomen. Soft and nontender. Heart, lungs, and major organs looked good so far. Extremity injuries were obvious but non-life-threatening. He wasn't in any immediate trouble, so they could work him up to rule out any less obvious trauma with scans.

"Zoey," Emmett said, "let's get him to CAT scan—"

"I'm on it." Zoey flashed her a smile. "I'll take care of the laceration—"

"You two need to be in Maguire's meeting," Honor said, glancing at her watch, "five minutes ago. We've got this. There's nothing urgent surgically."

Emmett said, "We still have to rule out chest and abdominal—"

"We've got this," Honor repeated, indicating her ER residents. "Phillips, Armand, get an ortho consult. Order head, chest, abdominal CTs. Then one of you close up the laceration."

"Hey," Zoey said brightly, "I don't mind hanging around to close that up. In case you get busy."

"Not necessary." Armand, a small wiry guy, carefully but determinedly edged in front of Zoey. The ER residents were every bit as aggressive about catching cases as the surgical residents. "You don't want to miss your meeting."

Zoey glared.

"Come on," Emmett said before Zoey decided to arm wrestle the ER resident with the ER chief standing right there. The ER chief who happened to be married to Quinn Maguire, the trauma chief *and* the director of their surgical training program. Not a great idea. Sometimes it was better to play nice.

"Fine," Zoey muttered.

Emmett pointed at Armand, who didn't even bother to hide his smirk. "But if there's anything on the CT, he goes to trauma."

"Fine," Armand said.

Honor grinned. "We know the drill, Dr. McCabe."

Emmett shrugged. "Worth a try."

Honor made shooing motions. "Don't be late for your meeting, now."

Knowing when she'd lost, Emmett nodded. Once they were out of earshot, she motioned to Zoey and said, "An accident? You told Blake I had an accident?"

"What would you call it," Zoey said with laughter in her voice.

"Last I saw you, you were sprawled on the floor with a hot blonde on top of you. I guess I could have told her that."

"Very funny." Emmett carefully blotted out the image of Sydney on top of her along with the sensation of Syd's fingers on her face. And their legs entwined…and…not a good idea. At all. "How about not saying anything at all."

"She knocked you flat on your ass."

"I'm aware," Emmett said as she headed down the hall toward the auditorium.

"Any idea who they are?"

Emmett shook her head. "Nope."

Not entirely true, but she didn't know anything about Sydney, really. What she thought she'd known about her once hadn't been enough to avoid the pain she hadn't seen coming.

❖

"You okay?" Jerry asked as they rushed through the unfamiliar halls.

"Yes." Syd's knee twinged with every step, but that was the least of her worries.

"Great entrance," Dani said dryly.

"Hopefully we won't run into them again right away," Jerry said.

Dani snorted but Syd couldn't find any humor in the situation.

"I'm afraid we're going to," Syd said. "They're surgical residents, after all."

"And she knows you," Dani said.

"No, she doesn't," Syd said, careful not to let her uneasiness show. Emmett McCabe. Here. She'd thought Emmett was headed for University Hospital across town. The last time they'd talked—well, they hadn't talked. They never did much talking about anything except surgery when they managed a few free hours at the same time. A few hours those few times. And then she'd been so thrown, so caught up in too many decisions, too many crises, to explain anything. Her world had spun out of control, and Emmett had seemed like part of a different lifetime. And she still was. Emmett was a stranger now—that's what Syd needed to remember.

"Well, she knows your name." Dani managed to nudge her shoulder as they sprinted. "What's that all about?"

"We met a long time ago, for about…five minutes." Not exactly true, but in the greater scheme of things, it might as well have been five minutes. Thinking of a few encounters as just a few minutes made it easier to keep things in perspective. Not even weeks, really, but a few nights over the span of a few weeks before her life had taken an abrupt turn in the road. Since then she'd been down more than a few roads she'd never expected to travel.

"She's hot," Dani remarked.

Syd shot her a look. Not that she could argue about the obvious. There were plenty of dark-haired, blue-eyed, bold-looking women in the world, but Emmett's personality matched her looks, and together they created a force that was hard to ignore. Effortlessly sexy and naturally charming was a tough combination to forget. But Syd had managed.

She'd never expected to see Emmett again, and thinking about her just reminded her of how much she'd lost. She'd very successfully relegated the brief interlude with Emmett McCabe to the list of other events in her past life that no longer mattered, and she'd just have to do the same thing again. She had more than enough to worry about just getting through the upcoming year.

"Let's forget it, okay? We've got more important things to think about." Syd stopped in front of the closed door with the plaque on the wall beside it announcing they had reached the Strom Auditorium.

The double doors were closed, but the murmur of voices coming from the other side was audible. She felt a little bit like a gladiator about to enter the Colosseum and tried not to think about the lions waiting on the other side. Silently, the three of them closed ranks. Jerry's shoulder touched her right, and Dani's pressed against her left. There'd be others from their program inside, trying to carve out a place in an unknown world just like them. But they were the seniors, the leaders, and they needed to set an example. They might be in a new program, but they were still responsible for their junior residents, and they couldn't leave their people adrift.

"Remember we're as good as anyone in that room," Syd said quietly. "No matter what happens, we need to have each other's backs."

"Right," Jerry murmured.

"Damn straight," Dani said.

Syd pushed the doors open, and they stepped through together.

CHAPTER FOUR

Strom Auditorium
PMC Hospital

Taking a deep breath, Syd pushed open the double doors and quickly stepped through into the auditorium. Just as quickly, she stopped to get her bearings. Like so much of what had happened in the last twenty-four hours, the surprises just kept coming. She couldn't prepare for the unknown, and being unprepared left her feeling vulnerable and out of control. Two things she hated and worked every day of her life to avoid. But she was a surgeon, and surgeons had to assess quickly, even in the midst of chaos. She took everything in with one quick scan.

She hadn't expected the room to be so big. She'd been in Off-Broadway theaters smaller than this place. Two tiers of seats flanked a wide center aisle leading down to the stage. The screen at the rear could stand in for an IMAX showing. A podium with the usual array of microphones and electronics occupied one front corner. Franklin hadn't had anything quite so grand, and bitterness welled in the back of her throat. PMC was bigger, brighter, and richer than Franklin. That was all. Shiny and showy didn't equal better medicine.

She hadn't expected so many people, either. At a fast glance she guessed the place would seat several hundred, and at least half the seats were occupied. She'd pictured the twelve of them from Franklin meeting with the program director in a conference room somewhere, maybe even going unnoticed for a day, like they had as interns. No one actually acknowledged an intern's presence for weeks sometimes. First years were transitory—interchangeable and easily replaceable. Well, so much for slipping seamlessly into the system. This looked far more formal and, she hated to admit, intimidating.

Beside her, Jerry grunted. "Time to swim in the deep end."

Dani muttered, "Looks like it's showtime. And we're the show."

"Yes, well," Syd murmured, "we all know how to swim." She pointed to a clutch of Franklin residents congregated in several rows about halfway to the front. "Come on, let's go sit with the small fry."

Aware of a few heads turning as they trooped down the aisle, Syd kept her gaze straight ahead. None of them were strangers to being evaluated. They'd all had their share of interviews, assessments, tests, and trials. This was just another one. Okay, maybe one that was a lot more important than many of the others they'd endured, but they *had* endured. And they would again. Several of their interns and junior residents looked up as they moved into an open row behind them, clear relief etched in their expressions.

"Do you know what's going on?" one reedy second year guy in nerdy glasses stage-whispered.

"Not anything more than you do." Syd leaned forward to give his shoulder a squeeze. "We'll find out together. Just hang in there."

He squirmed in his seat but nodded, his shoulders lifting slightly as if the presence of the older residents had given him courage.

At exactly 6:45, a dark-haired woman in maroon scrubs and a white lab coat strode onto the stage. Her lab coat was clean but wrinkled, as if she actually wore it to work in. It didn't hang on the back of a door to be pulled on by some administrator for show. But she was no administrator, and a bit of Syd's uneasiness drained away. Syd knew her. Quinn Maguire, the trauma chief and director of the surgical residency training program. Syd had taken Maguire's webinar on emergency management of airway problems, and she'd heard her speak at grand rounds at University Hospital when she'd been there. Maguire had an international reputation, and despite Syd's anxiety about being here, she was excited to be able to train with her. She wanted a career in peds surgery, and handling pediatric trauma was a big part of taking care of children. In major trauma centers, the pediatric and trauma surgeons often worked together. She wanted to get as much trauma experience as she could in preparation for her peds fellowship. If she somehow managed to secure one after all of this.

Emmett. Emmett had been responding to a trauma alert when Syd had knocked her over. Even as a medical student, Emmett had said she wanted to do trauma, and it looked like she hadn't changed her mind. They might end up sharing cases. They might end up— No, she was getting way ahead of herself. She had no idea what she'd be doing

here, and until she did, imagining anything, worrying about anything…
hoping for anything, was an exercise in disappointment. She needed to
remember what she'd learned the hard way—deal with the moment,
in the moment, and don't get caught in a web of hope and dreams that
could be swept away with no warning.

Maguire walked to the front of the stage, ignoring the podium and
the microphone.

"Good morning," she said without apparently raising her voice.

All the same, the room instantly stilled. She was a striking-looking
woman—jet black hair, athletic build, strong, commanding features.
She moved confidently, everything about her powerful and assured.
She reminded Syd a little bit of Emmett, another frivolous thought she
had no intention of dwelling on.

"Thank you all for making room in your busy schedules,"
Maguire said. "This announcement affects everyone in the department
of surgery, and I wanted everyone to get the information at the same
time so we can minimize rumors and baseless speculation. Not that
any of you are prone to gossip or conjecture." Maguire waited for the
laughter to subside, a faint smile adding to her piratical good looks.

"She's hot," Dani muttered.

"Shut up," Syd whispered. "You think everyone is hot."

"Not everyone," Dani said. "I don't think Jerry's hot."

"I'm wounded," Jerry grumbled.

"Stow it, you two," Syd said, grateful as always that she had the
two of them to remind her of who they were. Of all they'd been through
and how strong they were, together and apart.

Maguire looked over the audience that had neatly partitioned itself
into attendings on one side and residents on the other, with the Franklin
Twelve, as Syd was coming to think of her cadre, grouped behind the
PMC residents.

"Franklin Medical Center," Maguire said, "is one of the nearly
one hundred surgical training programs in the country forced to close
its resident training program due to the widespread decrease in federal
funding for advanced medical and other educational training."

A low murmur spread through the room, and Syd steeled herself.

"I want to stress this had nothing to do with the program's
accreditation or the standing of its residents."

Several PMC residents sitting a few rows ahead of Syd and the
others turned and stared. What had been curious expressions at first had
grown hostile and suspicious. Syd kept her eyes on Maguire.

"The announcement of the cuts was precipitous and unprecedented, leaving the affected programs little time or avenue to secure alternate funding. Fortunately, the American Board of Surgery and the National Board of Medical Examiners held emergency meetings just last week to approve the expansion of select training programs. We are one of those programs."

The room was so still Syd was sure her pounding heartbeat must be audible ten rows away. Maguire might as well have been handing out daily OR assignments.

"We will be adding twelve new residents to our program, three in each year, one through four, commencing immediately."

The quiet shattered and a roar erupted as people began shouting questions. Maguire settled her hands into her lab coat pockets, looking as relaxed as if a hundred people weren't shouting a hundred different questions at her.

The PMC residents sounded like a cageful of raging wolves.

Are you fucking kidding me?

We have to share our cases with twelve more residents?

What about the call schedule?

How do we even know they're even good enough—

"Yeah," a woman's voice cut through the din, "after all, that's a community-based program. Don't tell me they're anywhere near as good as we are."

Dani shot up in her seat, and Syd grabbed her arm. "Not a word."

"Fuck that," Dani said.

"It's not worth it."

"It's worth it if it makes me feel better," Dani said.

"You'll get your chance. All you have to do is show them how good you are."

"All I have to do is tell them to go take a flying—"

"Not today," Syd said grimly. "Today we keep our heads down until we know what we have to fight."

Dani folded her arms and stared daggers at the lithe redhead who'd made the comment as she turned to give them a cold, condescending sneer.

"She's hot," Dani said under her breath.

Jerry smirked. "She'd tear your throat out, Tiger."

"Not scared," Dani said.

Maguire finally held up a hand, and once more, the room quieted, although the low hum of voices didn't completely disperse this time.

"I know this will be an adjustment for everyone," Maguire said, "residents and attendings alike. But our census shows we have enough patients system wide and ample cases to provide appropriate training experience for everyone. There will be a revised organizational schedule for the various surgical services incorporating our new Franklin residents available later today. I expect our present residents to extend themselves to their new colleagues in explaining how our services run and assisting them in any way possible during the transition."

"My ass," a male voice barked.

"No way," a female resident said just loud enough to be heard by those around her, but her comment didn't carry down to the stage. "I'm not babysitting anybody."

Maguire went on, "Will the Franklin residents please wait here. The rest of you, we have a surgical service to run. Let's get to it."

Maguire turned and walked off the stage, taking no questions. For a moment, no one in the room moved, and then everyone surged at once. Clumps of people clogged the aisles as voices rose in question or complaint. The doors behind where Syd was sitting banged open, and Emmett hurtled in, followed by the blonde who'd been with her outside the trauma unit earlier. The redhead who'd been making all the snarky comments met them in the middle of the aisle a few rows from Syd.

"What did we miss?" Emmett said.

The redhead shot another incendiary glare in Syd's direction. "You won't fucking believe this."

❖

"What are you talking about," Emmett said, shifting so people could get around her to the exit.

"Un-fucking-believable," Sadie repeated.

"Come on, Matthews," Zoey said, "what's the deal?"

Sadie inclined her head toward a group of residents Emmett didn't recognize, except for one. Syd stood at the center of the scrum with everyone looking at her. Apparently she was their leader. No surprise there.

"Come on." Emmett tipped her head toward the back of the auditorium and threaded her way through the slowly moving, murmuring throng to an out-of-the-way corner. "Well?"

"We just picked up twelve new residents, three in every year,"

Sadie said. "Their interns are going to be second years along with our second years."

"Wait a minute," Emmett said. "Every year? Three new residents a year all the way through?"

"Yup." Sadie almost smiled. "Including fifth year."

Zoey's eyebrows climbed. "How the hell are they going to do that?"

Emmett shook her head. She couldn't see it. That would make eight residents in the fifth year. That was a big program for any hospital, and all eight would have to meet the minimum caseload to sit for the boards. That was a lot of cases. "There's got to be some mistake. Maybe they're holding them all back a year or something."

Sadie laughed, just a little smugly. "Um, that wouldn't solve anything. Except for your year. Of course."

Emmett sighed. "Come on, Sadie. Give me a break."

"Nope. Too easy." Sadie shrugged. "Anyhow, that's not the way Maguire put it. According to the chief, we've got plenty of patients to go around."

Zoey snorted. "There's never enough patients to go around."

"Yeah, well," Sadie said, raising her voice, "the cases at PMC belong to PMC residents."

"Cut it out, Sadie," Emmett said. "They're not the enemy."

"Says who." Sadie made a face, her shamrock-green eyes flaring. "Oh, wait—more names for your one-nighter list."

Zoey snapped, "Grow up, Sadie. Like you didn't know—"

"Enough, already," Emmett said. "This is not the place."

"Fine." Sadie abruptly swiveled and beelined out the door.

"She is really in a twist," Zoey said, laughing softly. "What did you do to her—hit her with your megaton charm bomb?"

"Oh, leave off," Emmett said.

"Can't help myself." Expression suddenly somber, Zoey said, "So, what do you think?"

"If Sadie's right, that explains what all those new residents are doing here, but I don't get why Syd is here. She—"

"Ha! So you do know her. Come on, spill it."

Emmett grimaced. "Not now. Besides, it was all a long time ago, and I don't really know anything about her."

Zoey gave her a long, hard stare. "You've got history."

"No, we don't. Like I said, I was a medical student, and she was an intern. Our paths crossed while I was interviewing for first year spots. I barely knew her."

Zoey's brow wrinkled. "Well, that doesn't make any sense then. If she was a year ahead of you, she shouldn't be here. Unless she got held back for some reason. Maybe she failed her boards."

"No. Syd was a superstar." Emmett glanced past Zoey and locked eyes with Syd. She hadn't meant to, but her gaze had traveled in that direction as if pulled by a magnet. Which was bullshit. She was just curious. Who wouldn't be? All the same, she couldn't look away. "You had to be the best to get into University…"

"What?"

"Nothing," Emmett said. Nothing was making sense. Syd had been an intern in one of the two best surgical training programs in the city, hell, in the entire country. PMC rivaled the University Hospital program for the caliber of the attendings and the caseloads but didn't have quite as much research money as University Hospital. Hence, PMC fell a notch below University in prestige, for all that mattered. So why was Syd part of this group from Franklin? Franklin's program was well-known for its strong community roots and wealth of surgical experience in everyday cases, but not much in the way of the unusual, once-in-a-lifetime cases they routinely saw at PMC. "Like I said, I don't know anything."

"Well, I think you're about to."

"Huh?" Emmett said absently, watching as the dozen Franklin residents slowly made their way toward the back of the auditorium.

A voice from behind her said, "McCabe, my office."

Emmett didn't need to turn around to recognize the speaker. "Okay, Chief."

Maguire moved past her and stopped the group of Franklin residents just as they reached the foyer at the rear of the auditorium. Emmett and Zoey hung back, watching. Maguire shook hands with everyone, said something Emmett couldn't quite make out, and snagged one of the second year PMC residents who was also loitering nearby. A minute later, the PMC resident, wearing a reluctant expression, led the Franklin residents away.

Zoey laughed. "Looks like Watanobe got snagged to play tour guide. If he misses the hernia he was supposed to do this morning, he's going to be pissed."

"Probably a lot of people will be pissed for a while," Emmett said.

The Franklin residents disappeared, all except one. Syd and Maguire left together.

"Uh-oh," Zoey said. "Looks like you better get going or you might get left behind."

"Have I ever mentioned you are a pain in my ass?" Emmett said.

Zoey's grin widened. "Frequently. Call me as soon as you're done?"

"Yeah. I hope this doesn't take too long. I've got a case."

"You hope," Zoey said.

Shaking her head, Emmett hustled out and jogged down the hall in the direction of Maguire's office. She had a feeling whatever was about to go down was going to ruin her day.

CHAPTER FIVE

Before Emmett made it halfway down the hall, a horde of PMC residents descended on her.

"Are we really going to have three more residents in our year?" a second year asked, a panicked expression on her face. Three or four other junior residents, all of them looking so young Emmett was sometimes surprised they were even doctors, talked over each other in a chaotic downpour.

"Are they going to cut three of us—do you think they'll do it right away?"

"Will they—"

Emmett couldn't remember being so fresh-faced, wide-eyed, and green. When she had arrived along with twenty-four other first years, she'd been scared and exhilarated and raring to prove herself. She remembered being more sure of herself than this bunch, but maybe that was just self-flattery tinctured by time.

She pictured herself that first morning in early summer, sitting in the Strom Auditorium where she'd just been, feeling dwarfed by the size of the room, surreptitiously checking out the other first years, taking stock of her competition. Those two dozen eager, bright-eyed newly minted doctors were her rivals, and they all knew it. They all accepted it. They'd been forged in the fires of cutthroat competition since college. Premed had been a shark fest, everyone vying for the highest grades, the best recommendations, a chance at a stint in the best research lab, and choice summer externships in hospitals and clinics. Then came medical school and the fight to stand out on clinical rotations, the race to be the first one with the answer on rounds, the one who never went home from the hospital, the one with the flash. She'd had the flash, but she'd had the will and the grit to sacrifice too. Okay, and maybe she had a bit more of the shark to her. She couldn't apologize for that. When you were elbow deep in a living person, fighting against the odds, you needed a bit of the shark.

The junior residents looked younger by the second as mass anxiety grew into rising hysteria. Time to yank them back from the edge.

"You heard the chief this morning," Emmett said sharply. "Nothing's changed—yet. Same ground rules. There's always room at the top. So *be* on the top. You've all got services to get to. What are you doing standing around in the hall?"

A ripple of unease shivered through the crowd, feet shuffled, hands disappeared into pockets, and shoulders hunched. She couldn't offer them consolation or encouragement. That wasn't what they needed. She couldn't change the circumstances, and if they were to survive, they'd have to find their own way to climb to the top of the pile.

"Yeah but…" one of the second years said cautiously.

"What, Reynolds?" Emmett fixed the brunette with a hard stare. Reynolds was probably the weakest in her year. Smart, but she lacked confidence. Self-doubt was a cardinal sin for a surgeon. One of the first of many tenets the senior residents taught the first years was that a surgeon could be wrong, but never uncertain. Hesitation in an emergency killed far more often than a confident decision that might turn out to be wrong later.

Simple rules to live by. To survive by.

"If you want to make it through this program," Emmett said, her gaze taking in each one of them in rapid-fire, "then you better hit the floors, find the cases, and prove you know what you're doing. Things just got a lot harder. Sink or swim, people."

Backs stiffened, gazes sharpened, and the baby sharks pivoted and took off at a run. Emmett watched them go. The senior residents would have to be watching them a lot more carefully from now on. A whole new batch of fish had just been dumped into their waters, and the battle to stay alive was going to be bloody.

She had a fight of her own to win, and she picked up her pace. As she rounded the corner to the chief's office, a wave of déjà vu washed over her. Her midsection still ached from the shot she'd taken from Syd. Her whole body still vibrated from the sensation of lying under her on the floor, arms and legs entangled, the scent of…rosemary? yeah, rosemary wafting over her.

"Hey, Gary," she said to the hipster behind the desk in front of the chief's closed office door. "The chief wanted to see me."

Gary lifted a brow, his gaze sharp behind his Warby Parker frames. "She's waiting. Go on in."

"Thanks," Emmett said, her throat suddenly and unexpectedly dry. Maguire was her secret idol. Maguire was the reason she was here. She'd had a good shot at a place at University Hospital, but Maguire, young, aggressive, hard driving, and with a reputation for being fast and fearless in the OR, had won her over. That's what Emmett wanted to be—fast and fearless, the best of the best. With Maguire at the helm of a strong surgical department that was still small enough for residents to matter, and plenty of cases to give her all the surgery she could handle, PMC had been her first choice.

Interviewers weren't allowed to tell a candidate where they stood on their acceptance list, any more than a candidate was supposed to say where they wanted to go, but everyone knew the code. Three other surgical heads, including the one at University, had indicated interest. Maguire hadn't given her any sign as to where she stood. None of the catchphrases—*We think you're a strong candidate for a program like ours, You'd make a great fit here, We expect you will rank highly anywhere.*

After the interview when they'd shaken hands, all Maguire had said was, "Think hard about what kind of training you want. Anyone who comes here will be asked to do more than they ever thought they could and will have to work harder than they would anywhere else, because the only way to be the best is to give more than you think you have to give."

Emmett had known immediately this was her place.

Her place.

She knocked on the office door, heard Maguire tell her to come in, and entered the chief's corner office. Windows on one side overlooked the wide tree-lined avenue that fronted the medical center, and out the adjacent side a view of the parking lot and a rolling expanse of green park stretched for two blocks surrounding the hospital. PMC sat in the middle of a residential neighborhood, unlike the Center City hospitals. PMC was part of the community, and most of the staff lived nearby. PMC offered the best of both worlds—a high-powered trauma center and top-tier medical school, right where people actually lived. Another thing Emmett loved about the place.

Two chairs sat in front of Maguire's broad dark oak desk. A pile of journals sat in one corner next to a stack of patient charts, her laptop occupied the other, and two green file folders placed side by side filled the center next to a steaming coffee cup. Emmett eyed those two green folders, an uneasy feeling settling in her gut.

"Have a seat, McCabe," Quinn Maguire said.

Syd already occupied the left-hand chair and Emmett took the right. Maguire leaned back in her black swivel office chair and took a sip of her coffee.

"Introductions. Emmett McCabe," Maguire said, nodding to first Emmett, then Syd. "Sydney Stevens."

Emmett turned to Syd and took her outstretched hand.

Syd's eyes met hers as their hands touched. Syd's fingers were cool and dry and strong as they clasped hands. Emmett searched her gaze for a sign of challenge, or anger, or some hint of recognition. Nothing but cool appraisal, which she would've expected from anyone. Starting from zero, then. And where else would they start? They were strangers, after all.

"Morning," Emmett said.

"Hello."

Syd smiled for a fraction of a second, and Emmett almost thought she heard *again* after the hello. Syd let go of her hand and turned back to Maguire, and Emmett mentally chided herself. Just her imagination.

"You're both fourth years," Maguire said.

The buzz in Emmett's head grew a little louder. She could count the times she'd had a private meeting with the chief on one finger. She didn't even need that one. She'd hoped, okay, expected a meeting like this when Maguire told her she'd be chief resident next year. This was not the picture she had in mind. She didn't need to look at Syd to feel the tension radiating from her still, tense form.

"We've got less than two months before the new first years arrive," Maguire said. "By then we need to have the Franklin residents integrated into our services so we can all concentrate on keeping the first years from drowning. I'll expect the senior residents to see that happens—all the senior residents."

Emmett nodded. Nothing new here—part of being a senior resident was teaching the juniors how to be residents. The attendings taught by sharing their experience, and by example. That's why the fight to get into the OR was so vicious—all the critical lessons happened there.

"Ordinarily," Maguire went on, "we wouldn't be making any announcements about the fifth year until next month, but this isn't usual circumstances."

Emmett couldn't even hear Syd breathing the room was so quiet.

"McCabe," Maguire said, "you were slated for the chief resident slot."

Emmett's gut tightened. The word *were* ricocheted in her brain like a gunshot. She waited.

"Stevens," Maguire said, shifting her gaze from Emmett to Syd. "According to your program director, you were to be chief also. Congratulations."

"Thank you, Chief," Syd said calmly.

"So," Maguire said, "we have an embarrassment of riches and a situation we need to resolve quickly for the sake of stabilizing our program." She leaned forward. "Our number one priority from this moment forward is to see that every PMC resident receives the best training possible. *Every* resident. This is the last time you'll hear me refer to the Franklin residents. The only residents here are PMC residents. I expect that to be the case with everyone."

"Yes, Chief," Emmett and Syd said in the same breath.

Emmett had a feeling a sword was hanging over her head. Four years of hard work and sacrifice. She'd known when she'd chosen surgery, the longest, most grueling, most competitive training program, what she was getting into. They'd all known. No, that wasn't true. No one could really know, no one could really be prepared, without experiencing the endless nights without sleep, the relentless pressure to excel, the constant need to make life-or-death decisions. They lived on the knife edge of failure—one wrong step away from catastrophe. Oh, they all knew what the textbooks said about diagnosis and treatment, they'd seen case after case, learned and studied and copied their mentors, but nothing could prepare them for the moment when they were alone in the midst of a crisis, when a patient's fate came down to what they said with no one standing behind them, no safety net, no do-overs. In that moment, when they needed to push past the fear and reach deep inside for the strength and courage to act, they were alone.

Emmett felt the loneliness now. Maybe Syd, less than an arm's length away, did too. She'd spent the last four years ignoring her needs and blocking out her pain and disappointment to earn this final mark of success. Now what? Her heart beat faster in her chest, but she kept her breathing as even and quiet as Syd's. Never show fear.

"We need to integrate our residents at every level, and it's the chief resident's responsibility to see that that happens." Maguire took them both in with her direct, unwavering gaze.

The sword was about to fall, and Emmett steeled herself for the blade.

"You both know the case requirements for you to sit for your boards—due to the unusual circumstances, we've received special dispensation for the fifth years who will have only been here for one full year. However, the two-hundred-minimum case requirement as operating surgeon for chief residents as well as twenty-five major cases as teaching assistant still stands."

Emmett mentally checked her surgical log. She was okay as long as she had her pick of cases the last year—at least she had been.

"I sat down with the other members of the training committee last night," Maguire said, "and we went through everyone's case logs, board scores, and evaluations in order to assign residents where they needed experience." Her gaze shifted to Emmett. "McCabe, you're a little heavy on trauma cases and light in peds surgery and transplant. You're also light on teaching cases."

"Uh…I figured I could count peds trauma as peds cases," Emmett said.

Maguire smiled. "Trauma trumps peds at this point, especially"— she looked at Syd—"since Stevens—all the *former* Franklin residents— are light on trauma."

Syd leaned forward, the first move she'd made since shaking hands with Emmett. "Franklin is a level two center, Chief. We all have experience with routine traumas, and all the seniors are ACLS and ATLS certified."

"I am aware, Dr. Stevens," Maguire said mildly.

"Yes, Chief." Syd sat back.

Emmett admired the move. Points to Stevens for standing up for her people.

"But," Maguire said, "I want every resident to have experience with major traumas. So here's the plan."

CHAPTER SIX

S yd was still processing when she walked out of Chief Maguire's office. The administrative wing was clear and quiet at the beginning of the day. No patients came down this hallway, and considering they were in the surgical wing, all the offices were empty. Everyone was in the OR. That was the only place a surgeon ever wanted to be. The printout of the new surgical service assignments dangled from her right hand. She didn't even want to think about what Jerry and Dani would say when she told them, let alone the junior residents. She stopped a few feet down the hall and looked at Emmett. "Does anyone really think this will work?"

"Someone must," Emmett muttered.

Syd couldn't imagine what Emmett was feeling right now. Short of being royally ticked off, that was. And really, she couldn't blame her. She would absolutely feel the same way in Emmett's place. Surviving a surgical residency was pretty much a tightrope act without a net, where the slightest disruption in balance could drop you into free fall. This was a damn big shift in everyone's equilibrium. But she couldn't worry about Emmett right now, could she? Emmett wasn't her problem, and none of this was her doing. She hadn't been responsible for the government deciding to cut funding for medical training programs by 60 percent, and she certainly wasn't responsible for PMC deciding to expand its program and take in the Franklin residents.

PMC had made a smart move. After all, everyone knew residents were inexpensive labor, and hospitals benefited from their presence. Residents got paid, sure, but not as much as salaried attending physicians, and hospitals always needed willing bodies to staff the shifts no one else wanted. Residents worked around the clock, and even though they weren't supposed to work more than twenty-four hours in a row without time off, they frequently did. If they didn't tell, who would know, and every resident was in a race to beat out all the others for the best cases and the most OR time. No one would report working over the mandated hours, especially not now when every resident would be scrambling to rack up the right cases. The cases that counted for the boards.

"What now?" Syd said finally.

Emmett leaned back against the wall and regarded her with hot, dark eyes. Eyes so dark the blue looked purple. Yep, she was pissed, all right.

"I guess the first thing we should do is round up our people and break the news."

"I don't know why Maguire didn't do that this morning," Syd said.

"I do." Emmett's face was a study in stony anger. "There would've been a riot."

"This isn't great for any of us, you know," Syd said, tired of bearing the brunt of everyone's frustration. *She* was just as frustrated and worried and angry too.

"Yeah, I get that. But you know, we weren't the ones getting screwed until an hour ago." Emmett blew out a breath. She hadn't asked for this, and no one had asked her how she felt about having her entire future potentially derailed. None of the PMC residents had a choice.

"Well, that certainly gives me and the rest of the Franklins an advantage." Syd snorted. "We had almost twenty-four hours to get over being screwed. But cheer up. You ought to start feeling better before long."

"Great." Emmett pressed her lips together. She knew somewhere in the back of her mind that this was no one's fault, but right now, her rational mind was not in control. All she knew was everything she'd planned and worked for had just gone up in smoke. Not only that, she was somehow going to have to learn to work with Syd, which not only felt weird, it felt dangerous. "Why are you even here?"

"What?" Syd narrowed her eyes. "I thought your chief made it clear—"

"No," Emmett growled. "Not about why the Franklins are here, why are *you* here? You were an intern five years ago. You weren't even at Franklin. You should be finishing up at University—"

Syd's chin came up and her eyes grew glacial. "I'm a fourth year Franklin surgical resident. Where I did my internship is ancient history, and not relevant."

And nobody's business.

Emmett blinked. She got the unspoken message loud and clear. The frost in the air made her skin itch. Any other day, with anyone else, she wouldn't have pushed, but maybe the past wasn't as over and gone as she'd thought. Syd had disappeared without a single word—she hadn't answered her phone or texts or returned messages. The hospital operators wouldn't page her. And Emmett had had no idea how else to reach her. Now here she was, acting as if they'd never even met.

"Look, it isn't as if I don't know—"

"You don't. You don't know anything about me. What happened years ago doesn't matter now. The only thing that matters is figuring out how to get through the next year."

Emmett stiffened. "Understood. You heard the chief—the residents need to get the new rotation schedules stat."

"Okay then. I'll page the Franklin…" Syd's lips tightened. "I'll page the new *PMC* residents, and you'll handle the others?"

Scorn laced her voice.

"Fine." Emmett looked at the time on her phone. "Frickin' hell. I'm going to miss my eight o'clock case. This is going to screw up the OR coverage all morning. I have to go."

"Do you think you could show me where the locker room is first?" Syd gestured to her T-shirt with the Charlie Brown image and frayed blue jeans sheepishly. "This is all I had in my locker at Franklin. I need scrubs."

"Yeah, sure." Emmett got it. Scrubs were armor. As good as a Superman cape. "Come with me."

As Emmett led her through a warren of hallways, Syd tried to imprint the route on her mind. She needed to learn the shortcuts as quickly as she could. She was suddenly responsible for half of all the residents in the training program, and the last thing she wanted to do was stumble around like a first year resident. She at least needed to *look* like she belonged.

"The locker room is across the hall from the surgical lounge," Emmett said, taking her up two flights of stairs to the third floor. "The TICU and the SICU—"

"Yes," Syd pointed to signs on the wall with arrows indicating the trauma and surgical intensive care units. "I got that. Who's in charge once the patients get there? Us or the intensive care people?"

"Good question."

Syd took hope when Emmett gave her a look that came close to suggesting they were on the same side.

Emmett went on, "We handle the wound care and immediate post-op fluids. The ICU docs will order meds and monitor general status. Don't let them touch any dressings, tubes, drains, sutures—"

"Are you kidding?" Syd laughed. "No chance."

"Exactly."

Emmett grinned, and Syd flushed as if she'd just been handed the game ball. Really. As if it mattered what Emmett McCabe thought of her.

"Okay, so…" Emmett slowed as they started down the hall. "Fifteen OR rooms, five dedicated to OB/GYN and labor and delivery. We keep one room empty on a rotating basis, so it will be open if a trauma comes in. If that one is in use, trauma bumps any case, any time."

"What happens if we get multiple traumas and need more than a couple of rooms?"

"If we don't have a room up here open, we can do anything except bypass downstairs in trauma admitting." Emmett shrugged. "I think if we had to, we could do that too."

"Okay." Syd's pulse quickened as she mentally reshuffled her picture of what she'd be facing. She'd seen trauma cases at Franklin, but usually isolated injuries in stable patients. Gunshots, fractures, blunt force trauma. This was going to be a whole new game. "What about attending coverage for trauma alerts?"

"There are two trauma fellows, and three rotating trauma attendings. You already know Maguire—she's the chief. Surgical residents and fellows do the initial assessment and resuscitation. If you get there fast, you can get the case."

"Sounds like a free-for-all."

Emmett grinned, and this time, the grin looked genuine. A happy, sharky grin. "Oh, it is."

The grin fooled Syd into forgetting she and Emmett still had major hurdles ahead and she let down her guard. "Look, Emmett, about all of this, I—"

Emmett's expression shuttered. "Let's get our people organized before we lose any more time. You can talk to your people in the locker room if you want to. I'll take my team to the cafeteria."

"Fine." Syd pushed open the door to the surgical locker room as Emmett strode away.

Your people. My team.

So much for no more *them* and *us*. Did Maguire really think it was going to be that simple?

❖

Honor stopped at the end of the bed where her second year resident was closing the laceration on the young man hit by a car. She automatically checked the monitors at the head of the table. All good. Time to clear the trauma bay before another emergency came rolling in. "You just about done here?"

Armand clipped the last suture in the row of 5-0 nylons he'd placed in the bicyclist's forehead. "Just waiting on the CT results, but his neuro check is fine. Ortho has him scheduled for an ORIF of the tibia fracture this afternoon."

"Good. Are you sending him to the floor pre-op?"

"As soon as I see the CT."

Honor nodded. "Good work." Spinning around, she nearly bumped into her wife. The first jolt of pleasure was familiar and never diminished by how many times she'd experienced it. "Hey. I didn't expect to see you down here this morning."

"Everything quiet?" Quinn asked.

"So far. Why? Something happening?"

"I'm about to head to the OR for a couple of hours. Just wanted to make sure everything was under control before then."

Honor frowned. Quinn wasn't one to worry about situations that hadn't happened yet. She dealt with realities, not possibilities. She slid her arm through Quinn's and tugged her away from the patient's bedside. "What's going on?"

Quinn blew out a breath. "This residency situation is going to destabilize things for a while. It's like dumping an entire bunch of interns into the mix, except they're not interns. All the same, the new residents don't know the facility, our routines, or each other. There's no cohesion."

"And I suppose the PMC veterans aren't exactly stepping up to lend a helping hand."

"Blame them?" Quinn grimaced.

"Of course not. You knew this would happen."

"I did, and we'll weather it. But it's going to be rocky going for a while."

"What's really bugging you?"

Quinn sighed. "It's not fair to any of them, and I know it, but I can't say it. They don't need sympathy—they need to dig their way back onto solid ground. And the only ones who can do that are them."

"You think any of them will jump ship?"

"There's a possibility some of the junior residents, especially the shaky ones, will go under with more competition..." She glanced around the trauma bay. "And some of them will have to be cut. We have enough room for everyone, but only if they manage to make it above the high-water line. We can't keep anyone who falls behind."

"Including the ones who have been here the whole time?"

"Including them."

"All of these things have already occurred to you. So what else is going on?"

Quinn's gaze deepened. "You always know, don't you."

Honor smiled. "You mean when something is bugging you? Lots of practice."

Quinn laughed. "Oh, come on. I'm not the moody type."

"That's true, you're not. Broody sometimes. Dark and twisty sometimes."

Quinn threaded her arm around Honor's waist and pulled her into an empty trauma bay, yanking the curtain halfway closed behind her. She kissed her swiftly. "I thought you liked me broody and twisty."

Honor caught her breath. They were married with two kids, but Quinn's touch streaked through her with as much heat as the first time. Every time. All the same, they hadn't had an encounter in the hospital for a long while. "I've missed this."

"At your service," Quinn murmured.

Honor kissed Quinn back, then pressed a palm firmly against her chest and pointed to herself with the other hand. "ER chief here. I have a reputation to maintain."

"Mm-hmm." Quinn pulled her closer, kissed her again. "You think I'm going to sully it?"

Honor laughed and stepped back. "You can sully it all you want at home. Tonight."

"Black belt test."

Honor caught her breath. "And how could I have forgotten that. God. I love my children. You think we could send them to camp?"

Quinn chuckled. "You'd be miserable within three days."

"Probably two. After the test?"

"It's a date."

Honor poked Quinn's chest. "And you're still broody. Why?"

"McCabe. She's…"

"Your favorite?"

"I don't have favorites."

Honor lifted a brow. Waited.

"Okay, I'm not supposed to have favorites. But she's my first pick for a trauma fellowship when she finishes, if she wants it. And I hope to hell she does."

"But?"

"I can't play favorites, no matter what I think. And she's going to have tough competition this year."

"From one of the Franklins?"

Quinn nodded. "Sydney Stevens. She's exceptional. Her board scores are higher than McCabe's, but not by much. They're both top tier there. McCabe has more trauma experience, but Stevens has more overall OR experience." She shook her head. "They'll be competing for choice of chiefs' rotations next year. I had to spell it out for them, and they're not happy. They're going to be bumping heads all year long."

"Competition is good for them. It will lift both their games. You've been there—you know."

"I know. And ordinarily I wouldn't mind some healthy competition, but the circumstances are unusual, and they're going to have to adjust pretty quickly."

"And you are going to have to let them figure it out on their own."

"I know you're right," Quinn said. "You'll probably see a lot of them down here. If they get too territorial—"

"I'll keep the bloodshed to a minimum," Honor said. "Go to the OR. We've got this covered."

"Thanks." Quinn grinned. "See you tonight."

"Oh yes, you will."

❖

Emmett paged Zoey, Sadie, and Hank stat to the cafeteria. They arrived out of breath a minute after she sat down with her third cup of coffee. Zoey dropped into a chair on her right, Sadie sat across from her, and Hank squeezed in on her left.

"So?" Zoey said. "What the frick is going on? What did the chief want with you?"

"All the services are being reorganized," Emmett said flatly. She spread out the sheet in front of her.

"What does that mean?" Sadie demanded. A strand of her flame-colored hair had come loose from her ponytail, and she pushed it impatiently behind her ear. That was Sadie, fiery and hot tempered. She'd been that way in bed too, which was probably why Emmett had broken her rule about repeats. More times than she'd meant to. She hoped she'd be able to smooth things over with a little more time, but today was not going to be that day.

"The Franklins—" Emmett grimaced. "The *new* PMC residents need to get up to speed as quickly as possible, and the chief wants the services integrated so those of us who have the most experience can make that happen."

"Hold their hands, you mean," Sadie said.

"Oh, come on," Zoey said. "Don't we have enough to do?"

"Well," Emmett said, "you're about to have a lot more."

"They're splitting up our service, aren't they," Sadie snapped.

"They're splitting all the services. So everybody just has to suck it up." Emmett couldn't complain in front of her junior residents, and especially not in front of a med student who just happened to be her little brother. "Zoey, you're moving to peds surgery."

"What?" Zoey shot up straight. "Why? I don't need more peds cases."

"No, but the chief thinks…" Emmett shook her head. She was the leader and had to set an example, even if she still smarted from hearing that Syd had topped her in the boards. Not by much, but still, she hated being second in anything. Maguire had tasked her and Syd to get this done, and she was going to get all her residents in line. "Dani Chan will be senior on peds, and you'll be her third year."

Zoey stared. "You have got to be kidding me. She'll be in charge?"

"Yep."

"That's crazy. She just got here!"

Emmett shrugged. "She'll be a fifth year in July. She needs the chief level cases. That's just the way it's going to be."

"Who's taking my place on this service?"

Emmett blew out a breath. "I'll still be senior with Syd Stevens and a Franklin second year."

Zoey laughed. "Oh, man, that ought to be fun. Two fourth years going after the same cases?"

"What about me?" Sadie said.

"You're going with Zoey." She glanced at her brother. "You're good. None of the med students will be affected by this."

Emmett stood before Sadie could have a meltdown. "Let's get to work."

❖

"Okay, everybody, gather around," Syd said when her fellow transfer residents arrived in the locker room. She gestured to the far corner behind the third row of lockers even though the place was deserted at just after eight. All the same, she wanted to have this discussion in private. "I have your rotations—interns, for now you'll be assigned to a first year slot and get your second year assignments at the normal time." She read off their names, the services to which the three of them would be assigned, and the residents they needed to contact. "Page your seniors, introduce yourselves, and get to work. You won't be doing anything differently here than you were doing at Franklin."

"You mean scut and more scut."

Syd smothered her smile. The classic intern lament never changed, nor did the senior resident's response. "Suck it up."

"Right, we're here to serve," one of the others murmured, and the three of them headed for the door.

"Okay, second and third years, listen up." She read out their rotations. "Morty...you're coming with me to trauma."

"Cool." The pale, stick-thin second year pushed his square black glasses up his nose and flicked a shock of lank dark hair off his forehead.

"They're not gonna let us do anything, are they," one of the third years said despondently.

"What you need to do," Syd said, as much to herself as to them, "is prove you deserve to be here. You know how to do that. Be the first one here in the morning, make sure you know everything about the patients for rounds. Review the cases that are scheduled for the OR and be ready to assist. And if you're not..." She anticipated their concerns. "If you're not assisting, be there anyway, answer questions, be as good as you know you are. Remember, there's always room at the top."

The last of the residents trooped out, and Syd said, "Morty—wait for me outside, will you?"

"Sure thing."

A minute later, Syd, Dani, and Jerry were alone.

"How bad is it?" Dani asked.

"We're about to make a lot of people unhappy today," Syd said quietly.

CHAPTER SEVEN

Emmett paused by the cafeteria table. Her team—her previous team—clustered a few feet away, staring at her. For a second she wondered if she'd only imagined she'd just given them new assignments. Maybe they were waiting for her to tell them she'd been joking. That wasn't it, though. They were waiting for her to tell them what they wanted to hear—that they didn't really have to make room for anyone new, that the playing field was already full, that they could ignore the new reality. She looked past the junior resident and her brother as if they weren't there and landed on Zoey. She cocked her head. *Well?*

"Sadie," Zoey said abruptly, coming to life as if someone had flipped a switch, "head up to the NICU and start on the patient charts. I'll meet you there in a few minutes. We'll need to round on the whole peds service."

Sadie made a face. "What about the new acting *chief?*"

Zoey shrugged. "I guess that's up to her. I'm not going to go looking for her." She shot Emmett a defiant glance as if to say, *I did my part. And that's all I'm going to do.*

Sadie grinned. "Good enough. Catch you in a few."

"Hank," Emmett said as her brother trailed out of the cafeteria after her, "I'll meet you in the trauma unit as soon as I can. See everyone again before we make rounds."

"Oh," he said, "okay. Sure."

When Sadie and Hank got far enough away, Emmett said to Zoey, "You're really not going to make things easy for the new guys, are you."

"And I suppose you are?" Zoey snorted. "Of course, *you* are still in charge on your service. I have to play wingman for somebody who shouldn't even be here. How would you feel if you were taking orders from somebody who just showed up, *and* you were supposed to show them the ropes at the same time?"

"Okay—I wouldn't be happy." Emmett turned in the direction of the trauma unit. "Everyone, including the interns, will have to deal with that on some level. I just think it's probably best if we don't complain too much in front of the juniors."

"Wow." Zoey stopped, looked up and down the hall, and pulled Emmett into one of the on-call rooms. The room, one of dozens just like it scattered throughout the hospital, was big enough to hold bunks, a desk, and a bookcase with a couple of reference books no one ever looked at. A stack of clean linens sat on an otherwise empty closet shelf. Housekeeping was supposed to change the beds, but since people were in and out all day grabbing naps, if someone wanted clean sheets, they changed the sheets themselves. Most of the time nobody bothered. Zoey clicked the lock, leaned back against the door, and folded her arms. Her smile flickered between a smirk and a scowl. "Okay, now you can drop the responsible chief-resident-in-waiting routine and tell me what you really think."

Any other time, Emmett probably would've unloaded her frustration and disappointment. Zoey was her sounding board, just like she was Zoey's. With only a year between them, they'd shared just about everything the place could throw at them—ridicule, overwork, uncertainty, and the highs of making it up the ladder, one rung at a time. Today felt different, and the distance between them was new. New and uncomfortable. But Quinn had pulled *her* aside, singled her out to explain what was happening and to ask for her help. Her and Syd. That felt weird too. Syd being here, being in the same position as her, like it or not, had thrown her a curveball. They were somehow on the same side and competing simultaneously. "We could both end up being chief."

"What?"

"Co-chiefs. Syd Stevens and I might both be chief residents next year."

"What?" Zoey's voice rose. "How is that supposed to work?"

"I'm not altogether sure just yet," Emmett said, although she had a pretty good idea what might happen. No one was ever equal when power was shared, no matter who said they would be. One of them would have to have the first say, the first pick of rotations and cases, and no matter how hard they tried to *look* like they were equal, lines would be drawn and allegiances formed. She didn't like it. Syd probably didn't either.

"What did you say about that?"

"Nothing," Emmett said. "Maguire said—"

"Please." Zoey shook her head. "Maguire spoke and of course you just took it." She let out a deep sigh, her expression softening. "Sometimes you're just too good a team player."

Emmett grinned ruefully. She wasn't so sure about that.

"So how do *you* feel about bringing your new rival up to speed?" Zoey asked.

"I don't know how I feel about it."

"You're kidding, right? How about pissed off and betrayed?"

"Okay, maybe pissed off. A little." When Zoey huffed, Emmett rolled her eyes. "Possibly a lot." She shot Zoey a frown. "But I don't think Maguire would have done this if she didn't think it would work."

Zoey rolled her eyes. "Listen, I know you think Maguire is God—"

"That's not true," Emmett said, even though on many levels, she sort of did. "But I trust her, and I know she wants us all to survive. So she has to think this could work."

"Oh, it will probably work, for most of us. The question is, which of us?"

"Come on, Zo," Emmett said with a sigh. "It hasn't even been half a day. We at least have to try."

"Do we? Why?"

Emmett's temper frayed. She'd hoped for a little backup from her best friend. "Because we don't have a choice. We have to do what we're told, remember? We're residents."

"Yeah, I know. But you know what?" Zoey's eyes got hard, something Emmett wasn't used to seeing in Zoey's carefree, come-what-may manner. "We don't have to make it easy for somebody else to take what we've earned."

Emmett got it then. Zoey was scared. Nervous and worried too. Just like all of them, just like her, even. And, she had to think, Syd and all the others too. She grabbed Zoey's hand and tugged her over to the bunk. They dropped down on it, landing shoulder to shoulder.

"Look," Emmett said, "nobody is going to pass you by. All the attendings like you, you're smart, and you're quick in the OR. You'll be fine. All you have to do is your job, and right now your job is to—"

"You know what I think would help a lot right now? Sex." Zoey kissed her.

Emmett laughed. "You always think sex is the answer to everything."

Zoey shrugged out of her lab coat. "Isn't it?"

They hadn't turned the lights on, and in the half gloom, her eyes gleamed like a cat's on the hunt. Even her voice was a purr. Emmett knew that tone—Zoey had switched to autopilot, and the only thing in her sights was the finish line. She wasn't quick enough to get out of the line of fire when Zoey made a sudden lunge, pushed Emmett down on the bunk, and straddled her hips. Zoey curled forward to keep from hitting her head on the underside of the top bunk and fisted the front of Emmett's scrub shirt. "I didn't get mine this morning, remember?"

Emmett grasped Zoey's hand as Zoey dragged her shirt out of her pants. "Oh. Hey. Timing. Bad timing, Zo."

"No such thing." Zoey yanked loose the ties on Emmett's scrub pants and tugged the scrubs lower on her hips. Her fingernails scraped over Emmett's abdomen.

Emmett twitched. "Zoey, come on."

Sex was Zoey's panacea—when she was happy, sad, worried, or scared. Sex was her go-to release. Some people handled all those feelings with a few shots of tequila or a fast ride on a motorcycle or something else to uncork the pressure cooker. With Zoey, it was sex. In celebration or despair. Sometimes with Emmett, and other times with whoever was there. Emmett was good with being Zoey's release valve, most of the time, and it wasn't as if she didn't have her own moments of blocking everything out with a few minutes of pure unadulterated physical pleasure. Zoey was just de-stressing the only way she knew how, and they both knew each other well enough to recognize that's all they were doing.

Right now, though, Emmett couldn't help her. Not like that. Her mind was elsewhere, and her body had checked out. She needed to find Syd. She had a service to get organized, patients to see, and Syd… She needed to stop wondering how this could have happened. How Syd could even *be* here. Emmett half sat up, but Zoey had her pinned in the narrow space with her knees on either side of Emmett's hips.

"Zoey, I gotta go."

"Two minutes," Zoey said, clearly not hearing her. She leaned farther down, a hand sliding under Emmett's waistband.

"I'm not kidding. I gotta go." Emmett caught Zoey's hand before she could get any lower and really distract her.

Zoey frowned. "You're really gonna play it straight, aren't you?"

"I'm going to take it one day at a time," Emmett said. "Starting with what Maguire asked me to do."

Zoey slid off her. "You know, sometimes you're just a pain in the ass. If I didn't love you, I might not be able to stand you."

"Yeah, I know that."

"Don't you ever get tired of playing by the rules?"

"Yeah." Emmett stood, tucked her shirt, and retied her pants. "Sometimes, I really do."

❖

Just as Syd had instructed, Morty was waiting for her right outside the surgeons' locker room. She had no doubt he would have waited there all day, calm and unruffled.

"You ready?" Syd asked.

Morty nodded vigorously, his Adam's apple bouncing. "Yep. Totally."

Syd smiled inwardly. Morty was one of the rare residents whose eagerness hadn't been tainted by a few years of relentless work. At first glance, he was often underestimated, appearing gawky and a little socially inept. She'd worked with him before, and she trusted him. He did his work, he never complained, and he had surprisingly deft hands in the OR. As awkward as he appeared elsewhere, he was graceful and at ease with instruments in his hands. As far as she was concerned, you couldn't ask for much more in a surgeon. She'd need a junior resident she could count on if she was going to be playing catch-up to McCabe on the trauma service. She didn't envy Dani with a service full of juniors she didn't know. Sloppy, lazy, or—worst of all—weak junior residents not only made a senior resident look bad, they were dangerous. She was about to become McCabe's right hand, and like it or not, she needed to be good at it.

"Come on," Syd said. "We should get our service in shape."

"The trauma intensive care unit is on this floor." Morty dropped his gaze for an instant before meeting hers again. "I should have gotten a list of the patients. I wasn't sure who to page, or I'd have that for you by now."

"I know you would. I'm not sure who else is going to be on our service, but I'll page the chief. That would be Emmett McCabe."

Morty didn't say anything, but his look held a question. A question she couldn't answer. She didn't know what kind of chief Emmett would be, and she couldn't explain to Morty why they were being assigned where they were. Theirs was not to question why—and that was never truer than today.

Emmett had given her her cell number, and she texted, *Ready to meet you. Where?*

A few seconds passed and she didn't get an answer. Shrugging, she glanced at Morty. "Well, we might as well start in the trauma unit. At least we can get a list of who's in there and go over their charts."

"Sounds good to me."

Syd headed in the direction indicated by the sign on the wall. They turned a corner just as a door labeled *On-call Room* opened and Emmett walked out. She was texting as she moved, and an instant later, a blonde followed her into the hallway, pulling on her lab coat. Emmett stopped short, a quick cascade of surprise verging on chagrin passing over her face. The blonde caught Syd's eye and grinned. The grin spoke volumes, even if the quick glance into the room Syd got hadn't given her a pretty good idea of what had been going on.

Syd schooled her expression. It was none of her business what Emmett McCabe did in the on-call room or anywhere else. It wouldn't be the first time she'd gone looking for a resident and found them indisposed. She was kind of surprised at the timing, considering everything that was going on, but then, this wasn't her playing field. She had no idea what the ground rules were.

Emmett flushed just a little, but her gaze remained flat and unapologetic. "Just got your text. The trauma unit is down this hall on your left. I'll meet you there as soon as I check that everything is covered in the OR."

"All right." Syd gestured to Morty. "Emmett, this is Morty Weiss. He's a second year."

"Right. Morty." Emmett held out her hand. "Good to meet you."

"Same," Morty said, sounding like he meant it. Syd suspected that he did, glad once more that she'd drawn a lucky number with him as a junior.

"Our med student is in the unit," Emmett said. "His name is Hank. He should be able to fill you in on all the patients. Morty, you'll be his direct supervisor. If you need something, he's your man. If he has a problem, he should call you first. Anything you can't handle... well, there shouldn't be anything you can't handle, right?"

Morty squared his thin shoulders. "Don't expect there will be, Emmett."

Emmett nodded sharply. "I'll see you there in a few."

While Emmett talked, the blonde lingered nearby, one shoulder casually braced against the wall. Syd was aware of the blonde's slow appraisal and wondered if her interest was personal or professional. Everyone was bound to be curious about the new people, but considering what she'd just seen, she wondered if McCabe's girlfriend, if that's indeed who she was, had some other kind of assessment in mind. She almost laughed at the idea she might be any kind of competition in that area. The last thing that ever might exist in her universe was an attraction to Emmett McCabe.

"Hi," the blonde said, stepping forward with a hand out. "I'm Zoey Cohen. You just took my place."

"I see," Syd said, shaking her hand. Interesting opener. Casual remark, subtle challenge, or warning? "Where did they move you?"

"Peds surgery."

With Dani, Syd thought. *Well, things are getting interesting fast.*

"You'll want this." Zoey held out a pager. "Trauma beeper. Text messages aren't always reliable in some areas of the complex. You wouldn't want to miss an alert."

"No, I wouldn't. Thanks." Syd took the pager, clipped it to her waistband, and motioned to Morty. "Come on, let's get going. We've lost enough of the day already."

"Right," he said and ambled after her.

From behind her, she heard Zoey laugh but couldn't make out Emmett's answer. Not that she cared. They'd just rounded the corner to the trauma unit when the trauma beeper vibrated. She checked and stopped in her tracks. *STAT trauma admitting.*

She grabbed the back of Morty's scrub shirt as he sailed past. "Change of plans, we've got incoming."

She pivoted and ran back down the hall toward the stairwell they'd come up earlier, sorting out in her head the fastest route to the trauma unit. Emmett had gotten to the stairs first and held the door open as she and Morty raced up. She grinned at them.

"Looks like it's going to be a busy day."

Emmett rocketed down the stairs and Syd flew after her, Morty galloping in their wake.

CHAPTER EIGHT

The charge of adrenaline coursing through Emmett's blood was the most exhilarating thing she'd felt all morning, even better than sex. She laughed inwardly. Sex was great fun, but the sensation only skimmed the surface—an electric shock, acute and sweet, dancing over her skin and swirling off into the air. Gone in a heartbeat. This excitement claimed every part of her, bubbling through every nerve ending in her body and injecting every fiber with anticipation. This call to action was her private pleasure, one that left her feeling lucky every single day.

Emmett slowed just enough to surge through the stairwell doors without knocking anyone down, and then she was running again. Shapes moved around her, people stepping aside, falling in line, rushing along with her to the brim of the same cliff. Slapping the button on the wall next to the wide double doors to trauma admitting was like screeching up to the edge of the abyss, teetering, about to fall and then…then she was inside and calm descended. As quickly as time had sped up during her dash to the trauma bay, now it slowed.

Bright lights, a milling throng, at first each body indistinguishable from the others, a cacophony of voices shouting, drowning each other out and yet each distinct through the utter stillness in her body and her mind. A long scan of the room—five beds occupied, one form beneath the tubes and wires and monitors smaller than the others. A kid.

In the eye of the storm, Honor Blake directing with the calmness and exquisite control of the seasoned conductor. Her voice somehow rose above all the rest.

"O'Brien, you've got trauma one—Kennedy, take two. Armand, take the child and call peds surgery."

She spun, spied Emmett.

"McCabe—bed three, crush injury to the chest, possible head and intra-abdominal injuries. Bed four, multiple extremity fractures, airway compromise."

"On it." Emmett headed for the injured, pointing as she elbowed a few of the gawkers who always showed up for a trauma alert out of the way. "Zoey, take—"

Emmett slowed so abruptly she nearly stumbled. Right. Zoey wasn't there. Her team had changed, and so had her responsibilities. Maguire had made that clear. Syd had to be brought up to speed on major traumas quickly. And Emmett, Maguire had pointed out with the merest tilt of her brow, needed more surgical teaching hours. Emmett was in charge, but the field was not entirely hers. She not only had to share, she had to play backup quarterback.

"Syd, take bed four while I check on bed three. I'll be there in a minute."

"Okay." Syd nodded briskly, looking cooler than she probably felt. A multiple trauma at a level one trauma center with patients who'd sustained immediately life-threatening, multisystem injuries was a lot different than stable patients at a level two, where the team had a lot more time to assess and treat, and a lot less chance for fatal errors.

Emmett resolutely turned to the patient in bay three and snapped, "Morty, you're with me."

"Yes, Chief." He jumped and was on her tail in an instant.

Points for him.

"So," Emmett said, "what have we got."

The ER resident, a second year, looked up, her eyes wide and just a little crazed. Adrenaline rush.

"Truck jumped the median, struck a passenger car head-on. This one's the van driver. Forty-five-year-old male, restrained, closed head injury, crush injury to the chest, possible intra-abdominal deceleration injuries. Hypotensive in the field, resuscitated with fluid. Oxygen sats were low on arrival, and he's unresponsive. I just intubated him."

Pretty standard for a car crash. Emmett scanned the monitors. Heart rate in the 90s, pressure hovering around 100, oxygen saturations holding but lower than she'd like to see. His lungs probably took a beating from a direct blow or the aggressive fluid management or both.

"Morty, what's first," she asked as she stepped up to the bed.

"Check his chest for breathing tube placement and bilateral airflow," he said. "CT of the head, chest, and abdomen if he's stable."

Quick and thorough. Another point for the skinny guy.

"Go ahead and listen and tell me what you think." As Morty pulled out a stethoscope, Emmett listened for herself, turning her head to check on bed four as she worked. That patient was a woman, late thirties or early forties, cervical collar in place, an air splint on her right lower extremity. Emmett saw Syd shake her head, say something to Armand, who hurriedly grabbed a stethoscope and stuck it on the patient's chest. Emmett needed to be over there, but she couldn't leave this patient yet.

"Good breath sounds both sides," Morty said. As he spoke, he palpated the unconscious man's abdomen. "His belly is soft, strong femoral pulses. If he's otherwise stable, he can go to CT."

"Good," Emmett said and checked his vitals again. His pressure was up a little from when she'd first checked, but everything else was about the same. She looked him over one more time—searching for that one thing she'd overlooked. The one thing that might make the difference between a save and a loss. "Any evidence of blunt head trauma?"

The ER resident shook her head. "No. No lacerations or contusions I could see. According to the paramedics, he was vocalizing but incoherent in the field."

Emmett narrowed her eyes. "What about on arrival?"

The ER resident shook her head. "No, nothing."

"Morty? What are we thinking?"

"He could have a deceleration brain injury. An intracranial bleed could cause his altered state of consciousness. Or it could just be a contusion."

Emmett quickly checked his pupils. Both were sluggishly reactive. "He needs a head CT and a neuro consult to clear his head and C-spine. There's nothing obvious in his chest and belly right now."

"Can I take him down for the CT?"

"Not until neuro sees him. Morty?" Emmett said, already moving around the bed toward Syd's patient. "What are you watching for now?"

"Drop in BP or O2 sats, change in heart rate. Further change in neuro status."

She smothered a grin. He was a smart one. He looked like he ought to be an accountant. "Good. He's yours. Stay with him. Make sure neuro sees him."

His grin widened, and she caught a flash of the shark in his eyes.

The one that swam at the outside of the herd, circling a school of smaller fish, waiting for the weak to fall away and then silently picking them off one after the other.

"Got it, Chief," he said and turned back to the ER resident. "Who's the neurosurgeon on call? How do I get them?"

She might not have to worry about that one. Leaving Morty to handle bay three, she checked on Syd. "Stevens, what have you got?"

"She needs a chest tube," Syd said.

Just like that. Not *I think she needs a chest tube*, or *maybe she needs a chest tube*, but clear and definitive. Emmett wasn't surprised.

"X-ray?"

"They're on their way, but her breath sounds are depressed on the right and her sats are not coming up on a hundred percent oxygen."

Emmett listened to her chest, an eye on the monitors. "Not much air movement on the right."

"Emmett, she's got a tracheal shift now," Syd said, a new urgency in her voice.

Emmett's heart rate kicked up. The situation had just moved from a controllable one to an emergency. If the patient had a tension pneumothorax, no air or blood was flowing normally, and that was a setup for a major crash.

Armand announced, "BP's falling, guys. We need to do something here."

"Somebody let Dr. Blake know this one's probably headed for the OR," Emmett said to the ER nurse before glancing at Syd. "You called it."

Pulling on gloves, Syd was already in motion. "I need a chest tube tray and a twenty-four French chest tube."

"What else?" Emmett's hands itched to do what needed to be done. Damn it, but teaching was hard.

"Fourteen-gauge Angiocath," Syd said, splashing Betadine onto the patient's right chest. "Where are they?"

"I got it," Emmett said and opened the sterile package, offering the needle to Syd.

Syd took it, pushed it between the fifth and sixth ribs along the patient's right side, and air whooshed out. Her pulse came down, her pressure started to come up, and her oxygen saturation rose.

"Nice," Emmett muttered.

Syd grinned for half a second before refocusing on the patient.

Honor appeared at the foot of the table. "You two on top of this?"

"Just about to put in a chest tube," Emmett said. "I wouldn't trust the Angiocath in this situation."

"Agreed," Honor said.

"She'll need a stat chest CT once that's in," Emmett added. "I'll call an attending."

Syd looked over at them. "Can we get a bedside portable ultrasound, look at her heart and great vessels? She could have a mediastinal injury. Save us some time."

Honor nodded. "Good call. Let's do that first before we let her go anywhere else. You're putting in the tube, Doctor…?"

"Stevens," Syd said. "Syd Stevens."

"Honor Blake." Honor turned as someone called her name. "Go ahead."

"You got that?" Emmett said quietly.

"I know how to put in a chest tube," Syd said softly.

"Right." Emmett gave her some space, checked to see that Morty's patient in bay three still looked okay, and glanced over her shoulder when she heard Zoey's familiar voice.

"The peds attending is in the OR," Zoey said to a small, intense-looking woman resident with slicked-back jet-black hair. "He said we can take Eddie here to CT if Honor says we're good to go."

"Anything for trauma?" Emmett asked, walking up to the bed.

Zoey laughed. "It's a peds case, Emmett."

The dark-haired woman gave her a questioning look.

"Emmett McCabe. I've got the trauma service."

"Dani Chan. We've got this here. Uh…thanks."

Emmett had a feeling that thanks pained her a little bit. She understood. Trauma surgeons had a reputation for moving in on other people's cases. Of course, that's because they were probably the best at handling whatever was going on. But she knew better than to step on the peds surgeons. Their chief took no prisoners.

"If you need a hand—"

Dani Chan straightened. "Nope. All good."

"Okay then." No thanks this time. Emmett nodded and caught Zoey's smirk. Couldn't hurt to try.

"Emmett." Syd's voice cut through the low level of conversation. Something in her tone—not panic, just a sharp warning—gave Emmett a jolt. She spun around. "What have you got?"

"Her pressure's falling," Syd said, lifting her stethoscope to her ears. "And look at her neck."

The veins in her neck bulged, and Emmett quickly checked the chest tube Syd had inserted. That looked fine.

Syd straightened. "Her heart sounds are muffled. I think she's tamponading."

"Fuck," Emmett muttered under her breath and listened for herself. She could barely make out the heartbeat. Fluid around the heart would do that. "We need that ultrasound."

Armand said, "I'll get it."

"Move, and get Dr. Blake."

"She's crashing," Syd said, and the beeping monitor and the flatline heart trace confirmed it. Instantly, she climbed onto one of the short stools near the stretcher and began chest compressions.

"What's going on," Honor said, rushing back to the bedside.

"Pericardial tamponade." Emmett grabbed the ultrasound gel from the cart and squirted it onto the chest for the ER resident, who slid the probe over the patient's chest.

"Armand," Honor said to her resident, "what do you see?"

"Um, just a second…wait, there!" He repositioned the probe and pointed to a dense layer around the heart. "Looks like blood in the pericardial sac."

"Sure does." Honor called to a nearby nurse, "Cliff, stat page cardiac and trauma. This one's got something going on in her chest."

"We ought to aspirate that," Emmett said.

"Yes." Honor nodded to Emmett. "Want to take Armand through it?"

"Sure." Emmett rummaged through the crash cart and came out with a large bore spinal needle and handed it to the ER resident. "Ever done one?"

"Seen one," he replied.

"Then you're ready," Emmett said. "Syd, hold compressions."

Syd relaxed, her gaze alternating between the resident who inserted the long needle into the patient's chest and the ultrasound that tracked the course of the needle advancing beneath the breastbone, angling up toward the shoulder, into the space around the heart. The EKG stuttered and spiked, no discernible rhythm, the electricity of the heart erratic.

"Runs of V-tach," Syd said.

"Okay, pull back just a little," Emmett said.

"Clear," Syd said as a normal EKG wave appeared.

"There you go," Emmett said as the needle pierced the sac surrounding the heart and entered where there should be no fluid, but there now was a layer of blood preventing the heart from functioning normally. "Aspirate that."

Armand pulled back on the syringe and a few cc's of thick dark fluid aspirated. "I can't get anything else out."

"Clotted," Syd murmured. "BP still forty palp."

"Trauma here yet?" Honor called to no one in particular.

"Not yet," Cliff called back, appearing at the bedside. "You need an instrument tray, Doc?"

"Looks like it. We're going to have to do a window." Honor sounded as calm as if she hadn't just suggested they were going to cut a hole into the patient's chest right in the emergency room. "Emmett, you're up. Ready for this?"

"Yes." Emmett snapped on fresh gloves and pictured the landmarks in her mind. Syd watched her. Honor watched her. Hell. Everyone was watching this.

"Take your time. We don't need to put the other lung down," Honor said, pulling on gloves to assist.

"Right," Emmett said tightly. No pressure. Right. She made the incision and spread the thin layer of fat and muscle right under the breastbone.

"Emmett," Morty called from the adjacent bay. "I think you need to see this."

"Can't," Emmett said without looking up from the incision she'd just made in the patient's chest. "Syd, go help Morty."

"Right," Syd said.

Syd disappeared just as Emmett snipped away a portion of the protective layer around the heart.

❖

"Morty," Syd said, trying not to be aggravated about missing out on the amazing procedure that Emmett somehow ended up doing on *her* patient. "What do you need?"

"His heart rate's down, and his pressure's up again." Morty shook his head. "Something's going on."

Syd assessed his vitals. If Morty had been anyone else, she wouldn't have been impressed. Everything was near normal at first glance. "Fill me in."

Morty quickly gave her a rundown of the patient's history and treatment so far. "But here's the thing—he was awake in the field."

Alarm bells rang. Almost before he'd finished speaking, Syd had her penlight in hand to check the pupils.

"His left pupil's enlarged and nonreactive."

"It wasn't a minute ago." Morty's voice climbed. "Crap, Syd, he's bradying down. Heart rate is fifty."

The ER resident instantly cranked up the head of the bed and said, "Starting hyperventilation."

"He's got a bleed," Syd said. "Did you call neuro?"

"Yes, he said he was on his way, but…"

"I don't think we can wait very long." Syd half turned. "Dr. Blake, this patient has an intracranial bleed, and he's—"

The patient seized, and Syd called, "Valium, I need ten mg of IV Valium stat and start a Dilantin drip."

A flurry of people gathered around the bed.

"Fill me in," a man with a deep baritone voice said from behind Syd.

She looked over her shoulder into the steady, dark eyes of a man who at first glance might've been Jerry's brother, a little bit older, and thirty pounds heavier. "Closed head injury. Recent, rapid onset of signs of intracranial bleeding. Left pupil's blown."

"Kos Hassan, neurosurge." As he spoke, he rapidly examined the patient. "You're new."

"Syd Stevens. Fourth year surgery resident."

He straightened, tucked his tie between the buttons on his snowy white shirt, and smiled. "Ever done a burr hole at the bedside, Doctor?"

"No."

"Well, you're about to."

Syd reached for a pair of sterile gloves, sweat trickling down the center of her spine. She'd actually only ever seen burr holes in the OR while observing brain surgery. But he hadn't asked her that, had he? Her hands were steady as she pulled on gloves. She could do this.

CHAPTER NINE

I heard a rumor you were getting started without me," Quinn Maguire said.

Quinn's words skipped over the outer reaches of Emmett's awareness like stones on the mirrored surface of a pond, barely casting a ripple. Nothing registered except the instruments in her hands and the open incision above the beating heart.

"Hi there," Emmett heard Honor say. "I thought you were scrubbed."

"I was," Quinn said, "till I got the message you were having more fun down here than I was. I left the fellow finishing up."

Fun wasn't exactly what Emmett had been thinking as she snipped away a postage-stamp-sized patch of pericardium from the underlying heart. Ordinarily, nothing separated the two structures except for a whisper-thin space. What she found now was a half-inch layer of congealed blood all around the heart. The buildup of clot constricted the heart in the closed space and prevented it from pumping normally. She was about to fix that by clearing away the clot. Only problem was, that blood had come from somewhere, and she had no idea if the bleeding had stopped. If she started the bleeding up again, what was she going to do down here in the trauma unit? Her pulse trip-hammered.

"Hey, Quinn?" Emmett cleared her throat. Crap, she sounded like a wimp. "Look at all this clot. There must be something big bleeding—a cardiac injury, maybe."

Quinn moved up close behind her and braced her hands on Emmett's shoulders. "Give me a look."

"Can you pull on those retractors, Dr. Blake," Emmett asked, leaning to her left to give Quinn a better view of the two-inch-square space she had made just below the patient's breastbone. At the depth of the wound, the thick cranberry-colored clot filled the space.

"Yep," Quinn said conversationally, "that's impressive. I bet you'll have to scoop some of that out by hand."

"It might stir up fresh hemorrhage," Emmett said. She didn't sound as wimpy that time but a queasy sensation settled in her stomach.

"It might. But she's not going to do well unless you get that out of there." Quinn squeezed her shoulder. "Go ahead and clear it, and then I guess we'll see."

Emmett's stomach cramped but the vomity feeling faded. Her legs were probably shaking, but since she couldn't feel them, she wasn't sure. Her hands, though, they didn't fail her. They were steady and as sharp as her vision. Everything was super clear as her focus narrowed until only the surgical field remained.

"Suction," she said.

"Here," Honor said and passed her the thin, flexible catheter.

Emmett carefully sucked away at the clot. Her first glimpse of the heart, beefy red and beating rhythmically—thank everything that was holy—left her in awe as it always did.

"Pressure's coming up," Armand said. "Sinus rhythm, but still slow."

"There's fresh blood," Emmett said as a trickle of new bleeding flooded into the field.

"Now's the time we move," Quinn said. "We've got a minute or two while she's stable enough to get her to the OR. I don't want to be handling a cardiac laceration down here."

"I'll call the OR and tell them you're coming," Honor said, stepping back from the table.

"And page the heart team," Emmett called while pressing a sterile pad over the incision she'd made in the patient's chest. No time to close that now.

Quinn grabbed the foot of the stretcher, Armand pushed from the front, and Emmett ran alongside, keeping the equipment and lines and monitors from tangling in the wheels or falling off. One of the ER staff raced ahead to hold the elevator.

"We'll get things set up for the heart team," Quinn said as the elevator doors opened. "But if they're tied up, we'll have to crack her chest."

"Absolutely," Emmett said, as if it was just another day instead of one filled with firsts. She was suddenly responsible for a whole new crop of residents, currently in the middle of an emergency she'd never handled before, and constantly unbalanced by the presence of a woman from her past she'd never been able to forget.

❖

Kos Hassan handed Syd a scalpel. "Do you know where you're going with this?"

She pictured the diagram from her trauma text in her mind, thanking genetics or just pure luck that she had an excellent visual memory. "Two finger breadths in front of the ear and two finger breadths above."

"All right. Where does that put you?"

"Temporal fossa," she said instantly.

"And what do we have to worry about in there?"

"Everything?" Syd laughed and hoped the neurosurgeon had a sense of humor. "Besides the brain? On the left side, speech and motor function."

"What else?" Hassan pointed at Morty, all the while arranging instruments on a tray with quick, efficient, seemingly automatic motions. "You, buddy, who are you?"

"Morty Weiss, sir."

"And who would you be, Morty?"

"Oh." Morty grinned that guileless grin. "A second year surgery resident."

"What are you worried about?"

"Middle cerebral artery?"

"Very good. You two are from Franklin, right?"

"We were, yes," Syd said.

Kos's laughter was a rumble. "Good point. Well, don't hit the middle cerebral artery, Dr. Stevens."

"No, Dr. Hassan. I won't." She hoped. She pointed to where she intended to make the incision. "Okay to start?"

"Perfectly."

Syd cut down directly to the skull, expecting the profuse bleeding that all scalp incisions made. "Morty, get those retractors in here."

Morty had anticipated what she'd need and already had the narrow right-angle retractors in his hands. He slid them into the incision and pulled back, stopping the bleeders with pressure and saving her critical time. She swabbed the area and looked at the skull, gleaming white under the bright lights. She didn't need a lot of exposure. The burr hole would only be about half an inch in diameter, and hopefully they'd only need one. Hopefully.

"Here you are," the neurosurgeon said, handing her the drill with the broad bone burr on the end. Drilling through the skull was the same as drilling bone anywhere else in the body. Bone was a hard substance, and the drill head generated heat around it as it penetrated. Heat killed living cells, and as dense as bone might be, it was still alive, and they didn't want to kill the skull. "Morty, you have to irrigate while I do this. Get a syringe of saline."

"Just a second." Morty sounded just a little bit breathless. "Okay, I've got it, Syd."

Syd spared a glance at Kos. "I'm starting."

"You've got the conn, Doctor."

Syd smiled at the familiar phrase. Her father had been a Navy doctor and her mother a Navy pilot. They'd both been out of the service since Syd and her siblings were young, but they never lost the language. She wondered what they'd think if they knew what she was about to do and quickly chased the thought away. No time for that now. No time for that at all.

"Here we go." Syd knew the principles. She knew there was an outer table of bone protecting a spongy vascularized middle and then another inner table of bone before getting to the tough fibrous tissue covering the brain itself. Not all that much protection, really, for the delicate spongy tissue packed with nerve cells and microscopic fibrils that carried the impulses that made the heart beat and the muscles move, and formed the thoughts and emotions and, if there was one, probably the soul of the individual. She started the drill and set it to the bone. Small pulverized bits of white dust shot into the air. "Irrigate, Morty."

The stream of saltwater washed away the minute particles and quickly turned pink when she hit the middle layer of the skull, and then clear again when she broke into the inner table. The resistance gave way and she instantly stopped the drill. The covering of the brain, a thick grayish envelope of dense tissue laced with blood vessels, instantly bulged into the wound.

"Quite a bit of pressure under there," Kos said in a steady, even voice. "Go ahead and cut that and give the brain a little bit of room to breathe."

Syd sliced into the dural lining and bloody cerebrospinal fluid gushed out. The CSF should be clear, not bloody, but the brain underneath pulsed in time to the patient's heartbeat, pink and healthy looking.

"Pulse is coming up," the ER resident said in a rapid staccato, her voice an octave higher than it had been earlier. "Pressure is coming down."

"Well, isn't that a pretty sight," Kos said.

Syd leaned against the table, her knees a little weak. She took the first breath she could remember breathing for what felt like an hour. "Is one hole enough?"

"It is for now, but we have to assume there's a clot somewhere. If it's epidural, we'll need to evacuate it. Since you've got such a nice, pretty little hole there," he said, "we might as well put in an intracranial pressure probe so we can monitor his brain pressures. If you don't mind, Dr. Stevens, I'll do the honors."

Syd chuckled. "I don't mind at all."

He already had the probe, a long thin needle connected to a transducer, in his hand. He threaded it through the hole in the skull, through the brain matter, and into the ventricle, the space deep in the brain where fluid cushioned the delicate organ as it moved about in the skull. He handed off the leads for the ER resident to connect to a monitor.

"Normal pressures," Syd said, watching the readout. Now she really could breathe again.

"I think we can take him down to CT now. If you're free, you can come along."

Syd checked the surrounding beds. Emmett and the woman Syd had been taking care of were gone. A tall redhead in a white lab coat and baby blue scrubs was conferring with Sadie and Zoey over the child in the last bay, and the ER residents were busy at the other two beds. "It doesn't look like they need us down here. I'd like to see this through."

He smiled, his eyes approving. "Well then, Doctors, shall we?"

Syd glanced at Morty, whose mouth tilted up into a triumphant grin. He was having fun. So was she.

❖

In the surgeons' lounge, Syd collapsed in an overstuffed chair that had seen better days. Actually, better decades. The dun-colored upholstery was worn black in places, some of the stuffing was coming out along the seams, and the arms sagged after undoubtedly serving as leg rests for generations of surgeons. The damn thing was so comfortable, she never wanted to get up. Morty handed her a can of Diet Coke and a bag of chips.

"Thought you might be hungry," he said, dropping onto the ugly mustard-yellow sofa adjacent to Syd's chair.

"Starving. Thanks."

"Me too," he mumbled around a mouthful of something orange that she thought might be cheese curls, but she didn't really want to think about.

"Are you like…" Morty laughed. "Are you like high right now?"

Syd dropped her head back, stared at the dingy gray tile ceiling, and laughed. "Totally."

"I mean, how cool was that?"

"Cool," Syd agreed. This feeling, this euphoric sense of invincibility, was what made all the misery worthwhile. Oh, sure, it didn't last, but like with any drug, at least so she imagined, just knowing the high would come again was addicting.

Morty swallowed another mouthful of totally non-nutritious artificial food. "And did you happen to see what Emmett was doing?"

"Oh, yeah," Syd said dryly. Emmett had moved in on her patient with the lethal efficiency of an apex predator—sleek and beautiful and deadly. And stolen her case. Forget the beautiful part too. The fact she was so damn easy to look at and charming and sexy just made it worse. "I saw."

"We were doing major procedures in the trauma unit."

"Well, we've done that stuff before."

"Sort of."

He was right. Sort of. She'd certainly put in any number of chest tubes in the OR and in the intensive care unit, but usually under much more controlled circumstances. She'd injected intracardiac epi during codes. But she'd never done what she'd done today. She'd never operated under extreme circumstances to save a patient's life. Circumstances when, if she'd failed, the patient would've died. She'd grown as a surgeon today in a way she never had before. She sighed. She'd known what she might have been giving up when she'd decided to go to Franklin, and she hadn't cared. Maybe her parents had been right. No. They weren't. She'd made the right decision then. The only one she could.

"You did really well today, Morty," Syd said. "You picked up what was going on with that patient, and if you hadn't—"

Emmett came through the door, a vending room sandwich in her hand. Her smile was bright. The energy emanating from her practically glowed.

"Hey, I was just about to call you guys." Emmett sat on the coffee table in front of Syd. Their knees nearly touched. Her dark hair was ruffled and a little sweaty. Syd blinked. Emmett looked good and the fact that she noticed was different. Different and totally not what she wanted.

"How's your patient?" Emmett asked, unwrapping her sandwich.

"Which one?" Syd said before she could stop herself. "The one I started with or the one I finished with?"

"Ah," Emmett said, taking a bite and looking as if the white bread and thin layer of turkey took effort to get down. She chewed, looked around, and Syd offered her soda.

"I'm done with it," Syd said, "if you don't mind sharing."

"Like I'm worried." Emmett rolled her eyes, took the can, and swallowed several gulps. "Thanks."

Seeming not to have noticed Syd's sarcasm, Emmett said, "The guy with the head injury."

"He's great," Morty said, sitting up straight. "The CAT scan showed an intradural hematoma, and Dr. Hassan is going to watch it for now. He's going to get a repeat CT in six hours if his ICP is stable."

"Did I see you getting ready to do burr holes over there?"

"Yep. Syd did emergency burr holes," Morty said. "Well, one, and Hassan put in an ICP monitor."

"Sweet." Emmett grinned at Syd, a spark of excitement and a little envy in her gaze. "Awesome, really."

Emmett's envy made Syd feel just a little bit better and exhilaration bubbled in her chest. Sure, she hadn't gotten to do the pericardial window, but she'd seen Emmett do it and knew she could. Instead, she'd done something she'd never done before, had never even *seen* under emergency circumstances. So as far as she was concerned, it was really a win-win. Not that she was going to say so to Emmett.

"Morty made a great save," Syd said quietly.

Emmett balled up the cellophane and cardboard wrapper from her sandwich and tossed it at the trash can. It hit the rim and fell onto the floor. Undaunted, she tossed the Coke can after it. "Two points," she said, standing and brushing crumbs from her scrubs. She picked up the wrapper and trashed it. "Morty, Hank is in the TICU checking on post-ops. Why don't you catch up with him and he'll go over the rest of the patients with you."

"On it." Morty was already on his feet and headed toward the door. He looked at Emmett the way he sometimes looked at Syd, as if he was a young, unseasoned hunter and she was the leader of the pack. But then, Syd thought ruefully, Emmett was his leader now.

"So," Emmett said, dropping into Morty's spot on the sofa and propping her feet on the coffee table. "We should talk."

Chapter Ten

Syd looked wary, and Emmett didn't blame her. Usually when someone started a conversation with *we should talk*, it didn't end up being a happy exchange. She ought to know—she'd had plenty of those the last five years. More often as time passed, and she'd usually been the one to start the conversation. She'd learned the safest route to avoiding misunderstanding and more drama than she ever wanted to experience was to be super clear right from the get-go. Even if sometimes she felt like an ass and a bit shallow saying she wasn't looking for anything except a friendly, mutual good time. She knew the reputation that approach had earned her—*player* about summed it up. She couldn't argue, even if she didn't agree. After all, actions meant a whole lot less than words, at least from the outside looking in.

Of course, Syd couldn't be expecting *that* talk, although she obviously expected something unpleasant. Emmett probably should have chosen a better way of leading into all this. But really, she hadn't even realized she was going to say anything until she'd picked up on Syd's reaction to what had gone down during the trauma alert. That and the niggling dissatisfied feeling she had too.

She hadn't been paying all that much attention in the moment—everyone was focused on doing their jobs, exactly as they should be. No matter what was going on personally—jealousies, relationship issues, healthy or unhealthy competition—when it came to taking care of patients, everyone worth anything at all set those things aside. Syd had done that, and Emmett had no doubt she'd keep on doing it. Just like she would. But the faint look of disdain and maybe anger Syd had directed at her, however briefly, had stung. Coming from someone else, even someone she cared about like Zoey, she might not have been as bothered. Throw a bunch of alpha dogs in the ring, and a little fur was bound to get ruffled. It wasn't her responsibility to smooth Syd's bruised ego, but she wanted to.

"Look," Emmett said, "this thing Maguire has us doing is an experiment. Maybe it's not such a great idea."

"Thing?" Syd said looking confused, and not helping her out at all.

Emmett ran a hand through her hair, let her arm fall onto the arm of the yellow sofa with a thud. "Putting the two of us together on the trauma service. Trauma isn't like most other services—it's not predictable. We can't look at the OR schedule at the beginning of the day and divvy things up or even *talk* about how to divvy things up. We have to take things as they come, in the moment."

"I get how trauma works, Emmett," Syd said just a little bit impatiently. "So?"

"So," Emmett said, "sometimes there's no time to discuss anything. We just have to do what needs to be done."

"I know this, Emmett. I'm not arguing it."

Emmett didn't usually have such a hard time expressing herself. Why was she walking on verbal eggshells with Syd? It wasn't as if Syd could just up and walk out on her. Her chest tightened. She could, though, couldn't she. Had done. Poof. Gone.

Emmett stomped out those thoughts. That was over and done. "So then you get why Honor handed that pericardial window off to me, right? I'm the senior on the service."

"Oh," Syd said dryly, "I know."

Emmett pointed a finger. "See there? I know what you're thinking."

"No, you don't."

"Oh, yeah, I do. You think Honor was playing favorites."

Syd half smiled. She *had* wondered if Honor Blake choosing Emmett to do the procedure had something more to do with the fact that Emmett appeared to be everybody's darling, and not just her being the senior resident. But she couldn't say it, couldn't complain about it. Certainly not now, and not to Emmett. They needed to get through the next month or however long this torture was going to last with the least amount of drama. She had no standing at PMC, and she couldn't be seen as a troublemaker.

"Look, it's not a big deal," Syd said.

"Honor wouldn't do that," Emmett insisted.

"Maybe not consciously." Syd sighed. "And so what if she did? It's an attending's prerogative to do what they want with residents, and they all do it all the time. When they don't want to worry about a patient at night, they discuss it with the residents they trust the most. When they know they're gonna have a tough case in the OR, they want the resident with the best hands to scrub in with them. And when there's a tough teaching procedure, they want the resident who isn't going to screw up in the middle."

Emmett nodded. "Maybe, some of the time. Sure. But all the good attendings are going to teach whoever's available, and Honor is one of the best teachers in the place. But seniority always counts for something."

"Oh, I know that." Syd paused. She'd been where Emmett was plenty of times—knowing she'd grabbed a case out from under another resident and suffering a fleeting pang of remorse. *Fleeting* being the operative word. They'd get their chance one day to have the pick of the cases. That's how the system worked. If you survived long enough, you'd reap the rewards. Emmett had nothing to apologize for. "Don't worry about it. You can't help it if you're the chosen one."

Emmett gaped. "What?"

Syd grinned, unexpectedly feeling better than she had all morning—except when she was in the middle of the trauma. When had that ever happened? "Well, if the crown fits—"

"Cut it out," Emmett said indignantly.

Emmett looked…cute. Oh, still attractive and sexy as hell, but some of that unpolished openness Syd remembered about her from their first meeting flashed across Emmett's face. Syd caught her breath and latched on to a quick change in subject. "What did you mean, that maybe Maguire's experiment isn't such a good idea?"

"We're way too close in experience to be on the same service. We need to be doing the same cases. Plus, it's a waste of talent."

Syd laughed. "You couldn't possibly know anything about my talent, so you must be talking about yourself. God, I don't remember you being so arrogant."

Emmett's heart pounded in her chest. She made sure her voice stayed light and easy. "I was a fourth year medical student. How could I be arrogant about anything? Besides, I didn't think you remembered anything at all about me." She should've stopped there, but she couldn't help herself. "I recall you were very talented, though."

Syd's face went blank, and Emmett mentally kicked her own ass. Syd had already been clear about the boundaries, even though they didn't make any sense to Emmett. She was supposed to act like nothing ever happened. That's what Syd wanted to pretend. Well, she'd never agreed to that.

"Maybe you don't remember," Emmett said, not caring about the anger that bled into her voice. "But I do. When we connected, it was like...fireworks. Rockets and firecrackers. Explosive, blinding."

"Emmett," Syd said quietly, "it was good sex, and it was a long time ago. Things like that, they die out as fast as those sparklers on the Fourth of July."

"Maybe." Emmett wasn't sure, and she definitely wasn't ready to believe it. She'd seen Quinn and Honor together plenty of times, just talking. There was heat there, for sure. Enough that she sometimes looked away, feeling a little bit too much like a voyeur, even though they weren't even touching. That's what she wanted, maybe, someday, when she was settled. A woman who lit the fireworks in her blood and wanted her to do the same. The only trouble was, only one woman had ever done that, and she'd just disappeared before they'd even had a chance to find out what was happening between them.

Fine then. If Syd wanted things strictly professional, that's what she'd do.

"I knew how good you were, work-wise," Emmett said, making a point to stress work, "just from talking with you that first day."

"You were just psyched about the interview."

"No. I mean, sure, I was. But that had nothing to do with...the rest." Emmett smiled, remembering how eager she had been on that first interview, and how cool it was that the resident assigned to take the medical students around the hospital was a surgical resident. A woman resident. Gorgeous and funny and confident. When Syd recounted tales of what her first year had been like so far, Emmett knew Syd was everything she wanted to be. Everything she *would* be in just a year. By the end of the tour, she and Syd had been deep in conversation while others in the group had wandered off. Somehow phone numbers had been exchanged, a date made for a drink, and a couple of drinks had turned into a night together. One night, all night, had turned into a few more stolen hours. Intense, riveting, consuming. And then...silence.

"I think you might have been too easily impressed," Syd said lightly, "but I appreciate—"

"Uh, hey, Emmett," Zoey said from the doorway. "I was about to page you."

Syd clamped her mouth shut, a veil dropping over her gaze.

Emmett shook herself and straightened up. How the hell long had Zoey been standing there? "What's up?"

"Fitzpatrick wants a trauma consult," Zoey said.

"On the kid from this morning?"

"Yeah." Zoey shrugged. "Abdominal CT shows a splenic tear with a pericapsular hematoma, but no active bleeding. She wants to watch it."

Syd said, "Sounds like a reasonable plan. Why the consult?"

Zoey glanced her way as if just noticing she was there. "The dad's a big-shot attorney, and considering the family got T-boned by an out-of-control delivery truck, this is going to be a big-money case. The consult shouldn't be too challenging."

Syd pressed her lips together.

"So it's a CYA consult," Emmett said.

"Mine is not to question why…" Zoey grinned and leaned against the doorway. "So, you do remember it's your turn to do dinner tonight? It would be good if you actually made it home so we could eat something besides cereal for a change."

Emmett flushed at Syd's raised brows and narrowed eyes.

Syd rose abruptly. "I'll page you when I've finished the consult."

"Thanks," Emmett called as Syd edged past Zoey in the doorway and disappeared. She appreciated Syd taking the consult without her needing to ask. That kind of job always fell to someone below the most senior resident. Which was Emmett. Man, that had to be hard for Syd to swallow.

"Kinda chilly in here," Zoey said, barely hiding her laughter.

"You enjoying yourself?"

"No, as a matter of fact." Zoey flopped on the end of the sofa. "I'm sick of peds already."

"So you decided to stir things up on my service?"

"Hey! I had a legitimate request."

"Since when have you cared about the dinner schedule?" Emmett said.

Zoey tapped her foot on the edge of the coffee table. "So what's the story with her?"

"No story." Emmett couldn't tell who she was angry at—Syd for dismissing the past as if it had never happened, Zoey for trying to dredge it up, or herself for caring. "No story at all."

❖

When someone dropped into a chair next to Syd at the peds ICU nurses' station, she expected it to be Zoey. Steeling herself for another subtly unpleasant conversation, she glanced up from the tablet where she'd been reviewing the child's CT scans, and her spirits rose. Smiling, she said to Dani, "Hey! How's it going?"

Dani took a quick look around and leaned in. "Weird. How about with you?"

Syd blew out a breath. "I vacillate between feeling like I've been dropped into a foreign country and having a really great time. The trauma alert this morning was…wild."

"I got a quick look at what you were doing," Dani said with a sigh. "Holy frick, you really lucked out. All I got was a watch-and-wait on my kid. Are you here seeing him?"

"Yes. I was just waiting for the repeat CT to finish the consult."

Dani waved a hand. "He's been stable. It's not going to show anything."

"Probably, but all the same, I ought to see it. So how's your day going?"

"Oh, just great." Dani made a face. "Both my junior residents are annoying. In fact, Sadie is downright obnoxious."

Syd frowned. "Sadie. She the redhead who was so bent about us being here this morning? Short, cute, and bitchy?"

Dani snorted. "That's a really nice way of putting it, but yeah. It helps that Zoey and Sadie don't seem to be crazy about each other. Sadie has someone else to snarl at some of the time." Dani cocked her head. "What?"

"Nothing," Syd said quickly.

"No, something. What? Come on, we need to stick together here."

"Zoey made a point of telling me I had taken her place on the trauma service. And she and Emmett are a thing."

"Really?" Dani's eyes gleamed. "Huh."

"Yes, well, they live together, and—" Syd stopped short of sharing the part about seeing Emmett and Zoey in the on-call room together, annoyed she was the teeniest bit bothered by that. She'd very successfully refused to think about Emmett for years and now she could barely stop. "Anyhow, they're tight. So I guess we'll just have to put up with the snark."

"Homicide is out of the question?"

Syd laughed. "I'd save that for extreme situations."

"They might have split us up," Dani said, "but it's still going to be us and them."

"No matter what, you, me, and Jerry are still a team." Syd squeezed Dani's arm. "Have you seen him?"

"No," Dani said, "but he's on general surgery. He's probably getting a lot more surgery than I am right now."

"Don't worry, it will come."

"Yeah, at least I get the pick of cases on peds." Dani grimaced. "Sorry. I wasn't trying to rub it in."

"Oh, I know."

"How's your *senior* resident?" Dani said, putting a sarcastic spin to the word *senior*.

"Emmett? She's fine." Syd rose. She did not want to think or talk about Emmett McCabe. "I'll wrap up this consult when the repeat CT is done."

"Hey, you okay?" Dani asked.

"What? Oh, sure. I'm fine." Syd was too weary to even complain. Not tired, just weary. The day already felt like it was thirty-six hours long instead of eight and four more to go before she could get out of there, if she was lucky. Trying to fit in at a new place on the fly and being faced with Emmett at every turn took all her energy. The last thing she wanted was to think about the past. Emmett had been part of a time she'd worked to forget every day for the past five years.

CHAPTER ELEVEN

Hey," Honor said when Quinn walked into the bathroom at a little after six, "you're home early."

"You too. Did you take Jack over already?"

Honor kissed her. "Yep. Linda has a split shift, and Robin was planning to feed the kids early so they could all watch *Brave*."

"Oh my God—again?" Quinn threaded her arms around Honor's waist and burrowed her face in Honor's damp hair. "Mmm, you smell good." She kissed her neck and started peeling off her clothes one-handed.

Honor laughed and arched her back, giving Quinn better access to her throat. "Got something in mind?"

"Shower." Quinn kissed her way down to Honor's breasts. "I was hoping for company, but you didn't wait for me."

"You didn't tell me you were on your way or I would have."

"I wasn't sure what time I'd get finished with that last case. Turned out to be easier than I thought."

"Just as well. We're not all that good about making quickies quick."

"True."

Honor kissed her and pushed her toward the shower. "How did everyone take the big announcement this morning?"

Quinn turned the shower on hot and stepped in. She left the door partway open. "Better than expected. No bodies have turned up yet. What did you think during the alert this morning?"

"Everyone stepped up. Really, it went as well as I could've hoped for," Honor said. "The new residents, at least the ones on trauma and peds surg, seemed very solid. Syd Stevens certainly is calm in an emergency."

"She was doing the burr holes." Quinn's eyes were closed and water streamed down her face and chest. Her shoulders and arms were finely muscled, her breasts the perfect size for holding.

Honor leaned against the vanity, enjoying the view. How was it she had seen this woman naked hundreds of times, and still she could catch a glimpse when she least expected it, and her heart would lurch. Right this instant, she could be quick. She stole a peek at the time. Damn it, they really didn't have time.

"Of course not," Honor muttered.

Quinn flung her head back, clearing the water from her hair. "Sorry? I missed that."

"Oh…" Honor unscrambled her brain. "I talked to Kos later in the morning about the neuro patient. He's stable, by the way. Anyhow, Kos was very impressed with Stevens. I think he might try to seduce her into neuro."

Quinn laughed. "Kos is always looking for the best residents to steal for neuro."

"Is she?" Reluctantly, Honor started to dress. No point torturing herself with what could have been. She smiled. Quinn *had* promised later. Still plenty of time for later. "Stevens. Is she one of the best?"

"All signs point that way."

"So we're going to be top-heavy for a few years. Emmett did a great job too."

Quinn flipped the dials off and stepped out, blindly reaching for a towel. Honor handed her one, and she briskly dried her hair and face. "Emmett always does a good job."

"You know," Honor said, grabbing a robe off the back of the door and replacing Quinn's towel, "it might be a good idea to plan some kind of get-together soon. Let the new residents get acquainted with everyone in a non-work situation. Might help with the integration."

"We've got the barbecue coming up like usual when the new interns arrive." Quinn pulled on the robe and cocked her head when Honor didn't answer. "What?"

Heat climbed up Honor's throat. "I was just thinking…"

Quinn moved closer, penning her in against the vanity. Her robe was open, her bare body firm and hot.

"Quinn," Honor warned.

"Yes?"

"We—"

A sharp rap on the door preceded Arly calling, "Hey, you guys. We have to go soon."

Quinn closed her eyes and groaned softly.

"Okay, honey," Honor called back. "We'll be ready." She turned Quinn around and gave a little shove. "Dress. Anyhow…about the residents. By the time the new first years arrive, all these residents have to be ready to work together. Right now they're strangers."

Quinn tied the robe. "So what are you thinking?"

"Maybe some kind of reception once a bit of the dust settles." Honor walked into the bedroom. "Hors d'oeuvres, drinks, a chance for people to walk around and talk to each other."

"All right," Quinn said, following. "I'll see if I can come up with some money for that. Just promise me you'll be there so I don't have to stand around by myself."

"I promise to rescue you." Honor laughed. Quinn was the last person to ever need rescuing from anything, but she liked knowing Quinn needed her. "So, do I need to worry about tonight?"

Quinn pulled on jeans and paused before zipping them up. "You mean Arly's test? No way. She's gonna be great."

"You'll look out for her, right?" Honor said quietly.

"Of course." Quinn kissed her. "Don't worry, Mom. She's going to be fine."

Honor sighed. "I know. Just promise me there won't be blood."

Quinn laughed. "It's Arly, baby. I can't promise that."

❖

Visiting hours ended at eight and the halls were quiet at a little after seven when Syd made her way on night rounds. Her last stop was trauma ICU. The ICUs allowed brief visits on the hour, and a few people usually waited in the family area for the next chance to spend a few minutes with a patient, but as the day wore on into night, families and friends left to go home and shower, grab a meal, or just take a much-needed break before returning to their vigils. No one appeared to be waiting as Syd slipped into the ICU. The lights had been turned down and the staff moved almost silently between the cubicles, the only sounds coming from the hissing ventilators and the beeping monitors. Far from being calm, the atmosphere always seemed a little charged, as if a storm might break out at any moment. Syd nodded to the occasional nurse or PA who glanced her way before going back to whatever they were doing. Her ID badge proclaimed her legitimacy, but since she wasn't on call and no one had paged her, making introductions was pointless. That would come in the middle of a crisis, when so many connections seemed to be forged.

A few more hours of anonymity suited Syd just fine. At the end of a day that now felt like several, she didn't have the energy to talk to anyone. She only wanted to check on this last patient, and then she was done. Funny, as tired as she felt, the idea of going home to an empty house and another dinner of takeout or frozen pizza didn't hold all that much appeal. Maybe that explained why she was still here when she didn't strictly need to be.

She stopped in the doorway of one of the individual rooms closest to the nurses' station, where the most acutely injured patients who needed even closer monitoring than all the others in the intensive care unit were placed. The patient was completely still, intubated and heavily sedated. A sheet covered his entire body, except for his face, which was partially obscured by the tape holding on the breathing tube and the white roll of gauze encircling his skull. The intracranial pressure wave on the monitor just to the right of the hospital bed cycled up and down in a steady rhythmic curve, each peak and valley following the beat of his heart and the subsequent pulse of the blood that flowed through his brain. ICP still normal.

Syd smiled to herself. The procedure she'd done in the emergency room had possibly saved this man's life—he wasn't out of the woods yet, and he had multiple injuries, any number of which could cause a lethal complication. But she had definitely saved his brain, and what was a beating heart without a mind and spirit to go with it? A surge of satisfaction pushed back the fatigue and stress of the long day. This moment, this rush of pleasure, was worth the price.

"He's looking good," a deep voice said from behind her.

Syd started slightly, registered who it was, and turned. "Hi, Dr. Hassan."

"Dr. Stevens." He smiled, his broad handsome face intelligent and intense. "That was a nice job this morning."

"Thank you." She glanced over her shoulder at the patient again. "I'm just glad it worked."

"Mmm," he murmured, his eyes traveling over the monitors and the patient as they spoke. "I just looked at his repeat head CT."

"Yes," Syd said, "me too. I didn't see any problems. I thought…"

"What?"

"I thought the edema around the hematoma looked improved."

He nodded. "Yes, so did I. That's probably from the drug regimen we've got him on along with the hyperventilation."

"I was wondering if we should increase the steroid dose. We've still got a little wiggle room."

"I was thinking the same thing myself," he said, "but since there's a little improvement, let's hold off on that. Keep it in reserve in case we need it."

"Okay."

"Anything else?" Kos asked.

"The ortho guys want to fix that open fracture in his right tibia as soon as they can."

"What did you tell them?"

Syd considered how to answer. Every question was a test of her judgment and her knowledge, and she was on totally new ground with every single attending in the hospital. Well, no point in waiting. She might as well let everyone know who she was. "I told them I'd check with you, but I didn't think he'd be ready for at least twenty-four hours."

"Good call." He leaned against the doorway and folded his arms. "So you've got one more year."

Syd's chest tightened. "Yes."

"What are your plans after that?"

"I'm thinking about a peds fellowship," Syd said.

"Good field," he said mildly.

"Yes." She'd always been set on peds. Why had she just said she was *thinking* about it instead of planning on it? Tired, that was all.

"You know," he said conversationally, "the thing about neuro is that everybody's got a head and a brain. Even kids."

"Um, yes." She laughed and for some weird reason, she wasn't tired any longer. "I guess that's true."

"Yup." He straightened, took one more look at the patient, and said, "Well, I've got to finish making rounds. Are you on call tonight?"

"Oh. No."

Looking surprised, he said, "You're here late, then."

"Not really. I just wanted to check on some of the patients before I went home."

He nodded as if that made perfect sense. "Well, good night, Dr. Stevens."

"Good night, Dr. Hassan."

She noticed he didn't write a note when he left, so she stopped by the station and added a post-op note to the chart. Now she could go home.

On her way to the locker room, she ran into Dani coming out of the elevator.

"Hey," Syd said. "You headed home?"

Dani shook her head. "No, I'm waiting to do an appy."

"Why?" Syd frowned. "Haven't you done about a million of them?"

"This one's on a four-year-old. And, you know…new guy."

"Wait, let me guess. Fitzpatrick is doing it, and you're bumping some lowly second year so you can operate with the peds chief?"

"Yeah," Dani said with a grin. "Fitzpatrick knows the family, and if she's gonna be doing it, so am I."

"Butt kisser."

"Damn right. You want to grab a coffee and hang around for a while?"

"Sure," Syd said, "might as well. I wasn't going to do anything at home anyhow and I'm starving."

"Let's hit the cafeteria, then."

Syd didn't mind hospital food. Most places actually tried to offer nutritious choices, and whatever was on the menu usually beat what she would have gotten from a drive-through. She ordered some vegetable lasagna and salad that looked pretty decent. Dani was a burger woman.

When they settled at a table in the mostly empty cafeteria, Dani asked, "So, what do you think about the situation?"

"I'm sorta trying not to," Syd said wearily. "Too many things I can't control. Today went okay, all things considered." She paused, catching the glint in Dani's eye. Surprise and a little envy stole through her. "You're having fun, aren't you?"

"Sort of." Dani attacked her burger as if she hadn't seen food for a week. Somehow she managed to put away more food than Syd and Jerry combined, and never seemed to gain a pound. Her metabolism always ran on overdrive, kind of like her energy level. She always burned hot. "There's a different vibe here, don't you think? Something in the air."

"Things are a bit more charged around here." Syd pictured Emmett for some reason, her attitude and drive. Emmett projected more than confidence. She carried herself like a gladiator about to enter the arena.

Dani grinned. "Yeah. It's a rush."

"So how is your service coming together?" Syd changed the subject along with her unruly images of Emmett McCabe.

Dani rolled her eyes. "They're smart—I have to give them that. But I wouldn't want to date any of them."

Syd laughed, and she hadn't thought anything could make her laugh through her bone-deep weariness. Oh, she'd been tired before, and she hadn't even worked a full twenty-four hours. After all this time, she could easily go thirty-six without starting to flag. But the day had brought up things she thought she'd put away a long time ago. Somehow, Dani still made her laugh. "You're already thinking about that?"

"Not really," Dani said. "Okay, maybe a little. You know how it is—you meet people and you know right away they might be somebody you wouldn't mind working with, but you wouldn't want to have a drink with them."

"I know what you mean." Syd's mind went instantly to Emmett. Again. She'd have a drink with Emmett. Actually, she'd *had* a drink with Emmett after knowing her only a few hours. She'd wanted to keep talking to her, she'd wanted to keep feeling the thrum of connection, she'd wanted to hold on to the excitement of discovery that had been almost instantaneous. The moment she'd met Emmett, she'd felt the way she always imagined she could feel with someone.

"Who knows," Syd said as casually as she could. "Maybe you'll change your mind when you get to know them better."

Dani snorted. "That is highly doubtful."

Dani's beeper sounded and she checked her message. Grabbing the last bit of burger, she crammed it in her mouth and stood up, taking her tray with her. "OR's ready, gotta go. See you later."

Syd waved. "Have fun."

Having no doubt Dani *would* have fun, Syd bussed her tray and headed back up to the locker room for the second time. She took the stairs instead of bothering to wait for the elevator, and as she started up, she automatically stepped to the right at the sound of footsteps rapidly descending. Emmett appeared on the landing ahead.

"Hey," Emmett said, stopping a few stairs above her. "I thought you went home an hour ago."

"Oh. No, I…what's going on?"

"Not exactly sure," Emmett said. "I just got a text from the chief to meet her in the emergency room."

"Do you want a hand?" Syd asked impulsively.

"You're not on call," Emmett said.

"I don't have anything else to do."

Emmett tilted her head, studied Syd for a second, and grinned. "Sure, why not?"

CHAPTER TWELVE

I didn't get a trauma alert," Syd said as she turned and followed Emmett back down the stairs. She still had her trauma beeper turned on, even though she wasn't technically on call. She was still there, after all, and a trauma case would give her an excuse to stay. The hospital was a world she knew, and one where she knew herself. PMC might have a slightly different geography than Franklin, but she recognized the culture and soon she'd know the terrain.

"There wasn't one." Emmett pushed opened the stairwell door and held it as Syd went through. "Maguire called me direct and asked me to meet her."

"So you're her guy, right?" Attendings didn't usually call residents except to give them an order or chew them out. A direct request to catch a case meant Maguire thought Emmett was the strongest resident available. And Emmett wasn't even chief resident yet. Yet. But that sure looked inevitable. Not that she was surprised. What surprised her was that Maguire had even taken the time to talk to her that morning at all or even entertain the possibility of anyone but Emmett being the chief resident next year. Right this minute, Syd didn't care. Maybe she would if she and the rest of the ex-Franklins survived in the brave new world.

She snorted.

"What?" Emmett shot her a look as they trotted side by side.

Hall traffic picked up as they got closer to the ER and trauma admitting with residents rushing past, transport moving patients in wheelchairs and gurneys, and the occasional visitor looking anxious and uncertain. Night and day weren't that much different once you left the patient floors. Oh, sure, there were peak hours for ER cases—first thing in the morning after people waited all night hoping to get better only to discover they felt worse, fender benders and more serious crashes during rush hour, and the inevitable weather-related accidents whenever it rained or snowed or got icy. But no matter the hour, major trauma centers were busy around the clock.

Syd said, "You know what I'm talking about."

"Maguire doesn't have a guy," Emmett said.

"And I guess that's why she called you personally," Syd said mildly.

"She probably figured I'd be here."

"Why are you? You're not on call, are you?"

"No." Emmett hit the button for the ER entrance. "But you're not either, and you're here."

"Yeah, but I'm the new guy. Not *the* guy."

Emmett laughed. "Sure, and guy or no guy, six months from now you'll still be here, waiting for something to happen. Won't you?"

Syd had to laugh too. "Maybe. It's a lot more fun sitting around here than anywhere else."

"Yeah," Emmett said with a sigh. "Funny about that, isn't it?"

Syd tried to pull back. Kidding around with Emmett was too easy, so easy she did it without thinking. And she didn't like doing things she hadn't thought out and planned ahead for. She'd done that way too much in the past, and all it had gotten her was heartache. Except once—but then, the hurt from that had never gone away either. "I guess it's an occupational hazard."

"For most," Emmett said as if she was turning the idea round in her mind. Almost as if she might regret not having much else in her life except work.

Syd understood. The same wondering whispers cropped up in the back of her mind every now and then too. Was the road she was on really going to be enough for a lifetime? She didn't want to think about that either. Definitely time to get back on nice safe neutral ground. "Besides, I wasn't in any hurry to ride the subway tonight, and Dani's doing a case."

Emmett perked up, that sharky glint that was so damn hot when it wasn't annoying racing into her eyes. "Peds has a case?"

"An appy."

"And Dani's doing it?" Emmett smirked. "Oh, yeah, an appendectomy's a senior resident's case, all right."

Syd kept a straight face. "Hey, nothing wrong with working hard."

Emmett narrowed her eyes. "Don't tell me Fitzpatrick is staffing it?"

"I—" She laughed. "Okay, yes."

"Nothing wrong with a little kiss-ass either."

Despite having said the same thing to Dani not thirty minutes before, Syd protested. "Like you never—"

"Never needed to."

"I'm drowning in bull right now."

Emmett raised a brow, and damn, she looked even hotter when she did. The glint in her deep blue eyes was joined by a ridiculous dimple to the right of her mouth. That dimple had been one of the first things she'd noticed. And right on the heels of that memory came the recollection of the buzz that had followed her first sight of Emmett. Then the buzz wasn't just a memory, and Syd mentally backpedaled. She so did not need this right now.

"I'm not even going there," Syd said flatly.

Emmett gave her a look as if she could feel the change in temperature and shifted the conversation. "So, where are you living?"

"In the Northeast," Syd said, her breath easing as the quagmire of unwanted emotions receded. "About five minutes from Franklin."

Emmett whistled. "That's going to be quite a haul down here every day."

"I know—we might have to do something about that." Syd sighed. "It was great…before. At least our landlord isn't much of a stickler for leases. We can probably give notice anytime if we ever get a chance to look for another place."

"I'll keep my eye out," Emmett said. "This time of year a lot of places open up in the neighborhood. An advantage to not being right in the city. But with a new crop of interns showing up soon, you'll have to move fast."

"Thanks, I appreciate it." Syd hesitated. Maybe getting Emmett involved with anything personal was a bad move. On the other hand, they *were* probably going to have to move. And trying to keep Emmett at a distance was hard enough when it wasn't something harmless like this after all. "We'll need a place big enough for the three of us."

Emmett treaded carefully with every word. Syd was finally talking to her, but teasing anything non-work-related out of her was tougher than finding water in the desert, and she didn't want to go too quickly. Still, curiosity was gnawing at her. Syd had walked into her life out of nowhere and opened a chapter in her past that had never been properly closed. Questions lingered along with regrets and a good bit of being pissed off too.

Right now, though, she was just enjoying talking to her. That instantaneous connection, the shared humor and understanding that didn't require explanation, had been the first thing that had drawn her to Syd. That and the feeling Syd was a kindred spirit—someone who loved the challenge of surgery as much as she did, someone who wanted to excel, a competitor and a colleague all rolled into one.

When she'd met Syd, the future had seemed so clear. She'd been so sure she'd end up at University and Syd would be there, a year ahead of her, someone to share the good and the bad with. When the connection had gone from conversation to physical intimacy almost faster than she'd been able to absorb, she'd been sure they would share much more than just their love of surgery. Then Syd had disappeared, and Maguire had tempted her with the program at PMC, and all of a sudden, she hadn't wanted to end up at University. She didn't regret her decision to rank PMC first, not for a minute, but now that Syd was here, she remembered how it had been...and how it might have been. She would have sworn she'd left it all behind, forgotten about it...mostly. But now, facing Syd, she was scrambling for any little bit of what had been. She kicked herself mentally. She was probably being a fool. In fact, she most definitely was being a fool.

"So you, ah, live with someone?" Emmett asked as casually as she could and braced herself for the reply. After all, almost five years was a long time. Syd probably had a girlfriend. Maybe even a wife. That would be good, right? Chapter closed. Over and done, finally.

"Jerry, Dani, and me," Syd said.

"Residents," Emmett said with a rush of pent-up air.

"Yes. We all started together, and you know how that is. You have to stick together at first because you're all just trying to stay afloat, and then you end up friends, and then...well, you know how it is."

"Right." Emmett gave her a long look.

Syd flushed. She hadn't meant to say so much. Emmett knew she'd started somewhere else before Franklin, that interning with Dani and Jerry hadn't really been her first time. And Emmett knew she was avoiding talking about it. She hadn't meant to reveal anything at all, and now she'd left openings for places she didn't want to go.

"There's the chief," Syd said gratefully as Quinn Maguire, Honor Blake, and a teenage girl in a dark blue T-shirt and martial arts pants came through the ER entrance. A bloodstained four-by-four was taped to the girl's forehead, and her left upper eyelid was almost swollen closed. Maguire had one hand on the shoulder of the teen, whose red-blond hair and deep brown eyes were a carbon copy of Honor Blake's. No question about that relationship.

Emmett picked up her pace, and Syd followed just half a step behind. This wasn't an ordinary ER consult. The three of them were clearly a family. Maybe Maguire didn't want anyone else there. After all, she'd called Emmett directly, and no matter what Emmett said, Emmett was clearly Maguire's guy.

"Hey, McCabe," Quinn said, "Arly here took a chunk of wood to the forehead. She's got a pretty good laceration and some debris that needs cleaning out."

Honor added, "She's going to need some sutures."

Emmett looked from Quinn to Honor. "You want me to get plastics?"

"No reason," Honor said.

Syd was impressed. Most parents, doctors or not, freaked out when their kids had facial lacerations. Even though the face healed better than any other part of the body and, in all but the worst cases, healed without too much scarring as long as the closure was clean and well aligned and the proper sutures were used. Of all the areas of the body, the face was the most forgiving. Still, any injury that might potentially leave a scar no matter how faint, especially to a girl—even though she'd never understood why that made a difference—was cause for frantic anxiety. Maguire and Blake had to be a little worried, but they didn't show it.

Everyone looked at Emmett, who took a step forward and held out her hand to Arly.

"Hey, Arly. I'm Emmett McCabe. I met you a couple times at the barbecues."

The girl smiled briefly and shook her hand. "I remember. You were a pretty awesome volleyball spiker. I think you almost nailed Quinn a couple of times at the net."

Emmett blushed. "Yeah, not intentional, I swear."

"So it's not a big deal. Just a scratch." Arly shot Honor and Quinn a look Syd had seen on a million teenagers that said, *My parents are making a big deal out of this, and they're embarrassing me.*

"Probably," Emmett said easily. "How about I take a look so you can all get out of here."

"Yeah," Arly said. "That's a plan."

Any lingering anxiety vanished as Emmett effortlessly connected with the teen. Emmett was good, very good, just as Syd had known she would be. All of a sudden, Syd wanted to be anywhere else.

"Well," Syd said quietly, "I don't think you need me here—"

"It's fine," Quinn said. "Maybe you could give Emmett a hand..."

"Of course," Syd said quickly. If Maguire wanted the full VIP treatment, she'd get it. Besides, Arly was a neat kid, and this time, she didn't mind playing assist to Emmett. Better that than suturing up the chief's daughter.

"I'll get her signed in." Honor touched Arly's cheek. "I'll be there in a few minutes."

"I'm fine, Mom," Arly said, just barely hiding her obvious affection beneath a patina of boredom.

"Hey." A very pregnant blond nurse in a powder-blue smock hurried over. "What are you guys doing here? Arly, what happened, baby?"

"I'm cool, Linda," Arly said. "Stupid board split weird and a chunk hit me in the head during my test."

"Oh, for God's sake." Linda shook her head. "And here I thought somebody got to you while you were sparring."

Arly looked affronted. "Are you kidding me? Nobody hits me in the face when I'm sparring." Arly caught Syd's questioning look. "Junior black belt test. I rocked it. Well, I was rocking it until that stupid board cracked in a million pieces."

"Hey, that's great," Syd said. "I didn't get to test until I was sixteen, so I never got my junior rank. You're what, fifteen?"

"Fourteen," Arly said. "Almost."

Quinn squeezed Arly's shoulder. "Quick learner."

Syd laughed. "Obviously."

"So do you still train?" Arly asked, her injury clearly already forgotten.

"Not as much as I'd like anymore. I don't have as much time."

"The dojo's only ten minutes from here. Maybe you could come by."

"Maybe." Syd glanced at Emmett. "I'll find us an empty cubicle and get set up."

"Thanks," Emmett said. "Could you grab some—"

"Three-oh Vicryl, six-oh Prolene?"

"Perfect."

"Hey, Arly," Syd said. "Do you want to come with me?"

"Sure."

Emmett hung back a few steps while Syd and Arly went ahead to a treatment cubicle. She lowered her voice and said to Quinn, "Her lid's pretty swollen. Do I need ophtho to check her eye?"

Quinn shook her head. "No. She had protective eyewear on for the board break." For an instant, she closed her eyes and let out a long breath. "We dodged a bullet, I think."

"I can get plastics here in fifteen minutes," Emmett said again. She had no pride in a situation like this. Whatever made the parents feel most comfortable was fine by her.

"Nervous, McCabe?" Quinn said.

"No. But you know…face and all."

"It's a straightforward linear laceration. Deep, but everything's favorable. Besides, I wouldn't let you do it if I didn't know you'd do a good job."

"Thanks."

"Great. Arly is a champ." Quinn clapped her on the back. "Just tell her everything you're going to do before you do it, and she'll be fine. So you good?"

"I'm good." As soon as she said it, Emmett realized she really was. She felt good in a way she hadn't in a long time. That was weird, but what the hell, why question it. "I better get going before Stevens steals my case."

Quinn laughed.

CHAPTER THIRTEEN

Need me in there?" Linda called as Emmett and Quinn walked toward the treatment cubicle.

"Nope, we're good," Emmett said.

"Great." Linda paused, put a hand on her lower back, and grimaced. An instant later she strode briskly in the direction of the ER admitting area. "I've got a boatload of walk-ins to get processed. Yell if you need anything."

"Will do." Emmett pulled the curtain aside, looking after Linda. "I thought she was a flight nurse."

"She is," Quinn said. "Honor grounded her until after the delivery." She smiled at Arly. "Doing okay?"

"Yep." Arly shifted and peered past Quinn. "Where's Mom?"

"Paperwork."

"Oh."

Syd had already opened the suture tray, and Arly sat half propped up on the stretcher, a sheet pulled up to her waist, her hands folded in her lap. She looked totally comfortable. Syd had removed the gauze covering Arly's laceration too. A couple of inches above her left eye, a three-inch horizontal gash ran across the center of her forehead. The wound wasn't bleeding now, but as Quinn had said, it was pretty deep. Quinn had been right about it being favorable too—the laceration couldn't have been in a better spot or orientation to heal with minimal scarring. The knot of tension in Emmett's midsection eased a fraction.

"We can wait for your other mom," Emmett said.

Arly shook her head. "She'll be here."

"If you're sure," Emmett said.

"Totally." Arly sounded calm and cool. Then she frowned. "My only *real* problem is, I didn't get to finish my test. I could have." She shot Quinn a half-wounded, half-affronted look. "But Quinn wouldn't let me."

Quinn leaned against the wall just inside the door. She shook her head, clearly unfazed by Arly's outrage. "Arly, you'd have had a hard time sparring with blood running in your eye."

"It wasn't bleeding that much."

"Didn't have to be," Quinn said. "Blood means you're done. You know the rules."

"Yeah," Arly sighed.

"Okay, you're going to want to hold still a second," Syd said. "I want to put some Betadine around the laceration so Emmett can get started. This shouldn't hurt." As she worked, she added, "No point giving your sparring partner an advantage, you know. Especially during your black belt test."

"I suppose." Arly was silent for a second. "Okay, yeah. I get it. But I could have—"

"You can test again in two weeks," Quinn said.

"Are you sure?"

"That's what Sensei said, right?"

Arly angled her head to stare at Emmett. "The stitches will be out by then, right?"

Emmett pulled on gloves. "Long gone."

"Here you go," Syd murmured, handing Emmett a syringe with a twenty-five gauge needle attached. "One percent lidocaine with epi."

Syd indicated the bottle on the counter and Emmett leaned down to check the label. She'd seen even the best of them grab the wrong drug in an emergency, and if she hadn't drawn a medication up herself, she always double-checked. Because if she administered it, she was responsible. No one else.

"Hey, Arly," Emmett said. "Are you allergic to anything?"

"No."

"Have you ever had lidocaine before? It's—"

"A local anesthetic. Yup. Once." Arly grinned at Quinn. "That's how my parents met."

"Is that right?" Emmett carefully did not look at Quinn. This could get embarrassing fast. "I'm going to inject this now. It might sting for a couple of seconds." As she started to infiltrate the edges of the wound, she said, "So what happened—the first time?"

"I had another cut on my face."

Arly didn't even wince as Emmett moved from the edges of the laceration into the deeper tissues. Quinn was right—she was a champ. A half-inch splinter of wood was immediately visible buried in the subcutaneous layer, but otherwise the wound looked clean. When Emmett was done injecting the local, she capped and handed the syringe to Syd, who disposed of it. "Thanks, Syd…if you want to head out—"

"That's okay," Syd said quietly. "I'll stay."

"Thanks," Emmett repeated. Syd didn't need to stay, and she certainly wasn't getting anything out of assisting on something as simple as closing a laceration, but it was nice having her there. Emmett felt comfortable doing what she was doing, but still, Arly was a VIP patient. Her parents couldn't get any more VIP. Maybe Syd knew she'd be a little nervous, even if she'd never let it show.

"So Quinn sewed you up then, right?" Emmett asked, hoping to distract Arly as she slowly extracted the sliver of wood.

"Yeah—hey, is that the wood?"

So much for distraction. Emmett held the mega-splinter up between the forceps. "That's it."

"Just in time," Honor said from the doorway.

"Wow, Mom," Arly said. "Pretty cool, huh?"

"Oh, totally." Honor lasered in on Emmett. "Did you get it all?"

"I'm going to check again, but it looks like it." Inwardly, Emmett smiled at the first sign of a nervous parent. Honor and Quinn were both doing really well, considering nobody liked to see their kid hurt, and two docs used to handling emergencies themselves must be struggling not to take over. She cleared away the small bit of clot from the depths of the wound and carefully checked for any other slivers of wood.

"Just that one piece," she said, looking from Arly to her parents. "Everything is clear. All we have to do now is put in a row or two of stitches, and you're outta here."

"So anyhow, Quinn fixed me up last time," Arly went on, obviously warming to her story, "and my mom fell for her right away."

Quinn coughed.

Honor laughed. "I think that's probably TMI, baby."

Arly grinned, and despite the fact she was practically a carbon copy of Honor in looks, there was something about the grin and the glint in her eye that reminded Emmett of Quinn. Emmett caught Arly's eye and raised a brow. Arly looked pleased with herself.

"Sparring then too?" Emmett tied the first suture and Syd leaned in and cut for her. Med student work, and Emmett appreciated again that Syd'd hung around. Anyone else, she might've thought they were trying to score points with the chief, but she couldn't imagine that was Syd's style. She was just doing it to be nice, or maybe…Maybe she wanted to hang out with Emmett. Emmett's stomach tightened at the thought. Maybe?

"Soccer," Arly said.

"Huh?"

"I got hurt playing soccer." Arly laughed. "Then Quinn started coaching our team so she could see my mom—"

"Hey, Arl," Quinn said, "it's not too late for us to sign you up for summer camp in Canada, you know."

"Yeah, okay," Arly said with an exaggerated sigh.

"Okay," Emmett said, straightening. "All done. I'm going to put some Steri-Strips on this which you should leave in place…" She glanced at Honor and Quinn. "Well, I guess you know what to do with that."

"We'll take it from here," Honor said, squeezing Arly's foot beneath the sheet. "Thanks."

"No problem." Emmett smoothed out the last Steri-Strip, wrapped up the instrument tray, and took off her gloves. "If you need me to check it again for any reason, just let me know."

Arly swung her legs over the side of the stretcher, preparing to jump down, and Quinn stepped in, murmuring, "Take it easy."

"I'm good," Arly said, but she put her hand on Quinn's and eased off the stretcher. Quinn's arm came around her shoulders, and for just a second, Arly leaned into her.

Emmett stopped at the nurses' station to write up her part of the chart, and Syd joined her.

"Nice kid," Emmett said.

"Yeah, she's super."

"Thanks for hanging around. I appreciated the moral support."

Syd leaned her arm on the counter and gave Emmett a look. "I doubt you needed it."

"You know how it is with patients like that. Talk about doubling up. Double the pressure, more like it."

"Oh, I know," Syd said. "I had the chief of medicine in the ER one night with a lacerated tendon. He was chopping carrots, slipped, and cut a distal flexor tendon."

"Oh, man. At least it wasn't the chief of surgery."

Syd rolled her eyes. "You'd have thought it was. I mean, I get it. Nobody wants to have a finger out of commission for six weeks, but by the time I was done repairing it, I had half the hospital in the room."

Emmett whistled. "You did it in the ER?"

"I got lucky—I could see both ends. I called the hand guy who was covering that night, and he was tied up at another hospital and told me to go ahead."

"Nice," Emmett said. "Nothing better than being handed the reins by an attending. Guy do okay?"

"He did. Believe me, I was following him through rehab every step of the way."

"Well, this was nothing to that."

"Hey, kids are tough, awake like that. No matter how together they are." Syd shook her head. "And with both parents in the room, both of them emergency docs? Least I could do was to make sure you didn't get into trouble."

Emmett laughed. Syd was actually teasing her. After the day they'd spent circling each other, she felt as if she'd just run a track full of hurdles and was crossing the finish line. Pleasure zipped through her. "Oh, right. Because, you know…putting in a couple sutures is so challenging."

"In a kid, sure can be. Maybe you should think of peds surgery," Syd said, then throttled it. What the hell was she talking about? She didn't need more competition. "You were really good with her."

"I thought about it," Emmett said. "I really like kids. But the parents…" She waggled her hand. "They can be hard to deal with. So no."

"You're right about that." Syd understood that all too well.

"Oh," Emmett said, scrawling her e-sig on the tablet, "and when you get the young ones, the babies, and you know they're not going to make it? Nope, I don't want to have to deal with that all the time."

A chill spread through Syd's chest. A cold so deep for an instant she couldn't move. "Yeah, well, part of the job. Right?"

"I guess," Emmett said, closing the chart. "Anyhow, I'll stick to trauma. What about you, where are you going after next year?" Emmett asked casually since every time she probed even a little bit, Syd closed the door on her.

"I don't know," Syd said. "I haven't quite decided. Maybe trauma."

"Huh," Emmett said, trying to look unfazed, "really."

Syd laughed. "No. I like the rush, but I don't really want to spend my life putting in chest tubes and taking out ruptured spleens."

"Come on," Emmett said in mock outrage. "We do more than that. Ruptured aortas, emergency trachs, bowel injuries. Plus, the resuscitation and—"

Syd held up a hand. "You don't have to sell me."

"Not to mention pericardial windows," Emmett said, taking a chance that Syd wasn't still ticked off about her taking that case in the morning. Not that she'd actually taken it. It had been handed to her, after all.

"Yeah," Syd said archly, "but while you were making a teeny little hole in the belly, I was *drilling* one in the skull."

Emmett smiled. "Yeah, that was cool."

Syd nodded thoughtfully. "Yeah, it was."

"So," Emmett said, "you heading home now?"

Syd sighed. "I guess I better. I'm on call tomorrow night, and I should probably get out of here for a little while."

"I'm about an eight-minute walk from here," Emmett said carefully, picking her way through a minefield. "I've got a car. I can give you a ride home."

"Oh," Syd said quickly, "that's really nice of you, but—"

"You do realize you're nowhere near the subway line, right? You'll have to grab a bus to get there?"

"On second thought," Syd said, "a ride sounds perfect."

❖

After Emmett dropped her off, Syd was too wired to sleep. The trip that had taken her, Dani, and Jerry almost an hour during morning rush-hour traffic had sped by in less than half the time after nine at night. Emmett had been strangely quiet the whole ride and let her out in front of her house with a quick *see you in the morning*. A second later she was gone. Syd was grateful she hadn't had to say much. Emmett had an almost mystical ability to get her talking about things she rarely thought about, let alone spoke of, without her even knowing she was going to say anything at all. She chalked her inattentiveness up to the crazy events of the day, certain she'd have a better handle on things in the morning.

When morning arrived a little after four on the heels of uneasy sleep and tangled dreams, grumpy didn't begin to describe her mood.

She walked into the bathroom she shared with Dani and turned on the shower, resolved to stop worrying about Emmett and to concentrate on getting herself and her fellow residents back on track.

As the warm water sluiced over her face and down her shoulders, she admitted that might be easier said than done. Every time she let the weariness sneak in or relaxed her guard just a tiny bit, Emmett seemed to slip past her barriers. The past-Emmett and the present-Emmett blurred into one, no matter how many times she told herself they were completely different people, just like she was. She didn't need that kind of distraction at work, and she definitely did not need the encroachment of the past into her life now, not after she'd so carefully and consistently shut it down.

She twisted off the water, stomped out, and grabbed a towel. "Done," she muttered. "Done with thinking about what's over and done, and done with thinking about Emmett McCabe." She stared at her face in the mirror and pretended she didn't see the shadows under her eyes. Slightly bedraggled and definitely not at her best. She narrowed them and glared. "You've been through all this once, and that was enough. Hear me? Done."

"Hey!" Dani called from the other side of the door. "Did you score already?"

"What? No!"

"Then who are you talking to?"

Syd wrapped a towel around her torso and opened the door. "Myself. What if I had been in there with someone?"

"I would have opened the champagne, because it would have been like the first time ever."

"We don't have any champagne," Syd grumbled, refusing to let Dani draw her into another conversation about the state of her nonexistent sex life. She twisted around Dani and hurried down the narrow hall to her room. Dani trailed along and waited in the doorway while Syd pulled on faded navy Franklin sweats and a matching tee.

Syd eyed her roomie. "What are you doing up so early?"

"Hungry," Dani said. "That burger was, like, a year ago."

Syd shook her head. Of course. "So are you cooking?"

Dani grinned. "There's cereal."

"Tell me it isn't Cap'n Crunch."

Dani's grin widened. "Nope. I'm on a health kick. It's Grape Nuts."

Syd made a face. "I'm not eating that stuff straight out of the box. And we probably don't have any milk."

"I think there might be pizza," Dani said as they walked downstairs to the kitchen.

"Please." Syd set up the coffeepot, and the promise of caffeine lightened her mood enough for her to feign civility. "How'd the case go last night?"

"It was fun." Dani swung her way onto the counter, settled in with a box of cereal between her knees, and methodically poked handfuls into her mouth.

Syd winced and tried not to watch. She found the remains of a loaf of bread in the refrigerator and made a slice of toast. She checked the half-empty jar of jam and decided since she couldn't see anything white or green on the surface it was probably okay. Pulling out a chair at the table, she sat down to eat. "Who did you make an enemy of?"

Dani made an innocent face. "I have no idea what you mean."

Syd snorted. "Whose case did you steal?"

"Oh. Sadie's."

"That's a way to win friends and keep your service happy," Syd commented.

"Sadie," Jerry said, walking into the kitchen looking like Syd's twin in his Franklin sweatpants and T-shirt. "She's hot."

Dani laughed. "Trust me, bud, you do not want to go there."

"Why not?" Jerry stuck his hand into Dani's cereal box and managed a handful before she pretended to yank it away.

"Because"—Dani held up a finger—"one, she's a right royal... witch, and"—holding up a second finger—"two, she's got a thing going for Emmett McCabe."

Syd coughed on a bite of toast that went down wrong and hurried to get a cup of coffee to hide her outburst. Zoey and Sadie. Emmett got around. Maybe their brief affair had just been one of many.

"Not what I heard," Jerry said. "The thing with McCabe is a flameout. Besides, Sadie's bi."

Syd turned with her coffee and leaned against the counter, feigning casual she didn't feel. "And how do you know all that?"

Dani smirked. "I overheard one of the OR nurses talking about Sadie and McCabe."

Jerry shrugged. "One of the PMC guys told me."

"Really, Jer?" Syd said. "You've been bonding with the *guys* by discussing the female residents and who they're sleeping with?"

Jerry looked from one to the other. "And you two haven't?"

Dani and Syd spoke simultaneously. "Of course not."

"Don't worry, I never talk about you two."

"Not if you want to live," Dani muttered.

Jerry laughed, poured coffee into a travel mug, and headed for the hall. "Gotta shower. Be ready in ten."

"So," Dani said, fixing her own coffee. "You believe it? About McCabe and Sadie?"

"Don't know, don't care," Syd said. "All I care about is getting the cases I need and staying far away from everybody else's drama."

"Good luck with that," Dani said.

Syd didn't need luck. All she needed was to remember what she'd worked for, for the last five years. She pitched the dregs of her coffee in the sink. "See you at the car."

Chapter Fourteen

Syd's decision to keep her conversations with Emmett McCabe limited strictly to surgery, to focus on the present and leave the past where it belonged, really wasn't all that hard to do when she was too damn busy for the next few weeks to do anything but work. Every surgery resident from intern on up recognized the new order of things, and a not-so-subtle pervasive aura of competition permeated every encounter. Residents ignored the hundred hour per week limit, stayed well past their in-house on-call time, haunted the ER and trauma admitting area trolling for new cases, and scrambled to be the best informed on rounds and in the OR.

Syd got to the hospital before five every morning, and even Dani, who was a master at sleeping until the last possible moment, wasn't complaining about leaving the house at the butt crack of dawn. Dani and Jerry were just as determined as Syd to outperform their PMC counterparts. Syd doubted she actually *could* outperform Emmett, but she was going to be damn sure she wasn't in her shadow. They were both fourth years, and maybe Emmett's experience with tertiary referral cases and major traumas surpassed hers, but she'd done more cases overall. She had the numbers, and she had the advantage in OR experience.

Her days settled into routine, as much as anything about surgery could be routine. She met Morty in the ICU at five and reviewed the a.m. vitals, overnight labs and X-rays, and notes from consulting services involved in her patients' care. If new problems had arisen during the night, she made sure Morty had ordered appropriate follow-up tests. Then she paged Hank for floor rounds. Hank turned out to be a sweetheart and a smart student, and even though she didn't really need to see the stable patients before rounds with Emmett, she liked teaching

Hank and he was super grateful. Med students were like puppies. Willing to do anything for attention and eternally bonded to their pack leaders. Training a med student guaranteed she'd have a resident who would have her back for life.

She made sure to stop by the OR and double-check the board for any after-hours add-ons or cancellations before heading to the cafeteria. Emmett would decide who scrubbed on which cases, but she wanted to make sure she was up to speed on all of them. By the time she, Morty, and Hank met Emmett in the cafeteria for formal rounds at six, the service was buttoned up. So far, Emmett had been fair in the allocation of cases, even though she could have taken all the majors for herself.

Today they only had two cases scheduled, and Syd was hoping Emmett would offer her a choice, as she sometimes did. She wanted to get in on the exploratory laparotomy scheduled for ten. The patient had been showing signs of sepsis and they'd ruled out everything except possible small bowel ischemia. With the rising white count, persistent fevers, and a suspicious collection on the abdominal CT, Quinn had decided to take a look. It was the kind of case where anything might happen—a gangrenous gallbladder, perforated small intestine, an abscess from almost any source.

She finished her second coffee just as they ended rounds. Now was the time, before Emmett assigned anyone to the cases.

"Hey, Emmett—"

"So, Syd," Emmett said, looking pleased, "I've got a lead on a place for you."

"Really?" Syd mentally shifted gears. Dani and Jerry agreed moving was a good idea, but no one had the time to look for a place. Syd was more than ready never to ride down Broad Street with Dani at the wheel again. For some weird reason, she still wasn't sleeping very well, and the transportation situation was getting to be a real problem for all three of them. They were rarely ready to leave the hospital at the same time, and with only one car, she and Jerry were often left spending the night in the hospital or braving the subway system in the middle of the night. Neither one of them liked doing that.

"Right about now, I'd be willing to live in a trailer." Syd narrowed her eyes. "It's not a trailer, is it?"

Emmett laughed. "No, but…"

"But what?"

"Well, I don't know how much you've seen of the neighborhood around here, but a lot of places are twins, you know, connected?"

Syd frowned. "I know, same for the Northeast. Why?"

"Because the place that's opening up is the other half of the house where I live."

Syd carefully put down her coffee. "Where you live. With Zoey and..."

"And me," Hank chimed in eagerly. "That would be so cool."

"Right. So cool." Syd pressed her lips together. So, so not cool.

"Well, I know the landlord hasn't listed it yet, so," Emmett said, "if you're interested..."

No. No way did she want to live practically in Emmett McCabe's lap. No, no, and no. Syd swallowed. "I'll talk to the others as soon as I can and let you know."

"Sure," Emmett said a little hesitantly, as if she'd expected Syd to be a lot happier than she appeared to be.

Any other time, Syd would be ecstatic someone else had done the legwork. Dani and Jerry would be too. A place within walking distance, big enough for all of them, would be perfect. Except for that one little glitch. Attached twins weren't known for their soundproofing. She could just imagine sharing a common wall with Emmett and Hank and Zoey. Emmett and Zoey. No, no, definitely not. But it wasn't fair to Dani and Jerry to just dismiss it out of hand, either. She didn't really even have to ask them. If they could afford it, they'd definitely want it. So was she going to hang her friends up just because she might possibly overhear a strange noise and imagine something that might not even be happening? She wasn't given to flights of fancy. It wasn't as if they'd all be sharing backyard barbecues or anything. God, she hoped not.

"Really, thanks," Syd said, trying to sound more enthusiastic.

Emmett's pager sounded and she checked it. "Hold on everybody, that's the chief." She dialed an extension and waited a couple seconds. "McCabe...Morning...Okay, sure...Uh-huh. Right. I'll get someone up there to get him ready."

She ended the call and glanced at Syd. "That was Maguire. The OR just called and they moved up the ex lap to eight opposite the triple tubes. We'll have to cover them both."

"Okay," Syd said. Now she'd probably end up doing the triple tubes, which was really a second year resident's case, but...not her call.

"Why don't I take Morty and we'll do the triple tubes," Emmett said. "You can scrub with the chief."

"Really?" Syd straightened. "Sure. I better head up to the unit and get him ready to go. We saw him on rounds this morning, but I'll check nothing's changed."

Emmett smiled. "Go ahead. I'll be around if you need me."

Syd rose and lifted her tray. "Thanks, Emmett."

"No problem. Hank, why don't you go with Syd."

"Okay," Hank said eagerly and jumped up to join her.

"So," Syd said as she and Hank double-timed through the halls, "what do you think we might find?"

"Well…" Hank launched into a pretty decent differential diagnosis.

"Good," Syd said as she hit the button for the intensive care unit. "Let's say you find an abscess. Then what?"

"Um, drain it, and maybe put in a percutaneous drain?"

"Maybe?" Syd shook her head. "There are no maybes in surgery."

Hank frowned. "Okay. If the bowel's not involved, we leave it alone. If there's perf or a lot of inflammation so that we can't tell, then we do a proximal colostomy to divert."

"Good," Syd said. "So you're sold on surgery next year?"

"Totally."

"Any thoughts about what you're going to do?"

"I was thinking I'd stick with general. I kinda like doing a little bit of everything." Hank paused. "What do you think?"

"It's a good plan. You can always change your mind and think about a fellowship halfway through." She grabbed the patient's chart from the rack. "And you're staying here, right?"

He grinned. "Well, yeah. That's the plan."

"Well, yeah." Syd laughed.

A moment later Maguire came in.

"You scrubbing in, Stevens?" Quinn asked.

"Yes. His latest H and H is ten and thirty-one. White count eighteen thousand. Platelets were normal this morning. Lytes looked good."

"How about his blood gases?" Quinn frowned as she swiped through the patient's records. "His last chest X-ray looked a little cloudy on the right side."

"He had a repeat portable scheduled for this morning. I haven't seen that yet. His blood gases were normal, though."

"Hank," Quinn said, "head down to X-ray now and dig out that film. Bring it up to the OR with you."

"I'm on it," Hank said and took off.

"I'll see you in the OR," Quinn said.

"Right."

Syd went directly from the intensive care unit to the OR and checked the assigned room. The nurses were just opening the instruments on the back tables. Anesthesia was setting up their med pumps and checking their gas lines in preparation for anesthetizing the patient.

"Are we ready for an eight o'clock start?" Syd asked the circulating nurse.

"We should be," he said, opening a pack of sterile sponges and dropping it onto the scrub nurse's table. Syd waited while the two nurses opened the band holding the stack of sterile lap pads together and counted them individually. The scrub nurse then continued counting the instruments.

"What size gloves do you wear, Doctor?" the circulator asked.

"Sevens, thanks," Syd said. "And our student wears an eight."

"Thanks," he said absently as he pulled gloves and opened them onto the table. He poured sterile saline into two basins and left to get another pack from the autoclave. Syd walked back to the holding area to check if they'd called for the patient.

"We're about to call for him now," the charge nurse in the pre-op area said. "We'll be taking him straight back."

"Okay, thanks." Syd circled back to the ICU to help transport the patient.

By the time Quinn started the scrub, the patient was anesthetized and Syd was prepping the abdomen. When she'd finished draping, she stepped around to the left side of the table, the traditional location for the assistant when the surgeon was right-handed. Quinn would stand on the right-hand side.

Quinn came through the doors, bumping them open with her shoulder and keeping her hands up in front of her so any water would drip off her elbows and not down onto her sterile hands. The scrub nurse dropped a sterile towel over her outstretched arm and she dried off. As she walked to the table, Quinn said, "Stevens, come around to the right."

Syd's heart did a little jog in her chest, but she didn't let her excitement show. She stepped up to the table, Quinn moved across from her, and Hank slid in next to Quinn. The scrub nurse moved her tables up next to Syd where she could pass Syd the instruments with no one in between them. Their shoulders touched. Surgery was an intimate affair.

"Are we ready?" Syd asked.

The anesthesiologist said, "Looking good."

"Midline incision," Syd said, looking up at Quinn.

"Sounds good to me," Quinn said.

Syd held out her hand. "Scalpel."

The scrub nurse slapped the knife handle into her hand. There was nothing quite as exhilarating as the feel of an instrument settling solidly in her palm, of closing her fingers around it and knowing that she now had control of everything that was about to happen in that room. She wouldn't be alone, and she couldn't do it alone, but the first move was hers, and with that, so was the responsibility. She put the knife two inches below the sternum and made the incision down the middle of the abdomen, curving gently around the umbilicus and stopping several inches below. With the sponge in her free hand, she pressed down on the edges of the incision and Quinn did likewise. They applied pressure simultaneously and the subcutaneous tissue parted enough that she could use the electrocautery to cut down through the subcutaneous tissue to the thin strip of dense fascia dividing the column of abdominal muscles. She lifted up with forceps, Quinn did the same, and she made a small incision entering the abdominal cavity. Cloudy yellow fluid immediately seeped out.

"Something's going on," Quinn said, her tone of satisfaction tempered with concern.

"You're right," Syd muttered. No matter what, it couldn't be good. Multiply injured patients were compromised in so many ways. Their immune systems were suppressed, their nutritional status weakened, and their healing abilities diminished. Something like this, an infection that a healthy individual could come back from without serious problems, could turn into a major life-threatening complication in a trauma patient.

Well, not this patient. He was hers now. Syd held out her hand, her eyes on the field.

"Scissors, please." Syd enlarged the incision, opening it wide enough to get the self-retaining retractors in. After that, it didn't take long to find the source of the problem, a large inflammatory mass partially hiding behind the colon.

"That's why we didn't see it at first," Syd grumbled. "It blended in with the colon."

"Probably ruptured at the time of the crash," Quinn said. "What do you want to do?"

"We ought to divert," Syd said immediately, using the suction to evacuate the worst of the infected fluid.

"I agree."

Syd worked quickly and efficiently, appreciating how good Maguire was at assisting. Only an excellent surgeon could make an excellent first assistant, anticipating what needed to be done because they already knew. By the time Syd stepped back from the table two hours later, the patient was stable and her tension gave way to a rush of triumph. She'd made a difference today.

The circulating nurse untied the back of her gown, and Syd pulled it off along with her gloves and dumped them in the receptacles.

"Hank, write up the post-op orders."

"Got it," he said.

"Nice job, Stevens," Quinn said as she shed her gown and gloves.

"Thank you."

"Call me if there's any problem."

"I will."

A second after Quinn left, Emmett stuck her head in the door and scanned the room. When she spied Syd, she entered. "Hey, we just finished over there. Morty did a really good job. How'd things go in here?"

"Fine." Syd filled her in as she helped the nurses move the patient into a bed for transport back to the ICU.

"Wow," Emmett said, lending a hand. "Great case."

"Yeah. It was."

"Listen," Emmett pushed one side of the bed as Syd guided the other through the OR and out into the hall, "we've got a couple hours before clinic and nothing else scheduled until then. How about we take a walk, and I'll show you the house. Then you can, you know, give your friends a better idea what the place is like."

Syd searched for a way to say no. "I should probably stick around and keep an eye on this guy."

Emmett's brows rose. "Why? He's stable, isn't he?"

"Yes, but…"

"The sun is shining," Emmett said in a light teasing voice. Her mouth quirked as if she knew she'd just delivered something impossible to turn down. And she was right too, damn her.

An hour's escape in the middle of the day at the height of springtime?

Syd laughed. "All right, let me just get this guy to the ICU."

"I'm headed over there too."

"Fine," Syd said. A walk in the sunshine in the middle of the day was novel enough to be enticing. The fact that she was going to take a walk with Emmett had absolutely nothing to do with her decision. Not a thing. It was all about the sunshine.

❖

"So," Emmett said as they walked out through the ER into noonday sunshine, "have you had much of a chance to look around the area?"

"No," Syd said. "I haven't really been out of the hospital much since we started."

"Yeah, I kinda noticed that. There seem to be an awful lot of residents around all the time."

Syd laughed. "Uh, yes."

"How's everybody doing?"

"You mean the ex-Franklins?"

"I meant the new PMC people."

Syd smiled. Emmett really was trying. "They're okay. I think the initial nerves are settling down, and the friction has been just the normal kind of personality stuff."

"That's good. There'll always be some people who don't exactly jibe."

"For sure."

Emmett shot her a look. "Problems?"

"No." Syd wasn't going to repeat Dani's complaints of how difficult Sadie was to manage. Smart, Dani allowed, but resistant to authority, especially Dani's. Not a terrible trait in a surgeon necessarily, but a pain in the behind when it was one of your junior residents. Syd wasn't about to mention Sadie by name, though, especially not if Emmett and Sadie had a thing. Had *had* a thing. Past tense. Maybe.

"Are you playing chief resident already?" Syd asked.

"No!"

Emmett's genuine surprise made Syd regret the offhand remark. Snark wasn't her thing. "Sorry. You've been really fair with all of us, and—"

"Hey, Syd," Emmett said, catching Syd's fingers for a second in hers.

Syd's breath caught, and she casually moved her hand away. "Yes?"

"The sun is shining."

Syd laughed, a lightness coming over her she totally did not recognize. What was she doing outside in the middle of the day? With

Emmett McCabe? She had no idea and right this instant she didn't really care. "All right. Next year is off the table."

"Deal."

They covered half a block in silence before Emmett asked, "Did you see the email about the reception thing?"

"I read it this morning," Syd said.

"You're going, right?" Emmett said.

"I was going to ask you if there was any way I could get out of it. Is it like, mandatory?"

"Well, it's out of the ordinary, which means Maguire set it up special. And that means we all better show. Pass the word to your people."

"Okay," Syd said. "I'm on call, though. So maybe—"

"Nope. Maguire has staff covering for us for the night of the reception."

"You're kidding," Syd said. "Staff are staying in house to cover *us*?"

"Yep."

"Wow," Syd said slowly. "I guess it really is mandatory."

"Guess so." Emmett grinned. "We're down this way."

Emmett led her onto a residential side street about seven blocks from the hospital. The houses were mostly attached twins, set a little way back from the sidewalk, most with small front yards, many with low picket or wrought-iron fences. Unlike the Northeast, where most of the trees had died or been removed over the years, this area was bursting with greenery. Maples and oaks and all kinds of shrubs, and azaleas and rhododendrons. Many of the front yards sported flower beds, and gliders adorned quite a few front porches. Children's swings and bikes populated many of the backyards visible down the wide paths between houses.

"It really is pretty here," Syd said.

"Especially in the spring," Emmett said. "It's my favorite time of year."

"Mine too," Syd said.

Emmett paused in front of a three-story Victorian twin painted a light green with pale yellow trim, its wide front porches divided by a low railing in the middle. The house wasn't any different than half a dozen others in the neighborhood, but it was well kept up and Syd liked it immediately.

"So this is it," Emmett said. "We've got the right side. The left side will be empty by the weekend. Med students had it before."

Syd groaned. "I hope they didn't trash the place."

"All girls, so that helps."

"Oh, believe me, I've known plenty of party girls quite capable of leaving a place in shambles."

Emmett grinned. "Is that right?"

That teasing note was back in Emmett's voice again. Syd arched a brow. "I am not speaking from actual personal experience, merely observation."

"Of course."

"I wish I could get a look inside."

"Layout's the same on both halves," Emmett said. "Why don't we go in my place?"

The sun was warm on Syd's shoulders, but that didn't explain the warmth swirling inside her. This was where she said no. She looked at Emmett and said, "Sure."

Chapter Fifteen

S o let me show you the backyard first," Emmett said, pointing down the grass and gravel alley that separated her house from its neighbor. She wasn't in any hurry to get inside, not when the breeze was so fresh, the sun was shining, and Syd was so relaxed. For the last couple weeks, Syd had been distant. More distant than usual, at least. She'd kept Emmett at arm's length since the day she and the others arrived at PMC, but lately their conversations had been strictly about patients. Nothing wrong with that, except the absence of anything else at all was so obvious Emmett kept searching her memory for what exactly she had said or done to push Syd even farther away. She couldn't come up with anything, but she wasn't imagining the no more teasing, no more casual talk of how everyone was doing—or not doing, no more *anything* except strictly what was needed to get the work done.

She missed those few brief moments of renewed connection, when Syd had relaxed and laughed and teased her about being Quinn's guy or accused her of practicing to be chief resident already. She hadn't even known how much she liked it until it stopped. And wasn't that the story of her life where Syd was concerned.

Of course, the obvious reason for Syd's attitude probably had nothing to do with her personally at all. They were competing for the same fifth year spot, and even though they didn't talk about it, Syd had to be thinking about it. *She* was. Maybe that was what all the coolness was about, the ever-present competition. She couldn't change that, but she wished she could. She *wished* she was only worried about Syd passing her by in the race to claim the number one spot—she couldn't really believe Maguire meant them to share it. No, she wished she didn't feel like she was the only one who remembered. The only one who wanted to go back.

"Who cuts the grass?" Syd asked.

The question plummeted Emmett back into the present and she laughed. "The landlord sends somebody around to do it."

"Oh, good," Syd said. "That's not something I want on my to-do list."

"Not into yard work?"

Syd chuckled. "Not hardly. There was one summer I was very into the gardener…"

Her voice trailed off and her eyes cooled the way they did when she didn't want to go wherever her memory had taken her.

"Girl gardener?" Emmett smiled.

"Yes, as a matter of fact." Syd shook her head. "I haven't thought about that in forever."

"First crush?" Emmett knew she was attempting to cross a minefield without a map, but she wanted to know. Wanted to know Syd.

"Not that I realized." Syd tilted her head, studied Emmett as if she was about to say more, then looked away. "It's a pretty nice yard."

And the moment was lost. Syd was back from wherever she'd been. But all the same, Emmett was happy. For a second, Syd had let her close. "Big enough for a volleyball net or something."

Syd gave her a look. "How many times have you put up a volleyball net out here?"

Emmett slid her hands into her pockets and shrugged. "Never?"

"Right. Because if you have time for volleyball, you are definitely not working hard enough."

"I'm very efficient."

Syd rolled her eyes and turned away. After a moment she said, "It's cool that the back porches connect, like in the front. At least there's someplace to sit out and have a beer."

"I do have time for that." Getting Syd to open up was like coaxing a cat out of a tree in a lightning storm—just when she thought she was making progress, Syd jumped farther out of reach. But she was damned if she was going to leave her out on that branch. "Why don't you bring Dani and Jerry around tonight to see the place and we can—"

"Quieter here too," Syd mused. She knew what Emmett was doing, and she could feel herself giving in to the gentle cajoling. Just like she always did when she spent any time at all with Emmett. She couldn't help being friendly, but she had to keep it casual, at least. She didn't need to tell anyone her life story, especially not Emmett. "The place we have now is right off the Northeast Extension, and there's always traffic."

"Not around here. Plenty of people walking around, a lot of people have dogs." Emmett pointed across the back fence and up toward the adjoining yard. "Quinn and Honor live on the street over there. You can actually see their backyard from here."

"Cozy," Syd said a little sarcastically. Everywhere she turned, barriers dissolved. How did anyone have a private life around here? As if anyone ever did in a hospital.

"Hey, it's nice," Emmett protested. "Neighborhoody."

"I don't know about you, but I'm not big on socializing with my attendings. It just feels weird." She wasn't big on socializing with anyone, really. She and Dani and Jerry lived together—that was different. They were family.

"Well, it's not like I'm having dinner with them or anything," Emmett said, "but a couple times a year the chief and Honor have all the residents over. Most of the attendings stop by. And Linda—the ER nurse from the night Arly got hurt?—she's a few more houses down that way."

"I guess this neighborhood is just an extension of the hospital," Syd murmured. Maybe moving here wasn't such a good idea after all. Did she really want to practically live with the people she worked with? Then again, since she rarely left the hospital except to sleep, what did that matter? What she really meant was did she really want to live next door to Emmett and risk bumping into her at all hours. Emmett and... whoever.

Emmett must have sensed her hesitation. "Come on, I'll take you through the house."

Syd checked the time on her phone. Weird, they hadn't been gone that long, but when she was with Emmett she totally lost track of the time. She never did that. "You think we should get back?"

"Nah. We've got at least forty minutes before clinic starts. Plenty of time."

"I want to grab some lunch," Syd said, suddenly wanting to get back to the safety of the hospital. Out here in the sunshine with birds singing and the breeze ruffling Emmett's hair, she felt exposed. She felt...alive. She felt more than she had in a long time.

"We've got pizza left from last night," Emmett said. "I can throw a couple pieces in the oven."

Syd could just say no, and they'd be back at PMC in a few minutes. "What kind?"

"Come on. Pepperoni, of course."

"What, no artichokes with olives and goat cheese?"

Emmett narrowed her eyes. "You're just trying to wind me up now, right?"

"Of course." Syd pivoted and walked toward the front of the house.

Syd's smile had been fleeting, but Emmett caught it, and a little heat stirred in her belly. She almost grabbed Syd's hand and stuffed her fist in her pocket before she blew it. That would be a mistake. She wanted to, though. Syd pulled at her like a wire stretched between them, ratcheting tighter and tighter every time they were near. All she had to do was see her and her heart banged at the inside of her ribs. She didn't want to believe that Syd didn't feel it, but she wasn't twenty-five anymore, and she wasn't that impressionable medical student who was so in awe of someone who'd made it to the next step, who was really a doctor, doing what she wanted to do. She wasn't that woman now, and she hadn't forgotten the ache that had lived inside her for a long time.

"So tell me about the rent," Syd said as Emmett fitted the key into the front door.

Emmett pushed the front door open and told her the details. "You cover the utilities."

"We can cover that," Syd said almost to herself. "And the landlord's decent?"

Emmett smiled. "More than decent. One of the GYN attendings owns the place."

"Wow," Syd said shaking her head. "No wonder no one's trashed the place, then."

"It helps."

The front door opened into a foyer that connected through an open archway on the left to the living room and down the hall to the kitchen in the back of the house. A staircase to the upper floor hugged the wall opposite the living room. Lots of tall windows let in light. The window trim and banisters were all original wood, as was the floor.

"Nice," Syd said.

"I'll put the pizza in before we go upstairs," Emmett said, "and it'll be ready when we get down."

"I feel a little guilty," Syd said.

Emmett paused, her heart suddenly fluttering. "Why?"

"Because I'm not supposed to be having fun in the middle of the day. I feel kind of like this is a jailbreak."

Emmett laughed, only slightly disappointed. If Syd was thinking anything like what she was thinking, she didn't want her to feel guilty for any reason at all. "There's no reason we can't have a lunch break. Plus we're three minutes at a run from the ER. If they needed us right away, it wouldn't take much longer than getting there from someplace else in the hospital."

"I know," Syd said. "I already thought of that. And the trauma alerts are always a few minutes before EMS arrives anyhow. It's just—I think I've forgotten how to have fun."

"It's easy to do."

"Forget?" Syd asked softly.

"Have fun, I meant," Emmett said just as softly. She wanted to add she'd be happy to help Syd remember, but she was back to walking on eggshells again. The invisible wall Syd had thrown up between them was crumbling, minute by minute. She was warring with herself, half of her clambering to be careful, the other half hopping around in celebration. Syd must've been reading her mind, because she suddenly headed toward the kitchen.

"We still ought to get going," Syd said.

"Right." Two steps forward, one step back. Sighing, Emmett followed, praying Hank or Zoey hadn't polished off the rest of the pizza that morning. She sighed in relief when she found three pieces in the box on the bottom shelf. She put them in the toaster oven and leaned back against the counter. Syd glanced around the kitchen with a curious expression. Emmett tried to see it through her eyes. A couple of coffee cups on the counter, no visible cookware. Not even much in the way of dishes in the glass-fronted cabinets. "We don't cook a lot."

Syd laughed. "Really? Don't I remember Zoey saying that one time about it being your turn to cook?"

"Uh...I don't think she meant—"

Syd waved a hand. "Never mind. I got the message."

Emmett froze. Amazing how fast the ice returned. "I don't think you did."

"Emmett," Syd said, "none of my business, okay? It's cool."

"It's not what you think." Oh, man, could that sound any worse? "I mean—"

"Hey, I don't think anything. Can I get a look upstairs? Because I'm ready to eat that pizza, cold or not, and I really do want to get back."

"Sure." Emmett couldn't figure out a good way to explain her relationship with Zoey. Most people didn't get it, and until now, she'd been happy to let them think whatever they wanted. But damn it, Zoey had sent a message and the one Syd had gotten wasn't right. And definitely wasn't the one Emmett wanted Syd to have.

She started up the stairs and paused before she reached the landing. She hadn't noticed it before, but it sounded like the shower was running.

Syd stopped one step below her. "What's up?"

"Someone's in the bathroom. I know it's not Hank, so I guess Zoey's here." Emmett frowned. "That's weird. I didn't think she was on call last night, but she must have been if she's home already."

"We should probably go," Syd said.

"No, it's okay. I'll just show you my room. Hank's is about the same size. Then we'll grab the pizza."

"Okay, if you're sure," Syd said.

"It's no problem. She doesn't bite."

"I wasn't worried about that."

Emmett wasn't altogether certain Zoey wouldn't bite someone, most likely her. She'd mentioned to Zoey the place next door would be empty soon and maybe she'd tell some of the residents about it, but she hadn't actually said who.

"So I'm down here at this end," Emmett said, pushing open the door. Her room was usually neat since she rarely spent time in it. Now that she saw it in daylight, it kind of looked abandoned. Not even a book or empty glass or pair of underwear anywhere.

Syd peered over her shoulder. "Are the other rooms this big?"

Emmett pulled the door closed. "Pretty much. Like I said, Hank's is at the far end and about the same size. We have two bathrooms, which is nice cause the guys can have their own. Zoey's is—"

The door opposite Hank's opened and Zoey walked out in a tank top and panties.

"What the fuck?" Zoey stared from Emmett to Syd, her bewildered expression rapidly turning to annoyance. "Having a nooner, McCabe?"

Emmett flushed. "Hell, Zoey. I didn't know you were here."

"Obviously."

"I was just showing Syd the house—"

"Uh-huh."

The bathroom door opened and a woman Emmett didn't know stepped out, wrapped in a towel and nothing else.

"Oh," the stranger said, taking in the group with an embarrassed smile.

"Hi, Mitchie," Syd said dryly.

"Syd! I mean...Dr. Stevens...uh, sorry!" She jumped back into the bathroom and slammed the door.

Emmett looked at Syd.

"Intern," Syd said.

"Okay." Emmett blew out a breath. "Maybe next time give me a heads-up, Zo."

Zoey jammed her hands on her hips. "I'm not required to inform you who I'm sleeping with. Or when. If you're feeling left out, you're free to pencil me in anytime you want."

Emmett rolled her eyes. She hadn't been sleeping with Zoey lately, but that was never a regular thing for them anyhow. Maybe more regular than lately, but Zoey'd never kept track before. "Come on, Zoey."

Zoey glanced at Syd. "Sorry if this ruined your lunch plans."

"No," Syd said casually. "Not at all. I hope you don't mind if I have some of your pizza. That's all I'm interested in."

Zoey looked from Syd to Emmett. "I'm sure."

Emmett followed Syd's rapid descent down the stairs. "Jeez, I'm sorry about that."

"Not your fault."

Emmett grabbed the pizza out of the toaster oven, snagged a couple of paper plates from the cabinet, and handed Syd her slices.

"All the same to you," Syd said flatly, "I think I'll eat this on the way back to the hospital."

"Listen—"

"Hey," Syd said. "Zoey's house. I don't blame her for being ticked off."

"I was just gonna say, sorry it was awkward."

"It wasn't awkward for me," Syd said, heading out of the kitchen. "Zoey's not my girlfriend."

Emmett hurried to catch up. Great. Just great.

CHAPTER SIXTEEN

Syd used eating her pizza as an excuse not to talk to Emmett about their little run-in with Zoey and Mitchie. She hadn't been kidding when she'd said she was starving, so she didn't feel too guilty about the silence. Still, she made her one and a half slices of pepperoni last almost all the way back to the hospital.

"So what do you think?" Emmett asked when Syd polished off her last bite.

"Decent pizza."

Emmett shot her a look. "Not what I meant."

Syd hadn't thought so, but really—Zoey was not high on her list of people to think about, let alone discuss. Besides, she didn't think much about Zoey's afternoon assignation at all, actually. She'd been immersed in hospital culture since her second year in medical school and could think of half a dozen times when she'd been trying to find her resident, or even one of her attendings, who'd gone AWOL. After repeated pages, they'd show up either a little flustered or, more often than not, slyly triumphant. When time was limited and choices of potential partners restricted to the people you saw every day, relationships or casual hookups were going to happen when and where and with whomever. She wasn't even bothered that Zoey had somehow managed to hook up with one of the ex-Franklin interns so quickly. Zoey was attractive, if you liked long-haired blondes with taunting blue eyes. Syd didn't have anything against sexy blondes. She just tended toward the dark and intense types herself, when she tended in any direction, which hadn't been anywhere at all in a long time.

Probably that's what bothered her more than anything. Not that Zoey was getting some, or even that *she* wasn't, but that she didn't even think about it. Or at least when she did, it was fleeting, and quickly squashed. She'd made such a mess of things from the very beginning, and then what she might've chalked up to simple inexperience had turned into a disaster she still couldn't shake free of.

She didn't care when or with whom Zoey was enjoying some action, but she was curious about one glaring question. Why didn't Emmett get that Zoey was seriously jealous? Zoey so clearly acted as if Emmett was her territory, even when she'd just gotten out of bed with another woman. Syd had nothing against open relationships, either. Simpler in lots of ways for people who didn't have the time and emotional energy to put into a relationship, but if one person had a different view of it than the other, that seemed like a recipe for disaster.

Another sort of disaster she really wanted to stay far, far away from. Which accounted for her lack of any kind of anything, simple or not. Syd realized Emmett was waiting for her to speak.

"Are you talking about Zoey and Mitchie?" Syd slowed as they approached the hospital. No rush now. Their little excursion was just about over.

"Mitchie, huh? So you know her," Emmett said.

Nothing in Emmett's tone hinted at jealousy, and Syd was unexpectedly relieved. "I know Mitchie a little. She was on my service for a month early in the year. She seems smart and pretty steady and that's about all I know about her. I heard she was engaged to one of the other residents. Maybe she still is."

Emmett rolled her eyes. "Zoey does have a way of getting herself in the middle of things sometimes."

"Just to be clear, I'm not interested in getting in the middle of anything, and if Zoey thinks otherwise—"

Emmett held her hand up. "Whoa. You're going in the totally wrong direction. Zoey and I are not a thing."

"I know you say so, but I'm not so sure Zoey feels the same way."

Emmett look honestly befuddled, and Syd had to admit, it was charming. Emmett was anything but naïve or innocent, but sometimes she was maybe just a little bit clueless. That was so surprising and so... *cute*, Syd wanted to reach out and brush her fingers through the dark lock of hair that kept tumbling over Emmett's forehead. And if that wasn't insanity, nothing was. She kept her hands decidedly to herself.

"Zoey and I are friends. She's cool with that."

"Like I said—if you say so."

"Okay then," Emmett said. "If we can stop talking about Zoey, let's talk about the house. Did you like it?"

Knee-jerk was to say no, but Syd couldn't manage it. "I do like the place. I know Dani and Jerry will love it. I have to at least tell them about it before I give you a decision, but I'd say ninety percent they'll want to take it."

Emmett's smile was blazing. "That's great."

Syd shook her head. "I'm not totally sure that's true. Zoey doesn't seem to care much for any of us, and even though I don't expect we'll be sharing potluck dinners, we're bound to run into each other, coming and going. I'm not looking for an uncomfortable situation while I'm sitting out on the porch having a beer. Life is tough enough at work."

"I guarantee it won't be uncomfortable," Emmett said. "Really, you don't know Zoey very well, but I do. She's my best friend. Sure, she runs hot sometimes. She's intense. But she's a good person, and she doesn't have any reason to have anything against you guys. It'll be fine."

Syd had to take her word for it. Emmett wasn't the type to fool herself so badly, even if she might be blind to Zoey's different interpretation of *friend*. The place was perfect for the three of them, and she wasn't about to be scared off from a great thing because Zoey might not want to be besties. "All right. I'll let you know by tomorrow morning at the latest. I just need to track them down and get their go-ahead."

"That's great. I'll call—"

Syd's trauma beeper went off at the same time as Emmett's. She glanced at Emmett as they jogged toward the hospital. Emmett's eyes had taken on that sharp battle glint again. Yes. Their little excursion into the other world was definitely over.

As soon as they came through the ER doors, Honor flagged them over. "A bunch of teenagers were racing ATVs and a couple of them collided. We've got five incoming. Reports of multiple injuries in all five. Peds surgery is on their way." She looked around. "Where's the rest of your—"

Hank and Morty came breathlessly careening around the corner from the opposite direction.

"Here," Morty sang out, pushing his glasses up with one hand and nearly coming to attention. "We're here."

"Good, get geared up. They'll be here in a couple of minutes." Smothering a smile, Honor motioned for her ER residents to follow her out to meet the EMS vans.

"Okay," Emmett said as they all pulled on paper gowns and

disposable gloves. "Honor will triage as they come in—the ER residents will manage airways and cardiopulmonary resuscitation. Syd, Morty… we'll assess the chest and abdomen for surgical trauma. If you find something, get an attending or me. Hank—you're with Morty."

"Right," Syd said as Dani and her junior resident ran in.

Grabbing a gown off a rack as she stormed up, Dani demanded, "Anybody seen Zoey?"

Emmett glanced at Syd.

"Not in the last ten minutes," Syd said. Revealing Zoey's lunchtime activity wasn't going to help anything right now.

"I'm right here," Zoey said from behind Syd.

Zoey must have come in right behind her and Emmett. She'd probably also heard Syd cover for her.

"Great," Dani said, instantly turning to Emmett. "What have we got?"

"Some fun afternoon, huh?" Zoey grinned at Syd.

Syd couldn't help it. She laughed. Zoey did have a way. "Awesome."

❖

Emmett waited just inside the doors. Sirens coming closer announced the imminent arrival of the patients. Quinn wasn't on-site yet, but she wasn't worried. Plenty of help down here if she needed backup. Plus she had Syd. The two of them could handle most anything.

Zoey edged over and whispered, "What the fuck, Emmett? What were you doing at the house with Stevens in the middle of the day?"

"She was looking at the place next door," Emmett said, lowering her voice even though no one could possibly hear them with all the other noise. "How was I supposed to know you'd be there? In bed?"

"I wasn't *in* bed. Not then anyhow. What do you mean, looking at the place next door?"

"Claire and the rest of them are out of there this weekend. Syd, Dani, and Jerry are looking for a place closer to here. I told you I was going to mention the place to some residents."

"You didn't say it was them," Zoey hissed.

"I didn't think I had to." Emmett cut a look in Syd's direction. She didn't appear to be listening. "They'll probably take the place."

"Well, that will be cozy," Zoey said.

"What's your problem with them?" Emmett said.

"I don't have a problem with them. Other than the fact that we have to share our cases with them and do a lot of handholding."

Emmett shook her head. "I don't think that's it. So far there's been plenty of cases for everyone. I haven't seen you sitting around with nothing to do."

Zoey narrowed her eyes. "You haven't seen me at all since the whole bunch of them showed up."

"What? What are you talking about?"

"You're hardly ever home. When you're here, you're too busy for...anything."

"You're kidding." Emmett slowly shook her head. "Are you pissed because we're not sleeping together?"

"I'm pissed because we're not anything anymore."

"Zoey," Emmett said. "That's not true."

"Are you sure, Emmett?" With a shake of her head, Zoey turned away as the first of the trauma patients came rolling through the door.

❖

Syd went to meet the first stretcher as the doors swung wide. Armand fell into line along with the others pushing the gurney.

"Fifteen-year-old, closed head injury, possible C-spine injury, unresponsive in the field," the EMT pushing the gurney called out.

"Airway?" Armand asked.

"Breathing on his own."

Syd quickly listened to his chest and lungs while they were still moving. "Breath sounds are good, heart sounds regular."

"Armand," Honor said, "take him in one."

Syd dropped back as the next patient rolled in. This one was awake and screaming.

"I can't feel my legs. I can't feel my legs." A girl, fifteen or sixteen, long blond hair matted with leaves and mud, writhed against the gurney straps crossing her midsection, her eyes unfocused and wild. "Why can't I feel my legs?"

"Someone page neuro," Honor called. "Emmett—"

"I've got it," Syd said. She couldn't say why exactly, but ever since she'd treated the guy with the head injury with a burr hole in the

ER, she'd been drawn to the neuro cases. She'd scrubbed on a couple and the surgery had been fun, but the surgery was only part of it. The saves. When they came, they felt so fundamental. So…huge.

"Okay—trauma two," Honor said and turned away.

While an ER resident checked the airway and central nervous system status, a med student inserted a second IV line and drew bloods. Syd listened to the girl's heart and lungs.

"Chest is clear," she said.

"BP's eighty," the resident said. "Pulse ox ninety-two."

"Belly feels good too." Syd leaned over until she could make eye contact with the girl. "What's your name?"

Clouded green eyes skittered from side to side. "Why can't I move?"

"You're in the emergency room. You were in an accident. I'm Dr. Stevens." Syd spoke slowly and firmly. "You're strapped down so you won't fall off the stretcher. You're in the emergency room. We're going to take care of you. What's your name, can you tell me that?"

"Cindy. It's Cindy." She sobbed, her gaze slowly settling on Syd. "We crashed, didn't we?"

"Yes, you did."

"I told him to slow down. I told him. Oh my God. What about Kimmie? And Ry—"

"We'll find out about them in a little while. You first." Syd smiled as the girl's frantic breathing slowed. "Good. Cindy, do you hurt anywhere?"

"My back. Somewhere—somewhere in my back."

"Can you squeeze my fingers?" Syd slid her fingers into Cindy's palms. Her grip was weak, but she had shoulder and upper extremity movement.

Syd lightly touched her upper chest. "Can you feel me touch you here?"

"Yes?" Cindy said, some of the fear seeping from her voice. "My fingers are tingly, though."

"Okay, how about here?" Syd asked, slowly pressing points down the center of the girl's body.

"You're not touching me now, are you?" Cindy said.

Syd marked the spot on Cindy's torso where the sensory deficit began. Reflexes and voluntary movement below that level were all absent. She straightened. "Did we hear from neuro?"

"Not here yet. CT's ready for us, though," the resident said.

"I think we should take her down." Syd looked around for Honor or Emmett. Emmett was conferring with Quinn in bay four. Dani and Zoey were doing an abdominal tap in bay five. The curtains were closed around bay three.

"Dr. Blake?" Syd called as Honor strode by.

Honor pivoted in her direction. "Yes?"

"Probable spinal cord injury," Syd said, stepping a few feet away from the bed so Cindy wouldn't hear her. "Looks like high thoracic. She's cardiodynamically stable, but we ought to get the CT as soon as we can."

Honor moved to the side of the bed and listened to the patient's chest before asking her resident, "Signs are stable?"

"No tachycardia. Pressure's borderline low but steady. I'm pushing fluids."

"All right, then take her down," Honor said. "I'll have someone page neuro again."

Syd and the resident transferred all the lines to the portable monitors and pushed Cindy's bed out into the hall and down to the elevators. While they moved, Syd explained the CT to her.

"I'll see you when you're done," Syd said, moving to the booth to observe the scans as they were completed.

"Head and C-spine look good," she murmured as the tech transferred the first images to the monitors.

Kos Hassan walked in just as the CT tech started the spine.

"We meet again, Dr. Stevens," he said. "What have you got?"

"Cord injury from an ATV crash. Looks like..." She leaned forward as the computerized scans of the vertebral bones and spinal cord began to appear on the monitors. She pointed. "There. T4 fracture. The cord's really swollen."

"Hmm." Kos studied the images a few more seconds. "I think that's a hematoma pressing on the cord."

Syd looked at the scan in the area of the fracture again. "I see it. You're right. That's blood, not edema. Damn, I missed that."

"Well, you won't next time. Treatment?"

"Bolus with steroids and get her to the OR. The spine needs to be decompressed, possibly fused, before she loses more function."

"I agree. If we move fast, she may even regain quite a bit. Is the family here?"

"I didn't see anyone yet," Syd said. "What about an abdominal CT?"

"Symptoms?"

"No, but with a cord lesion it might be hard to tell."

"Make it fast."

"I'll let the OR know we're coming," Syd said.

"I'll see about family and meet you there. You are scrubbing, right?"

"Absolutely," Syd said.

Emmett found her at the scrub sinks twenty minutes later.

"Hey," Emmett said. "Heard you were up here. What have you got?"

"Spine fracture with cord compression." Syd kneed off the water and held her arms up, letting water drip into the big stainless-steel sink. "You?"

"Ruptured subclavian artery. Clavicle fractured and tore right through it. Major hemothorax."

Syd pictured the big artery behind the collarbone at the apex of the chest. Really tough place to get to. "You're planning to repair it through an open thoracotomy?"

"Vascular thinks that's the best way to get control. Quinn and I are going to open for them."

"Nice case."

Emmett nodded. "I'm taking Morty. You want Hank?"

"He should stay with you. He might not see another one. What about the rest of the injured?"

"One kid's got a spleen and a liver lac. Peds is bringing him up now too." Emmett grimaced. "The other boy has a brainstem infarct. Hassan said maintain life support for now, but he's not going to recover. Might be a donor harvest by morning."

"Oh, man, that sucks."

"Yeah, especially since he was one of the drivers and the other driver was his brother. They were showing off for their friends, I guess."

Syd could picture it. "Stupid kids. God, I feel old. What about the last one?"

"She got lucky. Two fractured femurs. Ortho's on that."

Syd shook her head. Ironic how the one facing months of pain and rehab was the lucky one. "Sometimes this job sucks."

"Yeah, I know." Emmett hesitated. "Catch you later for a drink or something?"

Syd met Emmett's gaze. The conflict there matched her own—she'd had to learn to accept the excitement of doing a challenging surgery when the reason for that enthusiasm was a tragedy. Sometimes the lesson still hurt. "Yeah, I'll see you later."

CHAPTER SEVENTEEN

The overhead spots glinted off the metallic sheen of the titanium plates and screws spanning the fractures in Cindy's spine. Syd blinked back a bead of sweat threatening to drop from her eyelashes. The tiny drop of salt stung for an instant. Her back ached from leaning over the incision. Sympathy pains, maybe.

"What do you think?" Kos asked.

"I think that's it." Syd's voice sounded raspy. No wonder. No amount of swallowing soothed her parched throat. She'd give a lot for a cold bottle of water. Cold anything, really.

"I think you're right," Kos said. "Double-check that all the screws are tight, and remember, finger tight. That's enough. Don't strip them out of the bone now."

"Okay," Syd said, unable to even contemplate redoing the fixation devices at this point. Her brain felt like oatmeal. If she had to refocus to start the procedure again, bits of gray matter would leak out her ears. But of course she would start again if she had to—adrenaline was a powerful stimulant.

Gingerly, she worked her way up one side of the system of tiny struts they'd attached along the vertebrae to stabilize Cindy's spine and down the other, cautiously setting each screw with a final twist. While she double-checked the hardware, Kos packed bone fragments into the crevices surrounding the fracture sites.

"They all look good." Syd spared her first glance at the clock all afternoon. Six forty. Afternoon had come and gone. She'd been in the OR six hours, but like always, she never noticed time passing when the case was as demanding as this one. She never noticed she was hungry or thirsty. Now that the push was over, she'd feel it.

"How are you two doing?" Kos asked, directing his question to

Dani and Sadie, who were working on Cindy's hip. A little over an hour before, Kos had pulled them in from peds surgery to help out. He'd decided the safest route was to stabilize Cindy's spine with everything they had available, including slivers of her own bone. Her fractures spanned several levels in the thoracic spine, and bone grafts would speed healing. Dani and Sadie had harvested the bone graft.

"We're ready to close if you've got enough bone," Dani said, cutting sutures for Sadie. "How do things look up there?"

"We're good," Syd said. "Thanks for the assist."

"Anytime," Dani murmured.

Kos said, "Okay, Syd, let's close."

Syd irrigated gently, taking care not to displace the bone grafts, and checked one last time for bleeding. When the field stayed dry, she looked over the drapes at the nurse anesthetist who'd taken over at shift change at three. "How's she doing?"

"Pressure's still borderline low," he said, "but vitals are stable."

"Are you going to keep the tube in," Syd said, "until we see how her lung function is post-op?"

"Was planning on it," the anesthetist said.

"Okay then," Syd said. "We'll need about thirty minutes."

"I'll start lightening her up," the anesthetist said.

Kos indicated Syd should close, and she worked quickly, suturing the deep tissue layers over the spine together. When she reached the superficial muscle layer, Kos stepped back from the table. "I think you can take it from here, Syd. My daughter's got a softball game tonight, and I promised I'd be there. I've already missed the opening pitch, but I ought to still catch most of the game. Page me if you need me."

"Okay, thanks." Syd flushed with satisfaction. She'd felt at home doing this surgery, even though she had less experience with neuro cases. The anatomy, the structures, appealed to her. And Kos trusted her to take care of his patient. He wasn't the sort of attending who left his patients at the first opportunity. More important than all of that, she might have given Cindy a chance to regain some of the use of her lower body. Possibly all of it.

"I'll let the family know how's she doing." Kos pulled off his gown and gloves. "Nice job, Syd. Thanks, everybody."

"Thank you," Syd said again.

As he walked out, Dani said, "Sadie, you can give Syd a hand closing."

"Sure," Sadie said flatly, sliding up into Kos's empty place.

Dani dropped out also and quickly stripped off her gown and gloves. "Page me when you're done. We still need to make afternoon rounds."

"Okay." Sadie reached for the retractors but Syd picked them up first.

"Go ahead, Sadie," Syd said, motioning for the scrub nurse to pass Sadie the loaded needle holder. "Three-oh Vicryl on the fascia."

Sadie's eyes above her mask widened for an instant and a second passed. She held out her hand, and the slap of the needle holder into her palm seemed to jump-start her. "Thanks."

They worked in silence, Sadie suturing and Syd cutting for her. Syd was tired, and she didn't know Sadie well enough to chat. Things didn't look as if they'd warmed up much between Dani and Sadie, but Syd had to give Dani credit. She'd let Sadie do the harvest and the two of them had managed to work together pretty seamlessly. Dani was a good teacher, and from what Syd could see from her occasional glance at their field, Sadie had good hands. Not surprising. All the PMC residents were sharp. But then, so were the ex-Franks.

"Let's do a running subcuticular Prolene on the skin," Syd said.

"Staples would be faster," Sadie said.

"I know, but it's a long incision and the scar will be better." Maybe it was the memory of Cindy's terrified voice in the trauma bay or maybe knowing what a long road Cindy had ahead of her even with the best-case scenario, but Syd wanted to at least give her the best scar she could. "You can manage to do it in under half an hour, can't you?"

Sadie snorted. "Like five minutes."

"That's what I thought. Go ahead."

As Syd expected, Sadie quickly and efficiently completed the skin closure. After they'd applied the sterile dressing, Syd said, "Is the bed in here? Make sure there's a gel pad on it."

"It's right outside," the circulator said. The ICU team had sent the special spinal care bed over, making it unnecessary to transfer Cindy more than once.

"Sadie, help her get that," Syd said.

Once Sadie and the OR team maneuvered the bed up next to the OR table, anesthesia took the lead. Syd and everyone else followed his instructions. At this point, the airway was the most important thing to protect. Cindy was not breathing on her own, and if her endotracheal tube became dislodged, she could arrest.

At anesthesia's command, they tilted her onto her side, her back toward the bed, placed a roller board along the length of her body, gently returned her so she was lying on the board, and slid her into the bed. Throughout the transfer, Syd kept a careful watch on how they moved Cindy's legs, hips, and torso to be sure they didn't place undue strain on the spine. Everyone waited while anesthesia double-checked the airway and made sure she was ventilating on both sides. Once he was satisfied, the team ensured all the lines were moved onto the bed and nothing remained attached to the OR table or the IV stands that might be pulled out as they exited.

Syd guided the foot of the bed, Sadie pushed with a hand on the side rails, and anesthesia kept watch on the breathing tube as they pushed Cindy out into the hall. The five-minute trip from the OR to the TICU was as critical as any part of the procedure they'd just performed, and Syd didn't relax until they were inside the unit and the ICU staff converged on the bed.

The anesthetist gave his report and Syd heaved a sigh, the tension draining from her shoulders. Thirty minutes later, she was satisfied that Cindy was stable. She reviewed the post-op orders, took one more look at Cindy, and decided she could actually leave. She was exhausted and exhilarated at the same time. She was also starving.

As she was leaving the unit, Dani and Zoey came in on rounds.

"Hey," Dani said. "You done?"

"Yes. Oh, hey—" Syd hesitated, considering how much she wanted to say in front of Sadie and Zoey. Well, they'd find out soon enough anyhow. "I didn't get a chance to tell you earlier. I think I've got us a great place to live. If you're up for it when you're done, I'll tell you about it."

"How far away?" Dani asked instantly.

"Six-minute walk."

"It's not a trailer, is it?"

Syd laughed. "No, it's a house. Emmett, Zoey, and Hank live in the other half of the twin."

Dani grinned. "Well then, hell, yeah. Because you know, we're all just one big happy family."

Sadie didn't say a word, but her expression suggested she'd like to bite someone. Definitely territorial, although maybe that was more about the ex-Franks moving in than whatever she had—or didn't have—going with Emmett. Zoey was harder to read. She didn't look ecstatic, more calculating, as if she was trying to figure something out. Whatever it was, Syd wasn't going to worry about it. None of the tangled relationships that somehow all led back to Emmett were her concern.

"If you see Jerry, tell him I want to give Emmett a decision by the morning. It's a prime place and we don't want to lose it."

"Hell, Jerry will be fine with it if we are. Say yes," Dani said.

"Okay, I will. I'll text you the address if you want to drive by later."

"You want a ride home? We'll be done here in half an hour or so."

Syd hesitated. She was more than ready to go home. She was off call, her patient was stable, and she'd had one long, hard day. But she'd told Emmett she'd see her later. Then again, Emmett wasn't even around. She could be in the OR doing another case for all Syd knew. She should just go home. "Page me before you go. I'll let you know."

"Sure," Dani said, motioning to the others. "Come on, let's finish up."

Syd headed to the locker room to get out of her scrubs. She had the place to herself while she washed her face and took a minute to repair some of the damage done to her hair by six hours of being stuffed into an OR cap. When she was dressed in jeans, sandals, and a short-sleeved T-shirt, she had no more reason to procrastinate. Leave or... She checked her phone. No text from Emmett.

Emmett was probably in the OR, so involved in some great trauma case she hadn't even thought about Syd at all. Or maybe she'd left. She probably forgot.

Before she could change her mind, Syd rapidly texted, *Still around?*

She got an instant reply.

Just coming to find u. U done?

Yes. Syd paused. Waiting. This was a bad idea, wasn't it?

Still on for a drink?

Syd stared at the screen. Her thumbs moved.

I'm in the locker room.

Don't go.

Syd slipped her phone into her back pocket. Well, decision made. No point second-guessing herself now.

Emmett showed up two minutes later. She'd already changed into tapered navy khakis and a pale blue button-down shirt with the sleeves rolled up. Along with her sockless loafers, she looked downright hot. Syd smiled.

"What?" Emmett said.

"Nothing."

"Come on, something."

"You wore that same outfit for your interview. Do you have anything in your closet besides blue shirts and navy pants?"

Emmett stared, a flush rising in her neck. "How do you remember that? I don't even remember it."

Syd felt an answering blush come over her. What the hell had she just said? "I don't know, I just remembered, I guess."

"Yeah?"

For a second, Emmett looked like she was going to say more, and Syd's stomach tightened. She was tired, tired from the day, tired, she realized, for a long time. She just wasn't ready to do anything about it.

"I think you owe me a beer," Syd said quietly.

"You're right, I do." Emmett let out a breath, some of the intensity bleeding from her gaze. "I was thinking cheesesteaks to go with it."

"Is there actually a decent place around here to get one?" Syd recognized Emmett was backing off, giving her some space. She ought to be happy Emmett was accepting her limits, respecting the boundaries she'd set, and she was. She *was*. She just needed to move. She needed out of the confines of the locker room, out of the hospital. When was the last time she'd really wanted to leave? She pushed out into the hall, Emmett following.

"Believe it or not," Emmett said, holding the stairwell door open for her, "there's a little place a couple blocks over on our way home. Makes great cheesesteaks and pizza. Sound good?"

"Yes." Syd didn't think too long about the idea of home suddenly being the same place for both of them. "Let's get out of here."

❖

"How about we eat out here?" Emmett said as they walked up the flagstone path to the front porch.

"Sure," Syd said. "I've had enough of being inside for a while."

Emmett put the sack of cheesesteaks down on the porch and pulled out one of the two six-packs of local microbrew. She twisted off the cap and handed a bottle to Syd. Even at a little after eight, a bit of heat and light remained, and beneath it all, the scent of spring. The last time she'd been out here like this had been Indian summer, months ago, and she'd been sitting with Zoey then. Fall and winter and early spring had come and gone, and she hadn't even noticed. Maybe she'd missed more than time passing.

"Nice of you to get food for everyone," Syd said.

"It'll get eaten sooner or later. Probably breakfast. Kind of an unwritten rule—anyone who picks up food has to get enough for everyone for at least two meals." Emmett laughed, sipped her beer, and tried to put her finger on the unfamiliar lightness rising in her chest. Contented, that was the word for the peacefulness that lulled her mind into a lazy sort of pleasure. The world had slowed down somehow, and she only noticed now because she was so used to it always going by so fast. "You ever feel like you're always running?"

Syd shifted on the porch until her back was against the white wooden post. Facing Emmett, she stretched her legs down onto the top stair and sipped her beer. Her knee almost brushed Emmett's thigh. "I suppose so."

Her distant expression suggested she was thinking about something beyond the hectic life of a surgical resident, and Emmett wanted to ask. She'd been wanting to ask a lot of things since the moment she'd seen her again, but she never seemed to find the right time. Now wasn't the time either. She didn't want to break their fragile harmony. "You want your sandwich?"

Syd laughed, and her melancholy faded. "Hell, yes."

Grinning, Emmett passed one over. Maybe it didn't matter. Maybe the past was really just best forgotten. She only wished she could. What was it they said, if you didn't understand the past you were destined to repeat it? She never wanted to do that again. She never wanted to be hooked into someone so quickly, so deeply, that when the connection broke, it was like a sharp hook being pulled through her flesh, leaving a raw wound that bled and never really healed. So she needed to be careful. She already knew that. She'd been careful for five years, after all.

"Dani and Jerry are in for the house," Syd said, spreading her paper wrapper on her lap and lifting her steak.

Somehow she managed to eat it without making a mess, something Emmett never really managed. She put hers down on the porch and ate leaning over the paper, hoping to catch the worst of the debris. "That's great. I'll call the landlord and leave a message tonight. Is it okay if I give him your number so he can leave you details about the security deposit and all that?"

"Sure," Syd said. "When do you think we can move in? We'll want to give notice to our property manager. We're month-to-month, and leaving a week or so early isn't going to be a problem."

Emmett laughed. "You really want out of there, huh?"

"It was great when we were at Franklin, but now…" Syd's voice trailed off.

"Are you guys unhappy here?" Emmett hesitated a second. "Are you?"

"You know, I can't speak for everyone, but I think Dani and Jerry feel the same as me. There's opportunity here, but we all feel we're a step behind. Playing catch-up is hard, especially when you're senior."

"I know what you mean," Emmett said.

Syd gave her a long look. "I don't think you do. You're where you wanted to be, and you were Quinn's pick, weren't you?"

"I don't know about it at first," Emmett said truthfully. For some reason, pretending anything at all with Syd felt wrong. "But she let me know pretty soon that she thought I had the chops for trauma. She's never offered me anything or guaranteed me anything, though."

"No, she wouldn't. She's not like that."

Emmett chuckled. "Quinn is…"

"Next to God?"

Emmett laughed. "Maybe."

"Honor's pretty cool too."

"Almost everybody is in love with Honor," Emmett said. "If you mean that way."

Syd smiled. "I can see that."

"Got a crush?" Emmett said lightly.

Syd shook her head. "No, I'd probably be more inclined toward Quinn."

Emmett felt a weird rush of jealousy. As if that could ever be a reality. Still, a surge of competition had the hair on the back of her neck prickling. "Oh yeah?"

"I was speaking hypothetically," Syd said archly. "I don't get crushes on people."

"I'm glad to hear that," Emmett said. She should stop there, but she was tired of stopping. "So it wasn't a crush, back then?"

Syd carefully folded up the paper wrapper and placed it beside her. When she met Emmett's gaze, even in the dim light, Emmett could see the laughter had been replaced by something dark. "You're not going to leave it alone, are you?"

"I can't," Emmett said, desperation curling in her depths. "I just don't understand what happened…to you, to us."

"Emmett," Syd said gently, "we never had time for there to be an us."

The gentleness was almost as bad as the silence. Emmett didn't want pity. She wanted anger or regret or anything that mirrored her own feelings.

"If that's true, then why do we both still hurt?"

"I don't—"

"Hey," Zoey broke in, "there better be enough to go around!"

Emmett jerked and looked down the street. She wasn't really seeing what she was seeing. A whole clump of residents, led by Zoey, streamed up the walk toward the porch. Sadie, Dani, Hank, Jerry, and Zoey. All of them together?

The shift in the atmosphere was immediate. The cocoon of intimacy she'd shared with Syd disintegrated and blew away on the cool night air.

"It just so happens," Emmett said, "we have steaks and beer."

"Which one has onions and mushrooms?" Zoey squeezed in next to Emmett on the top stair and reached for a beer as Hank and Sadie dug into the bag of food.

Emmett laughed. "They're labeled."

Dani and Jerry hung back, and Emmett said, "There's plenty, you guys."

"Thanks." Dani glanced at Syd. "We decided to walk over to check out the place, and we ran into these guys." She tilted her head toward Zoey, Sadie, and Hank. "You were right about it being close. It's great."

Syd stood and leaned against the railing. When Emmett had shifted to make room for Zoey, their shoulders pressed together, and the contact made her uncomfortable. The conversation with Emmett made her uncomfortable. How many times did she have to experience the same thing before she accepted being with Emmett took her places she didn't want to go? "I already told Emmett we were in."

Jerry stood on the path at the bottom of the stairs, half a steak in one hand, a beer in the other, and his head tilted back to survey the house. "It's a nice place. How many bathrooms?"

Syd laughed. "Enough so that we don't have to share with you."

"Thank God," Dani muttered.

"Yes to that," Jerry said.

Zoey glanced at Emmett. "So we're all neighbors now."

"Looks like."

"What about you, Sadie?" Jerry asked super casually. "Are you in the neighborhood too?"

She nodded. "I share a place with a couple other people in my year about three blocks that way." She pointed.

"Nice," he said.

"It's convenient." Sadie perched with one hip on the railing, her beer in her hand.

She managed to be on the outside of both groups, and Syd wondered if any of them were really her friends. She wondered too if Jerry had any idea what he was getting himself into. But not her problem. She watched Zoey and Emmett talking easily together and decided that wasn't her problem either.

"I'll take the ride home, Dani, whenever you're going."

Dani sighed. "Yeah, I know. It's just so damn nice out."

"Spring fever." Syd chuckled.

"Something like that, I guess." Dani's usual high energy was dampened for some reason.

"Well, take your ti—" Syd's phone vibrated and she pulled it out of her back pocket. "Stevens."

"It's Nalini, in the TICU. I know you're not on call, Dr. Stevens, but we can't reach Dr. Hassan, and the resident covering—"

"That's okay." Syd stiffened. "What's going on?"

Everyone went silent, watching her. They all recognized this kind of call.

"It's the spinal cord patient from this afternoon. Her pressure keeps bottoming out, and we've been pushing fluids, but it's not helping."

"Have you checked her H and H?"

"About an hour ago. It's a little lower than right after surgery. The on-call resident said that was just from the fluid push."

"Run another one. What's her heart rate?"

"That's just the thing—it's all over the place. First it's fast, then it's slow. The resident says it's neurogenic shock and just to keep her fluids running."

"Did they come by and examine her?"

"No, she didn't. She said she was tied up in the emergency room."

"All right, I'm coming. Page Dr. Hassan again. He must not have reception. And have the operators call his cell."

"Thank you," the nurse said, her relief obvious.

Syd pocketed her phone. "I gotta go back."

"What's going on?" Emmett asked.

"Problem with the patient from this afternoon. Her pressure's unstable." Syd was halfway down the sidewalk when she realized Emmett was coming with her. "You don't need to come."

"Yeah," Emmett said, "I do."

Emmett might not officially be chief resident yet, but she already acted the part.

CHAPTER EIGHTEEN

"Where's the resident on call?" Emmett asked as they ran. Her tone suggested she wasn't happy.

"Tied up in the ER," Syd said, "and Kos isn't answering. Cindy's hypotensive, and the nurses are worried."

"Who called?"

"Nalini."

"She's good. If she's got a feeling"—Emmett slowed, waiting for the ER auto doors to swing open, and then slipped inside—"I'd take it seriously. Our guys should know that."

"Maybe it's an ex-Frank. That's the downside of us being new here. Damn it—this shouldn't happen." Syd followed Emmett inside. She didn't have time to worry about who might have dropped the ball. Chances were a junior resident without much neuro experience was buried with scut and just came to the obvious conclusion. Patients with spinal cord injuries often had unstable vital signs—traumatized nervous systems were volatile and erratic. The central nervous system regulated everything—breathing, heartbeat, blood pressure—and when damaged, wild fluctuations resulted. But trauma patients often had more than one injury, and sometimes the nerve injuries masked the others. And that was exactly why you needed to be extra-suspicious when something seemed off.

"Doesn't matter who it was now," Emmett said.

Not now maybe, but it mattered. If a nurse called more than once, the very least a resident needed to do was go see the patient or make sure someone else did. Everyone missed things, but you should never miss a problem because you were too damn busy, or too tired, or too lazy to evaluate the patient. Emmett wouldn't let this go, and even if she did, Syd wouldn't. Cindy was her patient.

No one paid very much attention as they half jogged through the halls toward the elevators. Everyone had their own mission.

"Kos said he was going to his daughter's softball game." Syd waited impatiently for the elevator doors to open, stepped aside as a transport pushed out a cart full of supplies, and jumped inside.

"He'd answer his page if he got it," Emmett said, pushing the button for the third floor. "Maybe he's somewhere the cell service is wonky."

"That's what I thought too," Syd said as they turned the corner toward the TICU. For a second, she pictured rushing around another corner and crashing into Emmett, the two of them ending up on the floor with Emmett underneath her. That seemed so long ago now. The shock of seeing her when she'd least expected had made a tiny fissure in the wall she'd created to block out the worst time in her life, and the cracks kept getting bigger day by day. They worked seamlessly together, and when they weren't working, they just…connected. As much as she wished being around Emmett wasn't so easy, right now she was glad for it.

She didn't know the rules here, and no one knew her. She didn't have any power. If she'd been at FHC, she'd be trusted to make decisions in any kind of emergency. Here she might as well be an intern again. That stung, as much as she tried to tell herself that would change in time. She didn't have the time tonight, and if she needed to rely on Emmett's backup to do what needed to be done for her patient, she would. Her pride could hurt later.

The nurse who'd called her was still at Cindy's bedside. Her gaze passed from Syd to Emmett, her relief clear.

"Thanks for coming."

"Sorry it took a while," Syd said. Someone's ass really did need kicking. Patient care was a team effort, and when a nurse or PA or OR tech or fellow resident needed an assist, they ought to get it. Thanks shouldn't come into it. "How's she doing?"

"Her urine output is low, and I still can't get her pressure up." The tight-bodied, thirtyish African American woman frowned. "It probably sounds crazy, but she just doesn't look right to me."

"Doesn't sound crazy to me at all." Syd leaned over the side rail, checking Cindy's pupils. Normal, which she'd expected. Cindy'd had no sign of intracranial injury earlier. If something was going on, it was somewhere else. "Do you have a repeat H and H back yet?"

"Not yet. I sent it as soon as I got off the phone with you. One of the aides hand-walked it down to the lab. I told him to stay there until they ran it."

"Good."

Cindy's blood pressure was running in the eighties, bottom normal. Her heart rate was 110 to 120, her urine output less than 15 cc for the last hour. In any other circumstance, those findings would send up red flags that she was bleeding somewhere, but that could all be due to the cord injury too. Syd listened to her heart and lungs. Nothing there seemed off. When she palpated her abdomen, a chill ran through her. The muscles beneath her hand were distended and tense. She glanced at Emmett, who'd been hanging back, letting her work. "I think something's going on in here. See what you think."

Nalini said, "That's a change. I've been doing neuro checks every hour, and I always do a quick exam. Her abdomen was firm earlier, but not like that."

Emmett scanned the vital signs, listened to Cindy's abdomen with her stethoscope, gently palpated as Syd had done. "She had a CT earlier?"

"Yes. Right before we went to the OR. We didn't see anything."

"Maybe there wasn't anything to see then. We need to repeat it."

"We need to talk to Kos," Syd said, "if we're going to move her down for a CT." She gestured to Nalini. "Has he answered his page yet?"

"No. Do you want us to call someone else from neurosurg?"

Syd hesitated. Another attending wasn't going to know this patient, and she wasn't comfortable talking to someone she didn't know. Another reason why being in a new place was a problem, especially when she needed to make decisions. "Emmett?"

"I think we should call Quinn," Emmett said.

"If there's something going on in her abdomen," Syd said quietly, "that makes the most sense. If it's neurogenic shock and the CT of her abdomen is normal, we can go to pressors and push fluids. But if there's a bleed or perforation, we'll have to open her belly." Syd nodded, the plan unfolding and her uneasiness fading. "Nalini, page Dr. Maguire."

"Right away."

Emmett said, "I'll call CT and let them know we might be coming down."

"What if we can't get Quinn?" Syd said, stepping to the door and lowering her voice. Cindy most likely couldn't hear her, but who knew for sure? And besides that, she didn't want to advertise they were flying solo here.

"Your call," Emmett said.

"We'll take her to CT anyhow," Syd said instantly, "and notify whoever else is on call for neuro when we get down there."

Emmett grinned. "I like it."

❖

Arly countered the back fist coming at her chin with a forearm block, pivoted on her right heel, and whipped a high head kick as she spun in a fast, tight circle. Her opponent, a twenty-year-old male black belt, managed to partially deflect the blow, but his balance was off when he stepped back and he couldn't block the follow-up straight-arm strike to his midsection. His breath shot out with an audible grunt.

Arly followed her first punch with a knife strike to his neck, stopping just short of a full-powered blow.

"Time," the judge called. "Halt."

Arly shifted back into a ready stance, her eyes bright with excitement.

"Match to Ms. Maguire-Blake."

Arly bowed to her opponent, who returned her bow, quickly trotted to the side of the room, and returned to her ready position.

Quinn smiled inwardly. Arly was quick and fearless. Her opponent had landed a few points, but Arly never hesitated. She was confident and sure. Quinn had winced at every glancing blow, but then, that was only natural. She'd rather take the shot for her, but she couldn't. Arly needed, wanted, to fight her own fight.

"She's good, isn't she," Honor murmured from beside her.

"She is." Quinn grasped Honor's hand and squeezed. "She's great."

The black belt panel conferred for a few moments, and then the senior sensei called Arly forward. She snapped to attention and Quinn held her breath. Beside her, she could feel Honor tense as well.

"Congratulations," he said, untying Arly's brown belt. He slipped the black belt around her waist and tied it.

Arly's arms snapped to her sides and she bowed. "Thank you, Sensei."

He returned her bow. "Dismissed."

Arly raced over to Quinn and Honor. "I did it, did you see me?"

"Great job." Quinn slung her arm around Arly's shoulders as Honor circled her waist.

"Congratulations, honey," Honor said.

Arly took a deep breath. "I'm really glad I passed."

"Never a doubt," Quinn said.

Arly grinned. "Kino is really tough. I might've gotten lucky with that spin kick."

Quinn laughed. "You know what I always say—"

"Better lucky than good?" Arly shot back.

Honor rolled her eyes. "Luck had nothing to do with it. It's training."

"That always helps too." Quinn's beeper vibrated, and she frowned. "Huh. I better get this."

"I thought you weren't on call tonight?" Honor said.

"I'm not. Probably a mistake, but I ought to check."

"Go ahead. We're good here."

As Arly packed up her gear, Quinn stepped out into the hall and dialed the extension.

"TICU," a man said.

"Maguire. Someone paged?"

"Oh, right…hold on for a second. Hey, Nalini, I've got Dr. Maguire."

A few seconds passed. "Dr. Maguire, it's Syd Stevens."

"Hi, Syd. What's up?"

"Really sorry to bother you, but Dr. Hassan must be out of beeper range. We've been trying to get him. It's about a post-op patient from today."

"The girl with the spine fracture?"

"Right."

Quinn listened, mentally sorting options as Syd gave her a rundown of what had been happening. "So what do you think?"

"I think we have to be sure there isn't an intra-abdominal bleed. It could be neurogenic shock, but if we're wrong, and she crashes—"

"Have you called CT?"

"Yes, they can take us now."

"Do it. I'll be there in a few minutes."

"I'll call you—"

Someone shouted in the background. "She's crashing."

"I gotta go," Syd said and disconnected.

Quinn stuck her head back in the dojo and caught Honor's eye. "I gotta go."

❖

"What happened?" Syd said breathlessly as she raced back to Cindy's bedside.

"Her pressure dropped out," Emmett said.

"I can't get a pulse," Nalini said, letting the side rail down and opening Cindy's gown.

"Rapid V-tach," Emmett said and began chest compression.

"Give an amp of epi." Syd grabbed the defibrillator paddles. "Charge to one twenty."

As soon as Nalini had the pads attached to Cindy's chest, Syd applied the paddles. "Clear!"

She discharged the defibrillator and Cindy's body jerked. She tried not to think about what the sharp spasm might be doing to her spine. What mattered now was stabilizing her rhythm and getting her blood pressure back to a normal level, or it wouldn't matter.

Breathlessly, she stared at the monitor. The cardiac rhythm went from the sharp sine waves of ventricular tachycardia to the erratic blips of fibrillation. Cindy's heart was not beating, just fluttering in her chest, unable to pump blood.

"Charge to two hundred." Syd re-applied the paddles. "Clear."

Emmett lifted her hands and waited for the jolt of electricity to pass back and forth between the paddles. Syd watched the EKG. The rapid fluttering disappeared. Flatline.

Her stomach plummeted. "Give her another amp of epi and charge to three hundred."

She positioned the paddles one last time.

"Clear."

Syd waited, time suspended, her gaze riveted on the EKG. The alarm continued to sound, signaling the absence of a detectable rhythm. Syd's heart rate skyrocketed. A second later, a normal beat spiked on the flatline. Then another. And another.

They'd gotten her back.

"Pressure?" Syd asked, her voice hoarse.

"Pressure's sixty palpable," Nalini said. "Still can't get an audible."

Another TICU nurse appeared in the doorway. "The lab called. Her hemoglobin is seven."

"Down from ten earlier." Syd glanced at Emmett across Cindy's still body. "She's got to be bleeding. She's too unstable to take down to CT. We need to get her to the OR."

"I'll let them know you're coming," Emmett said and sprinted out.

Syd helped Nalini get Cindy ready for transport. She couldn't leave her side now in case she arrested again. Once they reached the OR, the surgical team guided the bed in and Syd went to scrub. Quinn arrived just as she finished scrubbing.

"What's the status?" Quinn grabbed a mask and tied it around her neck.

"We can barely keep her pressure up. We cardioverted her three times in the TICU. I didn't think we could risk having her crash in CT." Through the windows above the scrub sink, Syd watched Emmett and the OR team transfer Cindy to the table.

"What's your plan?"

"An open abdominal tap. If we find blood, we can convert to a laparotomy."

"Got enough help?"

"I can assist Emmett if—"

Quinn shook her head. "Why don't you start. Emmett can assist, and I'll just put my head in when you know what's going on."

"Right." Syd finished scrubbing, backed through the door and spun around as the scrub nurse held out a towel. She dried her hands. "Go scrub, Emmett."

Quinn followed her in. "Go ahead, Emmett. I'll get her prepped."

Emmett didn't hesitate. "Thanks."

Syd took a deep breath, slid her arms into a sterile gown, waited while the scrub nurse held up her first glove, and pushed her hand into it. By the time the second glove was in place, Quinn had the abdomen prepped and Emmett had returned. A minute later, Cindy's face was obscured by the green sterile drapes. Only the rectangular patch of her abdomen was visible.

Syd stepped up to the table, held out her hand, and said, "Scalpel."

CHAPTER NINETEEN

Scalpel in hand, Syd looked across the table into Emmett's eyes. Emmett looked back, her gaze warm and steady. Quinn was in the lounge if they needed her, but here at the table there were only the two of them. Sometimes all they had were seconds to act, mere heartbeats in time to make a save or lose a patient. Here everything hinged on trust as much as skill. More, sometimes. Here, trust gave you the courage to be more than you thought possible.

"Ready?" Syd murmured.

"We're good."

Syd had time for a fleeting thought before she lowered the blade. Here in this moment, they were good.

She made a two-inch incision starting right below the navel and moving downward. Emmett sponged the blood away and Syd switched to the cautery to divide the underlying fat and muscle tissue until she reached the thin covering of the abdominal contents. Emmett had the short right-angle retractors ready and inserted them into the incision, pulling them apart to give Syd enough room to safely divide the last barriers. Once she'd breached the peritoneal cavity where all the vital organs were contained, she planned to insert a scope to determine if there was any bleeding, even a small amount.

"Scissors," she said and held out her hand. The handle slapped her palm, she slipped her fingers around it, and she snipped the filmy fascia. Instantly, bright red blood welled up into the wound. Her stomach tightened.

"We've got free blood," she said evenly.

"Pressure's dropping," the anesthesiologist announced.

Emmett asked him, "Are you hanging blood?"

"Second unit," he replied.

Syd said, "Better call for two more. She was only seven to start and she's actively bleeding. And someone call Dr. Maguire."

"I'm here," Quinn said from the corner of the room.

Syd hadn't noticed her come in. Without looking up, she said, "We're going to need to extend the incision and get a good look around."

"Sounds like a plan." Quinn pulled a stool over near the wall and sat down. "Go ahead, let me know what you find."

Emmett said, "Can we get another suction up here."

"Knife." Syd started several inches above the navel, curved around it, and cut down all the way to the lower abdomen. Once she'd entered the abdomen, Emmett placed the self-retaining retractors and cranked them open. Instantly, the intestines ballooned into the field, moist and pink and healthy looking. A sheen of blood covered everything.

"Moist lap pads," Syd said.

She and Emmett quickly used the ten-by-ten cotton pads to cover the bowel, and with one hand, Syd pushed it off to the side so she could get a look at the other organs. The liver filled the right upper quadrant, glistening bluish-red and undamaged. Blood continued to pool in the deeper recesses, obscuring her view of the stomach and spleen.

"Can you give me a little more exposure in the left upper quadrant," she said.

"Hold on," Emmett said, repositioning her retractor and leaning back a little to open up the space where Syd needed to see.

Syd gently lifted the bowel to check the stomach and vessels entering from the aorta that lay along the spine. The stomach and spleen all looked good, but fresh blood dribbled down the left side of the abdomen and pooled in the pelvis. When she scooped out the last of the small bowel she saw it. Blood seeped out of the fan-like sheath where the small bowel attached to the posterior abdominal wall.

"She's got a tear in the mesentery right where the superior mesenteric artery comes in," Syd said, just barely able to visualize the area of damage. "Emmett, can you get a hand under the bowel and take some of the pressure off?"

The last thing she wanted to do was convert a partial tear in an artery or vein into a total one. The big vessels that nourished the entire small bowel came directly off the aorta—if they were disrupted, the hemorrhage could lead to rapid exsanguination.

Emmett gently slipped her hand beneath the intestines. "You'll need to open that up to see what's bleeding."

"I know," Syd said. And when she did, she wouldn't have much time to control the bleeding. "Dr. Maguire? I might have to clamp the superior mesenteric."

If she did, the entire blood supply to the small bowel would be interrupted. If the bowel died, so did Cindy.

Quinn ambled around the foot of the table and stood behind Emmett, one hand on Emmett's shoulder as she leaned over to peer into the wound. "Yep. Looks like you've got an expanding hematoma down there. Something sure is bleeding. Better look and see."

"She's going to need more blood," Syd said.

The anesthesiologist replied, "Hanging another one now."

"Satinsky," Syd said, holding out a hand for the noncrushing vascular clamp. She'd done bowel resections before—lots of them for tumors and infections. She'd repaired arteries and veins too. At Franklin, they saw hundreds of patients with diabetic vascular disease who needed bypasses to help blood flow to their legs. She'd done all the parts, but she'd never done this. Emmett was a good assistant and Quinn continued to observe. If she got into trouble, Quinn would be right there. Knowing that settled her nerves. She knew what she was supposed to do, and knowing that she was the one in charge, the one expected to do it, gave her the confidence.

"Emmett, can you open up the mesentery."

"Scissors," Emmett said.

Syd readied the clamp in one hand and the suction in the other. Emmett incised the tissue surrounding the vascular bundle. A gush of blood poured into the field.

"One of the vessels must be torn," Syd said, her breath coming a little faster. Passing the suction to Emmett, she squeezed the vessels between the fingers of her left hand, manually cleared away the fat encasing them with a sweep of her thumb, and slid the clamp around the artery and vein with her other hand.

"The vessels are clamped," Syd said. The bleeding stopped. The bowel turned a dusky blue. The countdown clock in her head started ticking.

"Can you see the tear?" Quinn asked.

"Not yet," Syd said. "Emmett, sponge below my fingers."

Emmett muttered, "There it is."

"I see it," Syd said. "A partial avulsion of the vein. I think we can get a suture in it without narrowing it too much."

"Give it a shot," Quinn said.

They had one shot. If the suture didn't hold, the repair would be ten times harder and would take too long. Syd looked up for the first time. "You've got a better angle, Emmett. Go ahead."

Emmett nodded. "Five-oh Prolene on a vascular needle."

The scrub tech passed Emmett the vascular forceps and suture.

"Scissors," Syd said.

Emmett inserted a figure of eight suture and tied it down. Syd cut the suture and released the clamp.

The artery pulsed.

The vein filled up.

The bowel turned a healthy shade of pink.

Syd smiled.

"I'll be in the lounge," Quinn said and walked away.

"Let's run the bowel one more time," Syd said, "then we'll irrigate and close."

"I'm seeing some arrhythmias here," the anesthesiologist said, a new tension in his voice that hadn't been there before.

Syd looked over the ether screen at the monitors, saw several irregular heartbeats.

"She had a run of V-tach earlier," Syd said.

"I know. I've had her on a lidocaine drip but she's breaking through. You might want to hurry things up."

"All right," Syd said, pouring warm saline into the abdominal cavity. "We'll need fifteen minutes at least."

The OR door swung open and Kos Hassan hurried in. "I just got my page a few minutes ago," he said, breathing as if he'd been running. He probably had. "Quinn said she was bleeding. What's going on?"

Syd filled him in as he stepped close behind her.

"Looks like you've got things under control," he said.

"She's not bleeding now but she's still unstable," Syd muttered, suctioning out the last of the irrigation solution. It was clear. There was no other indication of bleeding.

"Sponge count," she said.

The circulating nurse started the count, and when they had determined all the sponges were out of the abdomen, Syd began the closure.

"V-tach!" the anesthesiologist called.

Syd continued suturing. Her job now was to get the patient off the table.

"I've lost her pressure," the anesthesiologist said sharply.

"Emmett," Syd said.

"Got it." Emmett passed her retractors to the scrub nurse, pushed the drapes up toward Cindy's head to get to her chest, and started closed cardiac compressions. The field was suddenly bloodless. Cindy's blood pressure was too low to perfuse her tissues.

"V-fib," the anesthesiologist said. "Pushing epi."

"Paddles," Emmett said.

A second later, Emmett called clear, and Syd stepped back from the table, along with everyone else.

"Nothing," the anesthesiologist said.

"Charge to two hundred." Emmett shocked her again, and on the third time, her heartbeat returned.

"She's still hypotensive," the anesthesiologist said, "but I've got a rhythm."

"Skin staples," Syd said, needing to get the incision closed as quickly as possible.

Twelve minutes later Kos helped Syd and the anesthesiologist push Cindy's bed back into the ICU. Emmett stopped at the nurses' station to take care of her post-op orders.

"I'm sorry you couldn't get me," Kos said while the ICU team got Cindy settled.

"I didn't think we could wait," Syd said, "and Dr. Maguire knew the patient."

"You made the right decision. All the way down the line."

Kos stood opposite Syd on the other side of Cindy's bed. Cindy lay motionless, the ventilator breathing for her through the endotracheal tube, her heart supported by infusions of antiarrhythmics and pressors, her legs encased in compression sleeves to prevent clotting and possible embolus. Her vital signs were stable, but that wasn't what worried Syd now.

"What do you think those hypotensive episodes did to her spinal cord injury?" she asked.

"There's a good chance she's lost whatever slim chance she had to recover function. And considering the two episodes of prolonged cardiac arrest..." He shook his head.

Syd didn't need it spelled out—prolonged decreased blood flow might have destroyed brain function too. Cindy might never wake up. "Should I get the EEG tonight?"

"Let's give her until early morning so we're sure the effects of the anesthesia have worn off." Kos said. "And, Syd..."

"Yes, sir?"

"You did everything exactly as you should have."

"If I'd gotten another abdominal CT, we might've picked up the bleed before her pressure bottomed out."

"You had no reason to repeat it. The first one didn't show anything. These things happen with injuries like this."

"I know, but if I just—"

"Believe me, if I thought you'd missed something, I'd let you know."

"Thank you," she said, appreciative but unconvinced. "I'll be here the rest of the night to keep an eye on her."

"Call me if you need me. And get the EEG first thing in the morning."

"I will."

After Kos left, Syd double-checked that everything looked stable and joined Emmett at the nurses' station.

"What a case, huh?" Emmett said, putting Cindy's chart aside.

"I'm glad you came back with me," Syd said. "That was hairy."

"It went great, though."

Syd let out a long breath. "I guess. I keep thinking I missed something."

"I can't think what it would be."

"Neither can I." Syd sighed. "I'm going to find an on-call room and crash here tonight. Kos wants an EEG first thing in the morning."

Emmett nodded. "I might as well stay too. There ought to be a room free somewhere. You ready?"

"All right." Syd tried very hard not to think about sharing a room with Emmett.

❖

Waking up underneath Emmett was weird and uncomfortable, as if she was surrounded by quicksand with no clear path out. One step wrong and she might sink. Her brain was a bit fuzzy, but she was aware enough to know the disquiet was coming from her and not anything Emmett had done. Other than to be Emmett. Going to sleep with her in the same room had been just as strange and probably would've made her every bit as uncomfortable if she hadn't been so exhausted a few hours earlier. But she'd stumbled to the bottom bunk, curled up on her side after kicking off her shoes, and mumbled good night. She'd slept in her scrubs, not for the first time in her life. Emmett had clambered up above her, muttered something similar, and gone still. As tired as she was, Syd had lain awake for a few seconds, listening. She'd heard nothing from Emmett. Not a snore. Not even a sigh. No movement at all. She must've fallen dead asleep as soon as she got horizontal.

After that Syd didn't remember anything at all until opening her eyes a few seconds ago. She hadn't dreamed, and mercifully, she hadn't been paged. She hoped that meant Cindy was stable.

Carefully, she swung her legs over the side of the bed and felt around with one foot for her shoes. Slipping into her sneaks, she quietly made her way to the door and let herself out into the hall. Four a.m., an hour earlier than she usually started rounds, and a couple of hours before the place would really get busy. She wanted to get the EEG completed before things in the ICU got too hectic.

Mostly, she wanted to know if Cindy was coming back.

The lights were still turned down to night level, as if the patients would know or care if it was night or day. Everyone was either intubated or sedated. A few curtains were closed, screening the patients while the nurses changed linens or drew a.m. bloods or a resident performed a procedure. Nighttime in the ICU always felt like a held breath, as if anything might happen at any moment.

Syd made her way to Cindy's room opposite the nurses' station. Her roto-bed, specially designed for spinal injury patients, was easier to handle in a larger space—hence the solo room.

"Good morning," she said to the nurse, a different nurse than the one who'd called her initially.

If he was surprised to see her so early, he didn't show it.

"Morning. Are you the neuro resident?"

She wasn't exactly, but Kos had left her to take care of Cindy. "Yes. Syd Stevens."

"Roger Debakey."

"How's she doing, Roger?"

He grimaced. "All her numbers look good. Post-op orders said hold blood for an H and H greater than ten-thirty, so we're waiting on another unit until we get her morning labs back."

"What's her last count?"

"Ten-five and thirty-one."

"Good. I need to schedule an EEG. Who should I call to get someone up here now?"

He told her, and after a little bit of cajoling, she convinced the tech to come up right away. She examined Cindy while she waited. Like the night before, Cindy lay motionless, all her various vital functions supported by machines and medications. Her neuro exam was remarkable for the absolute absence of anything. Her pupils were fixed and dilated. Syd couldn't elicit any peripheral reflexes, although she wouldn't have expected any in Cindy's lower body because of her spinal injury. But the arms had reflexes too, and those were absent. Possibly she was suffering from depressed central nervous function because of the periods of lack of oxygen during the multiple episodes of cardiac arrest, and possibly the dysfunction was temporary. Cindy was young and that helped most of the time. Sometimes, though, immature systems, particularly where nerves were concerned, were even more sensitive to insult.

Bottom line, Syd just didn't know, but the EEG would tell her.

"Hey," Hank said from the doorway. "What are you doing here so early?"

Syd looked over her shoulder. "I've been here all night. What are *you* doing here?"

"Scoring brownie points."

Syd laughed softly. "Points tallied."

Hank walked over beside her. "What happened? Is this why you came back last night?"

Nodding, Syd filled him in.

"Next time, call me," he said. "I could have helped."

"Kind of above and beyond."

"I'm a little freaked I'm going to be done in a few weeks, and there's a million things I don't know."

"We'll keep you out of trouble." Syd walked to the nurses' station to wait for the tech. "I'm going to stay for the EEG. Can you round on everyone?"

Hank brightened. "Sure."

"I'll see you later." She knew by now he didn't need her along, and she appreciated him picking up the slack for her. The EEG tech arrived with a portable machine while she was charting a note on her exam, and she followed him into the room.

Twenty minutes later, she let herself back into the on-call room. Emmett was gone. The disappointment, a sharp jolt that swiftly came and just as swiftly went, was a surprise. As soon as it registered, she pushed it aside. She was glad Emmett was gone. Hiding out for a few more minutes in the semidark, quiet space—alone—was exactly what she wanted. She sat on the edge of the narrow bed where she'd spent the night and thought about nothing at all. Her body ached from the long hours of standing and the too little sleep. Her brain would've hurt if she hadn't shut it off already. Right now, she was content not to think about anything at all.

The door opened, and Emmett walked in.

"Oh, hey," Emmett said. "I thought you'd taken off. I grabbed a shower and checked the ICU, but they said you'd left."

"No," Syd said flatly. "Still here."

Emmett's hair was damp, doing that curly thing it did when it was wet, and she wore fresh scrubs. She stopped a few feet from Syd and leaned an arm against the top bed, looking down. "What's going on?"

Syd jumped up, feeling trapped with Emmett standing over her. "Nothing. I should probably shower too. It'll wake me up."

"What did the EEG show?"

"There's no activity." She heard her own voice, emotionless, robotic. She really was tired.

"Fuck," Emmett said under her breath. "No doubt?"

"We'll need a confirmatory EEG in twenty-four hours," Syd said. "I already ordered it. But it's not going to show anything different."

"Damn."

"I'm going to have the transplant team evaluate her later today. I'm not sure she'll be a donor candidate because of the arrests, but…" She shook her head. "She was talking when she came in."

"Syd," Emmett said, shifting ever so slightly, forcing Syd to focus on her. "You know you did everything right, right?"

"I'm not so sure about that," Syd said with a long breath. "Right from the get-go, I worried something else was going on. I just didn't worry enough."

"Hey," Emmett said sharply. "That's bull. If you weren't as good as you are, you would have missed what was going on last night."

"You don't know that."

"Of course I do. It's always been obvious how good you—"

"Emmett, don't. Not right now."

"Don't what?" Emmett said, sounding perplexed.

"Don't talk about things you don't know anything about. You don't know me, whether I'm good at this or not."

"That's not true—"

"Emmett," Syd said. "Just leave it alone for once."

The look on Emmett's face, the flash of confusion that always made her look just a little bit young, followed by a flash of hurt, twisted something in Syd's already battered insides.

"Oh, Emmett," she murmured, just before she kissed her.

CHAPTER TWENTY

For a second, Emmett stood paralyzed while an avalanche of sensation roared through her, tumbling and turning her until she was breathless and disoriented. Shock blanked her brain. Instinct galvanized her body. The drive, the primal hunger to keep Syd's mouth exactly where it was hijacked reason and logic. Syd's hot, insistent, demanding mouth was kissing her as if she was the answer to every damn thing Syd wanted—and that was all that mattered. Emmett didn't care where she ended up as long as the rush never ended.

Syd was kissing her. Finally. At last. Again. All else was secondary.

Emmett wrapped her arms around Syd's waist and jerked her close, their bodies colliding so hard she gasped, as much as she could gasp without moving her mouth a single millimeter away from Syd's. Syd's tongue teased her lips and she opened her mouth. A flash of heat ignited at the glancing touch, turning her insides molten. She slid a hand into Syd's hair to deepen the kiss and Syd pulled her in, matching hunger with hunger. Emmett gripped the back of Syd's scrub shirt and pulled it loose, bunching it up until she found the soft, warm skin at the base of Syd's spine. She stroked her, caressed the sweep of the hollow above her ass, and Syd moaned into her mouth. The sound exploded through Emmett like a gunshot. Her clit ached and her insides clenched. Syd tugged at her lip, her teeth a sharp promise of pleasure, and Emmett tilted her head, inviting Syd to explore, answering every teasing stroke with one of her own. Daring Syd to take what she wanted. Syd's teeth grazed her again and she groaned.

Take me flashed through her overloaded consciousness, clear and definite. *Take everything.*

"Come on, Syd," Emmett growled. "Don't fucking tease me."

"Why not," Syd murmured. She jerked Emmett's shirt out of her scrubs and scraped her nails up the middle of Emmett's belly to her chest.

Syd's hand closed around her breast, and Emmett stumbled back. Her shoulder hit the post of the bunk, her calves collided with the edge of the bed, and she dropped down, pulling Syd with her.

On her back now, Syd somehow straddling her hips, their mouths still fused, kisses fast and furious. Somewhere a bell chimed, a reckoning denying retreat. No going back. No matter. She never wanted to go back. She'd only ever wanted the past to be the future. Half sitting, Emmett grabbed the bottom of Syd's scrub shirt in both hands and pulled it up above Syd's breasts, pressing her face against the sheer fabric enclosing them. Syd arched into her, and Emmett fanned her hands over Syd's bare back.

Syd's flesh was hot beneath her cheek, her nipple a hard prominence beneath the satiny material. Emmett found a nipple with her mouth, closed around it, and Syd moaned.

Somewhere the chimes rang again.

Syd rocked against her, making her clit tense and pound.

"Take your pants off," Emmett muttered.

"Emmett." Syd gasped, shaking her head as if surfacing from a dream. "God, Emmett. No."

"Syd," Emmett moaned. "Come on."

Syd opened her eyes, awareness pummeling her like icy rain. Her phone rang again. She took in the on-call room, her shirt pushed up to her neck, her thighs on either side of Emmett's hips, Emmett's hands on her breasts, her mouth—

She jerked back, grasping Emmett's wrists. "Emmett. Emmett, stop."

"What?" Emmett shuddered, her eyes wide and hazy.

Syd looked away, afraid of what she might see there. Scrambling to her feet, she yanked her shirt down and tucked it in. "Somebody's trying to get us."

"What?" Emmett repeated, looking around as if she didn't quite know where she was. Or what she'd done.

"Check your messages," Syd said, more sharply than she meant.

Emmett jerked as if she'd suddenly found herself somewhere she hadn't expected to be. She sat up and ran her hands through her hair. "Syd. What the fuck?"

"I don't know…never mind," Syd said. "Just…check your page."

Emmett grabbed her phone and got to her feet, her shirt still untucked, the strings on her scrub pants untied.

Syd's stomach dropped. When had she untied Emmett's pants? Why had she kissed her? What could she say to her now when she was as lost as Emmett looked?

"It's trauma admitting," Emmett said, looking at her phone.

"I know." Syd backed toward the door. "I got it too."

"Syd," Emmett said quickly, as if knowing Syd was about to disappear. A thousand questions flickered in her eyes. "Just now—I mean, what—"

"Not now, Emmett. We have to go." She couldn't give her any answers—she didn't have any. No answers, no excuses, no idea what she was doing.

"I know," Emmett said softly. "Are you okay?"

She should've known Emmett would go there first before anything else. Emmett, who had only ever been honest with her. Emmett, who she'd walked away from along with everything else. Emmett, who didn't deserve to be caught up in her regrets and remorse.

"I didn't mean to do that," Syd said, knowing even as she spoke she was lying to both of them. Somewhere, she must have meant it or she wouldn't have done it. She just didn't want that to be true. She had been so much better not looking back, not remembering any of it. "I'm as surprised as you are."

"I sort of guessed." Emmett laughed, a short hard sound. She hadn't moved, probably sensing Syd would be gone if she did. "For the record, I'm really glad you did."

"We need to get downstairs," Syd said.

Emmett nodded. "Right. We do."

Syd reached behind her, found the door handle, and turned it. They didn't have time for any of this now, and she was glad. She stepped out into the hall, Emmett close behind her, and almost collided with Zoey.

"Busy night?" Zoey asked bitingly, taking in the two of them and the slowly closing on-call room door.

Emmett just shook her head. "Trauma admitting is looking for us. Got to go."

"Us too," Dani said, arching an inquisitive eyebrow at Syd.

The overhead system announced a trauma alert, and Syd bolted forward. As long as there was work to focus on, she could pretend the rest of her life wasn't spinning out of control.

❖

Honor and Quinn were already gowned and gloved in trauma admitting when Emmett, Syd, Dani, and Zoey hurried in. Hank and Morty barreled in a few seconds later.

Quinn glanced over. "Good, you're just in time. We've got a house fire, three rigs on the way, with two adults and at least two kids."

"Wow," Emmett said. "All one family?"

"Unknown," Honor said. "Reports are it's a single family home, fully involved, but who knows how many occupants there might be or how they're related."

"I hate burn cases," Zoey muttered too quietly for Honor or Quinn to hear.

Honor pointed to a couple of second year ER residents. "Lang, Sahir, you take the kids along with peds surgery. Make sure you have solid airways right away."

Dani motioned to Zoey. "You take Lang, I'll go with Sahir."

"Right," Zoey said with obvious reluctance.

"You good?" Dani asked quietly.

Zoey flushed, looking surprised. "Yeah, I just hate burns."

"Me too," Dani said, although Syd had never heard her say that before. "Grab me if you need anything."

"Okay," Zoey said, her brows furrowing as if she was trying to process something unexpected. "Uh, thanks."

"Emmett," Honor said, "you and your team handle the adults. Depending on the extent of burns, we'll either treat here or stabilize and transfer."

"Right." Emmett handed out gowns. "Hank—you're with Syd. Morty, with me."

Syd gloved up and got ready. She moved to one side, out of Emmett's line of sight. She wouldn't be able to pretend nothing had happened, that she'd forgotten about the kiss, if she had to look at her. Once the patients arrived, she'd be fine.

All three emergency vehicles arrived at once, and the stretchers rolled in one after the other, EMTs and paramedics calling out vital signs, status updates, and reports on emergency treatment rendered in the field. Syd and Emmett and the others descended on the stretchers and fell into step as they trundled in.

Emmett caught the first adult, running alongside the gurney into trauma bay one. The female patient had extensive upper body second- and third-degree burns with obvious facial and peri-oral swelling. She was intubated and unconscious. Wet gauze covered the burns that weren't in areas where IV lines had been inserted.

"She wasn't breathing when fire rescue brought her down," the paramedic said. "We got a tube in and started ventilating as quickly as we could. Never lost her pulse but her blood pressure's been borderline normal. She's on her second liter of lactated Ringer's."

"Do we have blood gases?" Emmett asked while listening to the patient's lungs.

"No," the medic said.

"I'll get one sent," Brinks, the ER resident, said. He drew blood from the brachial artery and took over the airway management from the paramedic. "Indira? Can you run this down to the lab—tell them we need it stat."

"On it," the ER tech said, taking the syringe with the arterial sample.

"Her lungs are wet," Emmett said, slinging her stethoscope around her neck. "And she's got crackles everywhere. Can you try suctioning the tube?"

"Sure." Brinks passed a flexible catheter down the endotracheal tube and connected it to suction. The mucus that returned was filled with gray particles.

Emmett turned to the medic. "Was this a flash burn? Because she looks like she's got soot in her lungs—which means she might have burns all the way down. If so, she's going to need a trach."

The medic's face was streaked with soot and sweat. She shook her head. "I don't know. Fire rescue didn't give us anything else—the kids were still inside and it was crazy."

"Okay," Emmett said to Brinks. "If her gases are bad she'll need an early trach."

"I can bronch her," Brinks said.

Emmett considered it. "If you try it, make sure we're standing by to trach her. If she's got burns in her airway and she spasms, you'll lose her airway."

Brinks blanched. "Right. I'll talk to Dr. Blake."

"About what?" Honor said, appearing as if by magic.

Brinks jumped and Emmett grinned. She knew by now Honor

always knew exactly what was happening with every patient in the ER and was never far away.

"Probably airway burns," Emmett said.

Honor listened to the patient's chest. Nodded. "What about the rest of her injuries?"

"I estimated fifty percent surface area burns," Emmett said. "Twenty percent are deep second, possibly third." She pulled up her calculator app and plugged in the burn formula to determine fluid management. "We're going to need to up her fluids."

"I'll speed up the IV," Brinks said.

"Good," Honor said. "We'll need to transfer her. They can do the bronch when she arrives. We don't want to end up doing an emergency trach down here and then sticking her in an ambulance for a ride across town."

Brinks looked crestfallen.

"You want me to call about the transfer?" Emmett said. She wasn't getting a surgery out of this case but was satisfied she'd done the job. "I want to check on the others."

"See how many more we have to ship," Honor said, "before you call."

"Right." Emmett slipped into the group surrounding the other adult, a middle-aged male with thick burns over most of his chest, shoulders, and arms. If she had to guess, she'd put him closest to the start of the fire. Maybe his clothes had caught on fire or he'd gotten burned trying to put the fire out. His fingers were frozen into claws, a sign they were dying from lack of oxygen.

Syd was about to incise the burned tissue encircling his arms to release the constrictions that were blocking blood flow and killing the muscles and nerves underneath. Quinn looked over her shoulder as she made the first cut.

"That's it, keep the incision midline and just go through the burn for now. If we need to go deeper, we can do that as a second pass," Quinn said. "What else are you looking for?"

Syd said, "The ulnar nerve by the elbow and the superficial radial at the wrist."

"Good."

As Syd divided the charred tissue, none of which was bleeding, the underlying tissues immediately swelled into the gap, and she said, "Most of this fat looks dead."

"Probably is," Quinn said. "We can debride it later. Emmett, get the Doppler and check flow in the digits."

Emmett grabbed the Doppler and slid the probe over the palm. "I've got flow to the fingers."

Quinn grinned. "Good work, Stevens." She turned to Emmett. "What have you got in one?"

"She needs to be transferred to a burn unit. She's got upper airway involvement, probably pulmonary too."

"See if either of the kids will need to go too," Quinn said.

"I'll get an update from peds and then call about the transfers." Emmett headed over to where Dani and Zoey worked on two preteens, both of whom were unconscious and intubated. "What's the status?"

Zoey checked the monitors and stepped away from the bed. "No direct burns but both of them have lousy blood gases and a lot of facial swelling. They were most likely trapped somewhere, breathing hot air and toxic gases."

"Will they need to be trached?" Emmett asked.

Zoey shrugged. "Not right now but maybe in a few days if things don't resolve."

"So we can keep them here."

"I'll check with Fitzpatrick, but yeah, I think so. It's mostly going to be critical care, and our PICU can handle that."

"Okay—I've got one to transfer, so I'm going to call."

Zoey looked over to where Syd and Quinn worked on the male patient. "I noticed you've made a new conquest."

Emmett felt a flush rise in her neck. "You don't want to go there, Zoey."

"Really? Since when did you get sensitive about that?"

"Let it go, okay?"

Zoey shook her head. "What's the big deal, Emmett. It's not like I haven't seen you play around before."

"I'm not playing around."

"Sure you're not." Zoey laughed. "Who are you trying to kid?"

"Nobody." Emmett let out a long breath. "Look, I gotta go take care of this transfer."

"Whatever you say." Zoey turned her back, and Emmett walked away.

Zoey had it all wrong. She couldn't be fooling herself, because she had no idea what was going on. She wouldn't even know where to start.

❖

Syd made the last longitudinal incision in the left arm, gritting her teeth behind her mask as she divided the dead tissue. Burns were horrible injuries. She'd seen a few at Franklin, but nothing like this. She hoped she never saw another one.

When she put the scalpel down, her hand was shaking.

"Good job," Quinn said.

"I'm just glad he wasn't awake for it."

"You probably saved his arm," Quinn said.

"But not his hand."

"Maybe even part of that too."

"I'll get splints for his wrists and hands," Syd said.

"Then you're outta here."

Syd frowned. "What?"

"You worked all night, right?" Quinn said. "Remember the thirty-hour rule."

"Yes, but I got some sleep." That was an exaggeration, but Maguire didn't need to know that.

Quinn shook her head. "It doesn't matter. It counts as continuous hours in the hospital. Besides, these patients are all set. As soon as they're ready to roll, you take off."

Syd sighed. "All right, you're the boss."

Quinn grinned. "That's true."

Syd laughed. She wasn't sure where she found the energy to laugh, because everything inside seemed hurt.

Emmett was on the phone when she left. Syd didn't say good-bye.

Chapter Twenty-one

The screen door opened and closed and familiar steps crossed the wooden porch. Zoey sat down opposite Emmett on the top step and leaned back against the post, a beer in her hand.

"Hi," Emmett said.

The sun had just settled beyond the tops of the maples bordering the far reach of the backyard, and a few golden rays cut through the green branches and dappled the bottom steps. The scent of grilling food drifted on the gradually cooling breeze. She must've been out here at least an hour, but she couldn't remember what she'd been thinking, if she'd been thinking anything at all. The beer bottle beside her ran with rivulets of condensation, and when she put her hand around it, it was warm. She'd forgotten about that, along with the time.

"Here." Zoey stood and passed her cold bottle to Emmett. "I'll get another one."

"Thanks," Emmett said.

A minute later, Zoey returned and resumed her seat, stretching her legs out toward Emmett. She'd changed into a red tank top and loose navy shorts, pushing the late spring weather a little, but after what had seemed like a very long cold winter, any hint of warmth was cause for celebration. Zoey sipped her beer and studied Emmett. Finally, she said, "So what's going on with you?"

Emmett sighed. "Nothing."

Zoey snorted. "That's why you're sitting out here pining?"

"I'm not pining." Emmett managed to laugh, because she probably was pining. That also probably explained why she couldn't remember what she'd been doing for the last hour since she got home. She could actually pinpoint the reason, if she was being honest—and why pretend anything else? When she'd finished in the trauma unit, she looked for Syd, but she was gone. Syd was good at that, disappearing. The disappointment still stung a little.

"Well, we can argue about what you're doing—pining versus not pining, and why," Zoey said conversationally, "or we can pretend nothing's going on and I can leave you to play all wounded by yourself. Then again, I suppose we could get really extreme, and you could talk to me."

"Are you trying to tell me I'm being an ass?"

Zoey smiled. "I was trying to be nicer about it."

"I'm sorry."

"For what?" Zoey put her bottle down and looped her arms around her bare knees. "What exactly are you sorry for? Being unavailable in bed? Being strange and uncommunicative for the last few weeks? Or sleeping with Syd Stevens?"

"I didn't sleep with her."

"Aha. See which one you answered first?" Zoey's gaze sharpened, a fox sighting the hare. "So why don't we start there. What's going on, since I think if you answered *that,* all the other questions will be answered too."

"Are you really mad we're not sleeping together?"

"Well, you're pretty good in bed—"

Emmett laughed. "Thank you."

"But I'm not exactly withering up and blowing away. I do have other options."

"I know that. And, you know, I thought we were good on…us with or without the physical stuff."

Zoey rolled her eyes. "We were, we are. It's not the absence of sex, it's the absence of you. Dummy."

"I'm sorry."

"You said that. Still the same questions."

"I haven't been clear enough in my own head to explain anything, I guess. And some things aren't just about me, so it didn't seem like I really could share them."

"Back to Syd Stevens again, right?"

"Right." Emmett drank some of her beer and considered why she hadn't said anything to anyone about knowing Syd before this. "Syd has always been there in the back of my mind, you know? Like an unfinished story."

Zoey sat up straighter, her eyes narrowing. "Come again?"

"We met before, when I was a med student."

"You and Stevens?" Zoey's voice had gone up an octave. "You have a history."

Emmett winced. It sounded bad, the fact she hadn't said anything to her best friend until now. "Yes. A complicated one. From a long time ago."

"And you never thought to say anything. For weeks."

"It wasn't just about me."

"Oh, come on. What could be so important you had to keep it a secret. You slept with her?"

"Come on, Zoey. I'm not going to talk about that."

"I'll take that as a yes." Zoey tilted her head, gave Emmett a piercing glare. "I'm not asking for the specifics—like I don't know what the details would be like or anything."

"I know. It's just…that's not what this is about."

"Okay, fine, if you say so. I'm still pretty much in the dark here. What exactly *is* it about?"

"It's about me, all right?" Emmett set her beer down, frustrated at not being able to sort out her own feelings, let alone talk about them to someone else. "It's my problem, okay? I just never got past it."

Zoey's lips parted. "Wow," she said after a long pause, her voice dropping back to normal. "You're serious, aren't you?"

"Yeah," Emmett said, finding it easier to say the words than she'd imagined, now that she'd started. "I am. I never forgot. Any of it." She shook her head. "I wish I had. Syd seems to have."

"And you never said anything about her all this time?"

"I told you—Syd deserves not to have her past tossed around with strangers."

"No," Zoey said, waving a hand, "I don't mean why didn't you tell me about her *now*, I mean *before* now. Before Syd showed up again. We've been friends for years—we've been sleeping together, for crying out loud—and you never mentioned this woman in your past."

"Because she was in the past," Emmett said sharply. "Over, done."

Zoey laughed and shook her head. "But not forgotten."

Emmett leaned her head back against the post, watching the first sliver of moon appear in the deepening skies. "No, not forgotten. And now I just keep remembering."

"What about her? What does she say about reconnecting?"

Emmett rocked her head from side to side. "Syd doesn't seem to want to remember anything."

"So…nothing happened last night? And that's why you're sitting out here ruminating."

Emmett gave her a long look. "I'd rather not talk about that."

"Okay," Zoey said agreeably, nodding her head. "We won't talk about it, which means something happened but maybe not as much as you would like to happen. Am I warm?"

Emmett laughed. "Warm enough."

"You know I love you, right?" Zoey said.

Emmett stiffened. "Zoey—"

"Not that way," Zoey said. "Not *in* love with you, but I love you. I'd like it if you didn't get your heart broken."

Emmett smiled wryly. "That already happened, Zoe. A long time ago."

❖

Dani walked into the kitchen and stared at Syd. "What are you doing?"

"I'm packing," Syd said.

"No kidding." Dani made a wry face as she took in the open boxes on the counters, the floor, and almost every other available space, and the foot-high stack of newspapers Syd had collected from around the house. "This is what you do with your time off? You pack and make the rest of us feel guilty?"

Syd shook her head. "I'm not trying to make you feel guilty. I was just restless, and we need to pack. We're moving in two days, remember?"

"In theory, I am aware. I'm trying not to think about the actual act." Dani snagged one of the remaining glasses from the cabinet above the sink, threaded her way between the boxes to the refrigerator, and pulled out a half-full bottle of wine.

"That's four days old," Syd pointed out.

"Time we got rid of it, then. Consider it my contribution to housecleaning." Dani poured a glass and hopped up onto the counter in her usual place. "Are you going to do laundry and clean the bathrooms next?"

"I don't know, maybe. Why?" Syd placed a plate she'd wrapped in newspaper into a box, carefully folded the flaps, and labeled it *kitchen dishware* with a black Sharpie.

"Because that's what you do when something is bothering you."

Syd turned and folded her arms across her chest. "Nothing is bothering me."

Dani sipped her wine. "Syd, no bullshitting here. This is your I'm-not-going-to-think-about-it behavior. Rare, I'll admit, but recognizable after all this time."

"You still want to move, right?" Syd said.

"Are you kidding me? I can't wait until I don't have to drive to work anymore. Of course I want to move. So does Jerry."

"That's good to hear. I haven't seen him enough to know what he's up to," Syd said.

"You're trying to change the subject, and it's not going to work."

Syd laughed. "I really haven't seen Jerry for more than five minutes at a time for two weeks."

"That's because he's busy banging Sadie." Syd rolled her eyes and Dani grinned. "Which means he wants to move even more than we do, because she's only a couple blocks away from the new place."

"He's going to have to pack his own underwear," Syd said.

"I'll tell him unless you see him first." Dani finished the rest of the wine and set the glass aside. "What about you, do you want to move?"

"Sure," Syd said and turned back to her packing.

"Into the same house as Emmett?"

Syd felt her shoulders tighten but kept on wrapping dishes. "We're not moving into the same house. We're moving next door."

"Uh-huh, with a shared yard and adjoining porch. It's very cozy."

"We'll hardly ever be there, probably never even see each other."

"I recognize avoidance behavior when I see it. When you're ready to tell me what's going on, I'll be all ears." Dani jumped down and gave her a quick hug. "She's hot, by the way."

Syd laughed. She couldn't help it. Dani had a way of slicing through emotional turmoil with humor, even though she suspected that was Dani's defense against the things she'd rather not feel. "She's very hot. I totally agree."

"Glad to hear your heart's still beating. So, you know, maybe you should worry less and just take what's out there to be had."

Syd braced her hands on the counter and stared at the row of dishes she still needed to pack away. She'd been trying not to think about Emmett all afternoon, and she'd been pretty much unsuccessful. The impression of Emmett's body against hers was still alive. The heat of Emmett's mouth, the taste of her, the desire for her still curled within her. Take what was out there to be had. Yes, she'd tried that once.

"I'm not very good at that," Syd murmured.

"I have a feeling McCabe could help you out there."

Syd laughed softly. "That's exactly what I'm afraid of."

❖

Emmett nursed a cup of coffee in the kitchen just after six a.m. She couldn't seem to sleep late even on a day off. Lately it was worse. Even when she did get to sleep, her dreams were restless and she woke up feeling tired. After all these years of broken sleep, she could usually grab a few hours of deep sleep day or night and wake up feeling halfway rested. For the last couple of nights, she'd dreamed of kisses that faded into elusive fragments, and awakened frustrated and tired.

This morning she had the house to herself—Zoey had been on call the night before and wasn't due back until midday. Hank had spent the night with another student, supposedly studying for finals, but she suspected there was more sex than studying going on. She'd done the same in his place near the end of med school, except her celebration had been haunted by what might have been if she'd been on her way to University with Syd still there.

Damn, it would be nice if everything in her life didn't remind her of Syd.

At the distant sound of a door slamming, she got up to see who had come home. A little company to get her thoughts off what—or who—was keeping her up at night would be good right about now.

The living room was empty. Frowning, she opened the front door. A car she didn't recognize, packed to the roof with boxes and black plastic bags, sat at the end of the walkway. The front door on the adjoining twin was propped open.

Pulse quickening, she hopped the railing and walked to the open doorway. "Hello?"

"Hello," Syd called back.

"Hey, it's Emmett." She didn't enter, waiting for an invitation she wasn't sure was going to come.

Syd appeared from the depths of the house, dressed in khaki shorts and a patterned cotton tank top. Emmett hadn't seen her out of scrubs more than a few times since she'd arrived, and then she'd been wearing jeans and T-shirts. She looked terrific. Her arms were toned, her legs long and lean. She'd actually gotten even more beautiful in the last five years. Emmett's throat went dry.

"Hi," Emmett said, "I didn't realize you'd be here so early."

Syd slid her hands into her back pockets. "Oh. Sorry. I didn't think about the noise. Did I wake you?"

Constantly.

Laughing, Emmett shook her head. "No. I've been awake for quite a while." She hefted her coffee cup. "I just made a fresh pot. Do you need some?"

"You have no idea," Syd said.

"I've also got day-old jelly doughnuts, pizza that's only twelve hours old, and Cap'n Crunch. That never out-dates."

Syd smiled. "I wouldn't say no to a jelly doughnut. Unless it's got anything tasting of banana inside."

"What do you have against bananas?"

"Nothing in theory, it's just that anything you eat with a banana in it tastes like a banana. So you might as well eat a banana."

Emmett shook her head. "Raspberry, blackberry, or apple cinnamon. Anything strike your fancy?"

Syd gave her a long look, and lust curled in Emmett's middle. She had to tell herself that she was just reading things into that smoky look in Syd's eyes. Maybe.

"Apple cinnamon."

"Come on back to the kitchen." Emmett led the way over the railing and into her side of the twin.

"Is everyone else asleep?" Syd asked in a low voice.

"Nope. All gone."

"Oh." Syd stopped just inside the kitchen door, looking a little uncertain.

Emmett poured a cup of coffee. "You want milk? That never outdates either."

Syd snorted. "Should I pass, or have you taste-tested it this morning?"

Emmett grinned and held up her cup. "It's safe if you trust me to tell."

"Hmm. Tough question." Syd wagged her fingers. "I'll risk it."

Emmett brought her the coffee and a jelly doughnut. She backed away, got a second doughnut she didn't really want for herself, and took a bite while leaning against the counter. Syd tasted hers and looked a little less spooked. She also looked sexy as hell with a smidge of white powder on the corner of her mouth.

Emmett's clit woke up with a vengeance. Feigning casual, she asked, "So where's the rest of your crew?"

"As far as I know, Jerry is…somewhere else."

"You mean at Sadie's?"

"That's my guess." Syd hesitated. "Does that bother you?"

Emmett frowned. "Why would it?"

"Uh, no reason, really."

"Sadie and I are not a thing, Syd. We were never actually a thing, so whatever you heard—"

"Sorry, totally none of my business."

"Well, I'm making it your business," Emmett said quietly. "We had a very brief thing that wasn't a thing, except maybe I wasn't as clear as I should have been. And that was over quite a while ago. Sadie's actually really smart and a little shy. That comes off as snobby sometimes."

"I'm glad. Jerry's a really nice guy and doesn't play games."

"What about Dani? Is she coming by?" Emmett tried not to sound hopeful. The idea of having Syd all to herself was about the most exciting thing she'd contemplated in forever.

"She's sleeping in."

"So they left you to move?"

Syd polished off the rest of the doughnut and rested against the doorway. "Well, to be fair, they did offer to do their share as soon as they were free, but I didn't see any point sitting around with a pile of boxes and nothing to do all day."

"I'm volunteering, then, because I'm sitting around with nothing to do, and I don't even have any boxes to look at."

Syd grinned. "You really want to spend your morning toting boxes? It's supposed to be seventy-five by noon. Isn't this supposed to be spring still?"

"Hey, no complaints here. It could be fifty in a couple of days." Emmett took Syd's empty cup and set it with her own in the sink. "Besides, you get to wear shorts."

"True," Syd said. "But still, it's going to be hot, dusty work. I don't think that place has been cleaned for a while, and I'm not unpacking stuff over there until it is."

"Oh no. I draw the line at vacuuming. I'll carry boxes, but I'm not cleaning."

Syd put her hands on her hips. "What, cleaning is women's work?"

Emmett crossed the kitchen and stopped a couple of inches away from Syd. "I do my share of housework." She grinned. "But that mostly means plumbing, fixing loose boards on the porch, and taking out the trash."

"Aha," Syd said, giving Emmett a knowing look. "Like I said, no women's work."

Emmett rolled her eyes. "I don't believe in dividing chores along presumed gender lines. I'm just good at plumbing."

"Well then, you can take the bathrooms."

"Considering it's mostly plumbing, I can handle it." Emmett grinned. Hell, she'd clean the whole place with a napkin if it got Syd to smile at her that way all day.

"Then consider yourself drafted."

Emmett got the smile she wanted, the special one Syd only shared when she was relaxed and enjoying herself. She was so beautiful Emmett couldn't breathe. She was pretty sure if she didn't touch her right now she'd never breathe again.

She leaned a little closer, watching Syd's eyes grow wide. Keeping her gaze on Syd's, she ever so softly, ever so slowly, brushed her thumb over the corner of Syd's mouth.

"You had a bit of sugar right there." Emmett eased around Syd and walked through to the front of the house.

A few seconds passed before she heard Syd follow. She smiled to herself and didn't look back.

CHAPTER TWENTY-TWO

Syd leaned against the bathroom door to admire the view. She'd never seen a woman look so sexy in a sweat-stained T-shirt and jeans with holes in strategically located positions. Was that a swath of red and navy stripes showing through rips over Emmett's right butt? The image of Emmett in red and navy briefs made her brain fuzzy. And then there was the way Emmett's dark hair clung to the back of her neck in ridiculously captivating ringlets in an incongruous juxtaposition of innocence and seductiveness. All that was nearly enough to distract her from Emmett's profile—almost. Viewed from the side, a lock of hair fell over Emmett's forehead in a thick bold slash, just brushing the arch of her dark brow. The angle of her jaw was as clean and strong as if it had been sculpted. The muscles in her bare forearms flexed as she braced herself on one arm and wiped down the last of the water from the floor. She had almost backed out as far as the doorway, and if Syd leaned over, she'd be able to rest her hand on the arch of her back.

The idea filled her with more excitement than she'd imagined was still possible—no, that she would've been *certain* was impossible if it hadn't been for the kiss just the other day. The kiss that somehow managed to linger in the nerve endings throughout her body, indelibly stamped on her brain in some way that kept replaying at the slightest provocation. Just thinking about reliving that kiss had her sliding her hands into her back pockets again, which seemed to be the only safe place she could put them with Emmett so close. Every time she caught sight of Emmett she had the urge to touch her, and since she had no intention of doing that again, she was going to be spending a lot of time with her hands in her pockets.

She cleared her throat, as much to dispel the tension of arousal as to announce her presence. "I think it's about time for a break."

Emmett glanced over her shoulder, a grin easing the perfect line of her jaw. "Really? Because I don't think I've suffered enough yet."

Syd laughed. "You are such a drama queen."

"I'm sorry? I've now cleaned two of the world's most disgusting bathrooms. Neither term applies to me at the moment." She frowned. "Or really, at any moment."

"How would you feel if I walked down to that deli and got us lunch?"

"I would offer to have your children."

Syd caught her breath, working on a smile. "Oh no. That's a bit extreme."

"That's how thirsty I am right now." Emmett tossed her damp towel into a nearby bucket and rose. Her gaze narrowed. "Why do you look so fresh? And clean."

"Well," Syd said, feigning guilt and struggling to hold back a giggle. Really, giggling? What was wrong with her? Emmett just looked so damn adorable all hot and grumpy, that was all. "I might've taken advantage of the clean bathroom down the hall to shower."

"I heard the water running," Emmett said, "but I thought you were cleaning the kitchen."

"I swear, that will be my first task as soon as we have something to eat."

"Pretty sneaky." Emmett abandoned her cleaning equipment and walked toward Syd. "I need ten minutes to shower."

Syd took a step back. Emmett was altogether too close. Even slightly sweaty, she was delectable. Another thought that was totally unlike her. She never thought of women as…well, she never thought of women as possible bedmates, really, and certainly not as something edible. And now she was, and she was really in trouble. She took another step back, all the way into the middle of the hall. "Chicken steak, no onions, mushrooms, peppers, and ketchup."

Emmett followed her retreat and her smile widened. "Very good. You were paying attention."

"Just a good memory," Syd said.

"Really?" Emmett said slowly, her voice dropping. "And I thought it was just me."

Syd bit the inside of her lip. Why was the ground so unsteady everywhere around Emmett? Why couldn't she manage to keep a safe distance? Emmett was all twisted up with so many things she didn't want to remember.

"I'll be going now," Syd said lightly, "so you can get cooled off. In the shower."

Emmett nodded, her smile turning rueful. She knew—she always seemed to know—the minute Syd retreated. Good. Maybe that's what they both needed. A little reality.

"I'll be back soon," Syd said, and fled.

The deli was nearly empty on Sunday afternoon, and fifteen minutes later, she was on her way back with extra steaks for everyone who might show up later. She'd learned those house rules already. She half hoped someone else would be home when she got there. Just the two of them alone might not be such a good idea. As soon as she thought it, she scoffed at herself. She had enough control not to repeat her admittedly insane, out-of-the-blue kiss. Of course she did.

She stopped at Emmett's first and called through the screen door. "Emmett?"

When she got no answer, she decided Emmett must indeed be a very quick showerer. After a quick stop in the kitchen to drop off the extra steaks in the fridge, she headed back around to her own side of the twin.

"Emmett?" she called as she entered.

"Upstairs in the front bedroom," Emmett said.

That bedroom, with its bay window shaded by a huge old oak, was the one she intended to claim for herself. Did Emmett know that? Maybe she should tell her to come down to the kitchen. One quick look decided her against that. The place was still half filled with boxes, and she wasn't really keen to eat off any of the surfaces until she disinfected the place. She dug out their steaks and put the others in the fridge for later. She grabbed a roll of paper towels from an open box of cleaning supplies and carried them upstairs.

"Sorry," Syd said as she walked into the bedroom. "It was Sunday, and they didn't let me buy any be—" She stopped just inside the threshold, taking in the impromptu picnic Emmett had spread out on the floor—a faded army-green blanket she didn't recognize, several paper plates, napkins, and, thank all the powers that be, two beers running with condensation in the heat. "I couldn't get any beer."

"I figured you wouldn't be able to," Emmett said. "And we deserve them."

"God, do we ever." Syd dropped down on the corner of the blanket, which was surprisingly soft against her bare legs, and put the steaks in the middle. Emmett sat on the opposite corner, the windows behind her open, letting in sunlight and spring breezes. Syd smelled freshly cut grass, early lilacs, and what appeared to be an ever-present scent in the neighborhood, barbecue. Something else caught her attention then, spicy and slightly tangy. Emmett. Something she'd showered in or put on afterward.

Aware of her racing heart, Syd glanced down at her steak and concentrated on unwrapping the paper, trying not to think about Emmett in the shower, about her muscles sleek and shimmering with a sheen of falling water. Her hands trembled. She wasn't having a lot of success banishing the images.

"Here," Emmett said, passing her a bottle of beer. "Eat something, you'll feel better."

Syd raised her eyes, found Emmett watching her intently. "I'm fine."

"Okay. Have a beer anyway."

Syd laughed softly. "That's a great idea."

They ate in companionable silence for a few moments, trained to eat quickly by years of never having enough time to eat. They were conditioned to take everything quickly—sleep, food, pleasure—when and where it was to be found. Sitting and relaxing was a foreign sensation. Funny thing was, sitting with Emmett didn't feel strange at all.

"Most of the hard work is done," Syd said after she'd finished her sandwich. "The kitchen is a disaster zone, though. They managed to keep the surface fairly clean, but if you look carefully, and believe me, I didn't really want to, there are certain things that ought to be declared health hazards. The microwave and the toaster oven are two of them."

"You know," Emmett said, leaning on one elbow, her legs stretched out along the edge of the blanket, "the better part of valor might be to toss them and just get new ones. They're not too pricey these days."

"I might decide that after I get a better look at them." Syd finished the rest of her beer and set the bottle down on her paper plate. "Believe me, I'm not above paying a little bit to avoid nightmares."

"Wise decision." Emmett wrapped up the remains of their meal and deposited everything except Syd's returnable beer bottle into one of the plastic garbage bags they'd been using while cleaning. She tilted her beer bottle to empty it.

Syd watched her swallow, thinking the movement of her throat was both vulnerable and beautiful.

"What?" Emmett said when she leaned over to put her bottle next to Syd's. The movement put her face on a level with Syd's.

Syd shook her head. What could she say? *I think you're beautiful? I think you're the only woman who's ever made me feel peaceful and excited at the same time? I wish we didn't have a past, and that I just met you?*

"Something," Emmett said softly.

"Hard to explain," Syd said.

"Maybe one of these days, then." Emmett glided forward as effortlessly as if she hadn't moved at all until she was inches away. "Maybe one of these days you'll tell me. But not today."

"No, not today," Syd whispered, her gaze locked on Emmett's as Emmett's pupils grew larger and darker.

Then Emmett's mouth was on hers, not questioning, not tentative, but as certain and sure and confident as Emmett was about everything else. Syd tasted the yeasty sweet flavor of new beer, smelled the tangy aroma of Emmett's skin, absorbed the heat of her mouth and the demand of her kiss. She grabbed on to her, one hand in Emmett's hair, the other twisted in her T-shirt. She clung to her, drowning in her. The floor was probably hard when she lay back on the thin blanket and Emmett moved over her, when Emmett's weight came down on top of her and Emmett's thigh slid between her legs, but she didn't notice. The rough surface of Emmett's jeans pressed against the soft skin between her thighs, but all she registered was heat and desire. All she felt was the length of Emmett's body, fitted into every curve and angle of her own, the weight of her, the heat of her, the perfect fit. She wrapped her arms around Emmett's shoulders, curved one bare calf over the back of Emmett's jeans, tilted her hips until they cleaved even closer together. Emmett's teeth were on her throat, grazing the undersurface of her jaw. Her tongue flicked out, teasing at the soft spot below her ear. One hand slipped between them, curved around her breast.

Syd's breath came so quickly she was light-headed. She bunched the back of Emmett's T-shirt in one hand, dragged it out of her pants, and ran her fingers over columns of muscle, along the dip above her ass, and down beneath the waistband until her fingers dug in to tight, toned muscles. Emmett's fingers slid beneath her tank top, captured a nipple between her fingers, and squeezed lightly until Syd whimpered. Emmett's growl speared through her, and need pounded between her thighs. She pushed at Emmett's pants, frustrated when she couldn't get them down.

"They're in my damn way," she gasped.

Laughing, Emmett lifted her hips and reached between their bodies, unbuttoning her jeans and opening Syd's shorts.

"Do yours," Emmett ordered, rolling off and pushing down her jeans in one motion. Whatever she'd had on underneath the denim disappeared. She chucked her T-shirt behind her. Nothing under that either. For an instant, Syd could only stare. Emmett naked was a glory.

"Syd." Emmett's tone was impatient as she tugged Syd's shorts down.

Galvanized, Syd yanked off her tank and her bra and grasped Emmett's shoulders. She pulled Emmett down, needing to cover her nakedness with Emmett's skin, needing to drown again.

Emmett was there, every firm, hot, glorious inch of her, demanding Syd let down the barriers between them and take her in. Syd couldn't say no. Not now, not when the need was so hard on her.

She opened for her, found Emmett's hand, and drew it down between her legs. She arched when Emmett's fingers found her, cried out when Emmett stroked her, and came apart when Emmett filled her.

So deep, so hard, so unexpectedly fast she couldn't breathe.

Emmett was everywhere, around her, inside her, kissing and stroking and soothing. The need only coiled again, tighter and deeper than before. Syd came again, for once not thinking, not remembering, not holding back a single emotion.

Syd took a deep breath, felt it shudder in her lungs, took another, pressed her cheek against Emmett's breast. Her face was wet. Emmett's heart beat hard and fast.

Emmett brushed away tears with trembling fingers. "Syd. Hey, baby. You okay?"

"Sorry," Syd whispered. "That was…unexpected."

Emmett sucked in a breath and let out a strangled laugh. "I'll say. You're amazing."

"I'm something," Syd said unsteadily. "I don't…I don't usually…I never…not like that."

"I want to make you come again," Emmett murmured. "About a thousand times. That's how beautiful you are."

"I don't think I've got too many more like that in me," Syd said.

"Oh," Emmett said, that arrogant note back in her voice. "I bet we can find a few hundred or so."

Syd tilted her head back, focused on Emmett's eyes. "I'm not altogether sure I can take that again."

Emmett took a long breath. "Okay. For now."

"Emmett..." Syd began.

Emmett kissed her. "Let's not talk."

"Mmm. Let's not," Syd whispered. Emmett's kiss was a reprieve, permission to go on not thinking for at least a little while longer. A moment later, Syd braced her hands on Emmett's shoulders, pushed her back, and murmured, "Thank you. Thank you for this."

Astride Emmett's middle, she framed Emmett's face and kissed her mouth, her neck, and the hollow between her breasts. Moving lower on the soft worn wool, she nestled between Emmett's thighs and rubbed her cheek over the soft skin of Emmett's thigh. She found Emmett's hands, linked their fingers, and took her with her mouth, drawing out their pleasure as long as Emmett would let her. When Emmett exploded, she drank her in. Drowning again.

For endless moments, Emmett was everything.

CHAPTER TWENTY-THREE

Syd smiled as Emmett's fingers drifted over her breast, tickling one second and sending electric shocks of arousal through her in the next. The bedroom had warmed as the afternoon sun slanted in, and she might have dozed a little. Or maybe she'd just turned off for a while. She had no idea of the time.

"I didn't snore, did I?"

"Not once," Emmett murmured.

"Oh, good. I thought maybe I fell asleep. Sorry."

Emmett laughed. "No complaints here. If I wore you out, I must be doing something right."

Syd rolled her eyes, the only part of her body she currently felt like moving. "Ego much?"

"Mmm. Just highly motivated."

Emmett's fingers were definitely not tickling her now. Syd's nipple hardened and her thighs tensed. She couldn't argue with the results. "I'd say coma is more accurate."

"Even better."

"We should probably get dressed," Syd said.

"Why?" Emmett asked lazily, tracing Syd's navel and making her shiver. "It's really nice just like this."

"We're naked in the middle of the floor," Syd said.

"I know. Sorry about that."

Syd finally got up the strength to turn her head. Emmett leaned on an elbow, grinning down at her. Syd frowned. "What are you sorry about?"

"The part where we're on the floor. You can't be too comfortable."

Syd stretched. "You know, I actually feel great. I don't know why. I ought to at least have blanket burn."

Emmett shifted over her, sliding one bare thigh between Syd's legs. "We could work on that some more if you want to. I ought to be able to deliver another episode of brain melt."

"No doubt, O spectacular one." Laughing, Syd pushed Emmett up and off. Emmett didn't go too far, and she was glad. She liked touching her even more than she liked Emmett's hands on her. She laced her fingers with Emmett's. If they started again, she wasn't sure she'd want to stop, and they might not be alone much longer. "I need a bit of a rest."

"Later then."

Syd sighed. Saying no was hard, especially when her body was saying yes. Loudly. "We really should get dressed. Someone's going to come home sooner or later."

"We could put a Do Not Disturb sign on the door."

"Oh yeah, that would be subtle."

Emmett shrugged. "Do we care?"

When Syd didn't answer, her grin disappeared and a serious look came into her eyes. "Do you care?"

"I don't generally like to make announcements about my private life," Syd said quietly. And she really wasn't up for Zoey walking in on them. Maybe there was nothing going on between Emmett and Zoey, but she doubted Zoey would be overjoyed to see them together. And besides, they weren't together. Why send the wrong message? Why complicate everything when everything was already so damn complicated?

"You mean you don't want anyone to know we've been together." Emmett's tone was cool and flat. The accusation Syd expected to hear, and probably deserved, was missing, and she had a momentary twinge of remorse. Damn it. Why did everything have to come apart so quickly? Her fault. Again.

Syd sat up, found her tank top in the pile of clothes on the floor, and pulled it on. Somehow, she felt better having a serious conversation when she wasn't naked, and it looked like serious was about to happen. She shouldn't be surprised by that. She and Emmett had just had sex. They could hardly pretend nothing had changed, and she couldn't just walk away without saying…something.

"I can't think of any reason why we need to tell our friends that we had sex." There, that was neutral enough. And slightly cowardly.

"Is there some reason to pretend we didn't?" Emmett pulled on her jeans and leaned back on the blanket, her arms braced behind her.

She hadn't bothered with the shirt, and Syd instantly forgot what had seemed important to discuss a few seconds ago.

Irritated at her lack of focus and plain old good sense, she shook the haze from her brain. "What is it you want, Emmett?"

"I thought I made that pretty clear," Emmett said. "I want you. A lot."

"I got that part of it." Syd couldn't help the quick smile. "And it was wonderful. *You* were wonderful. We had sex. It was great. I think you could probably tell."

Emmett smiled for an instant. "I thought so too."

"But? What else?"

Emmett was quiet for a long while. Eventually, she pulled on her T-shirt and sat forward, her arms resting on her knees, her hands dangling loose.

Anyone who didn't know her would think she was relaxed, but Syd knew better. Emmett radiated the calm stillness that came over her when she was waiting for a trauma to hit the admitting area. Syd knew because she felt that way too. Every muscle tight and vibrating, set to snap into action.

Finally Emmett said, "It wasn't just sex."

"How could it be anything else?" Syd said gently. "The way our lives are right now, we barely have time to do anything except work. The toughest year of our residency is coming up soon."

"It wasn't just sex because I've never forgotten you or the way I felt about you five years ago."

Emmett's gaze bore into her with effortless intensity, and Syd's stomach tightened. She'd known this was coming, of course. They couldn't avoid talking about what had happened forever. She'd just had hoped it wouldn't be so soon. "I'm sorry for the way things ended. You deserved so much better."

Emmett made a face as if that wasn't what mattered to her.

"I never should've slept with you then, either," Syd said quietly.

"Are you saying you shouldn't have slept with me today?"

"No…I don't know. Maybe." Syd blew out a breath. "I'm not saying this very well. Sex isn't simple with you. It never was."

"We never needed to have *the talk* back then." Emmett grinned ruefully. "We were mostly too busy ripping each other's clothes off to worry about talking."

"I know. And that was pretty much my fault."

"Oh, come on, Syd," Emmett said, the first hint of heat in her voice. "There were two of us there, remember? I was so…blown away by you, all I could think about was being as close to you as I could get. Every time I saw you, I wanted you naked." She ran a hand through her hair, shook her head. "Pretty much still do."

"Okay, so we've got some kind of chemistry."

"Understatement."

"Now is a bad time for chemistry experiments. You know that as well as I do." Syd rubbed her face. "Maybe not for you. Maybe it's just me, but making the switch here from Franklin, being in limbo over my position next year, seeing you out of the blue—it's a lot for me to handle."

"Okay then, we'll go slow."

Syd took in the room and gave Emmett a pointed look. They'd mostly gotten dressed except for their sneakers and sandals, but that along with the remains of the impromptu picnic and the rumpled blanket screamed *We just rolled around together*. "You really think so?"

"Okay, maybe not slow-slow, but we don't have to figure everything out right now. We slept together, and I'm really, really hoping we can sleep together again, but we don't have to know everything that's going to happen for the rest of our lives right away."

"You realize it's a really bad idea, with the two of us in competition for next year, and everything from before."

Emmett sighed with exasperation. "We could clear up the before part pretty easily. All you have to do is tell me what the hell happened. Where did you go? Why didn't you tell me? And why the hell didn't you call me once in all this time?"

"You see? That's a whole lot of whys." Syd stared at her hands. "It's not that simple."

"Why not?"

Syd took a long breath. "Because in order to explain, I have to talk about a lot of things I would just rather not. Things I've worked really hard to leave behind me."

"I'm not sure where that leaves us, then," Emmett said.

"Right where we are now," Syd said. "Where we probably shouldn't be, getting involved again."

"I was most of the way toward being in love with you back then, you know," Emmett said quietly. "I never stopped."

"Emmett, I didn't know. Everything—*everything*—happened so quickly, I didn't think. I didn't have time to think!"

"It's okay," Emmett said, a distant expression crossing her face.

She stood, gathered up the trash bag they'd filled earlier, and gripped it in one hand. "I don't expect you to feel the same, and I didn't tell you to put pressure on you. But I'm done pretending that I don't have feelings for you. And I'm not going through what I went through before. If you're not interested, I understand. But if you are, you're going to have to do something about it."

"What are you saying?"

"I'm saying you need to let me in or we don't have anywhere to go." Emmett stopped in the doorway. "I really hope you remember one of these days."

Syd closed her eyes as Emmett's footsteps faded on the stairs. When the house was quiet once more, she folded the blanket, stacked it by the door, and went to the kitchen to attack the boxes. If she kept busy, she could avoid thinking.

❖

Emmett retreated to the back porch after she left Syd's side of the house. She thought about having another beer, but it was only four in the afternoon and she didn't really feel like one. A beer was meant for relaxing, winding down, letting go of the pressure and stress. Since she only got home from the hospital every couple of days, enjoying a beer was a pretty intermittent experience. And nothing was really going to relieve the way she was feeling right now, and she wasn't sure she really wanted anything to.

Maybe feeling a little bit of the all-over ache, like a physical and emotional bruise rolled into one, she'd felt the last time Syd had pulled away from her would be a good reminder, or an object lesson, or something like that. The message sure was clear. Syd wasn't over the past and Emmett was part of it. As much as she wanted to help Syd deal with whatever still haunted her, she couldn't. Syd wouldn't let her. That's what she needed to accept. Syd didn't want her close. And being close was exactly what Emmett wanted. What she'd always wanted with Syd.

Not just the great sex, but the amazing way everything inside her seemed to communicate, to *fit*, so effortlessly with Syd's energy and passion and need and desire. All the things she'd never experienced with anyone else before or after. She wanted those things with a woman. She needed those things. Maybe she didn't deserve them, but she was willing to try to. She was willing to try.

Syd wasn't. Or couldn't.

Emmett wasn't even angry with her. How could she be angry at someone who was hurting? She sighed, watching a robin hop around the base of the big maple, busily, maybe even blissfully, going about the business of living. She'd been crazy to think that either of them, her or Syd, could just go on sleeping together without thinking about the future. She wasn't made that way. Syd sure wasn't. Living on sex was a lot of fun, and she hoped that it would be for the rest of her life, but during the in-between times, life was a lot of other things. Quiet moments, challenges, thoughts and feelings and, most of all, connecting.

The screen door opened and closed and footsteps approached behind her. Zoey sat down beside her and popped the top on a Coke.

"Hey. How was your day?"

Emmett laughed. "Interesting."

"Did you leave those steaks in the fridge? 'Cause I covet one."

"Syd brought them. They're for anyone."

"Oh yeah? Huh. I saw the neighbors had arrived."

Emmett tensed ever so slightly. "Yeah, Syd showed up early this morning to start unpacking."

"Dani's over there now too. Haven't seen Jerry." Zoey laughed. "Sadie is probably wearing him out."

"Good for them."

"Yeah. True." Zoey took a long pull on her Coke. "Not jealous or anything, but I'm glad someone's getting some."

Emmett stared into the yard. The robin was gone. "Your night go okay?"

"Pretty much." Zoey closed her eyes and let out a long luxurious sigh. "And I am not on call for the next thirty-nine hours."

"Any big plans?"

"Not really," Zoey said pensively. "You?"

Emmett shook her head. "No."

Zoey opened one eye and gave her a look. "So, what's going on?"

"Absolutely nothing."

"Absolutely something," Zoey countered.

"No," Emmett said flatly. "Nothing's going on."

The door behind them opened again. Emmett didn't turn, expecting Hank. No one joined them, and she held her breath.

"Hey," Syd said quietly.

Emmett's heart actually skipped a beat when she started breathing again. She wasn't sure that was a good thing, but as long as she didn't drop dead on the spot, she didn't care. Syd stood just outside the closed screen door looking uncertain. Syd never looked uncertain.

"Hi," Emmett said.

Zoey lazily glanced over her shoulder. "Hey."

"Zoey," Syd said quietly, "would you mind if I talked to Emmett alone. That is, if Emmett doesn't mind?"

"Of course I don't mind," Emmett said quickly.

Zoey's head swiveled between Emmett and Syd, her eyebrows rising. "I was going to head next door and see if you guys needed any more help, anyhow. Dani still there?"

"Yes," Syd said, her gaze on Emmett.

"See you guys later then," Zoey said.

"Thanks," Syd said quietly. She sat down on the top step where Zoey had been a few seconds before, turned toward Emmett, and clasped her hands around her bent knees. "You're right. You deserve to know."

Emmett shook her head. "You know what, Syd, I don't. It was a long time ago, and whatever happened was obviously really hard. You don't have to relive it now."

Syd's smile was pained. "I know—that's what I tell myself too. But we're here now, and maybe we shouldn't have slept together, but we did. For that, at least, I'm responsible. Just like I was then, and I was wrong to walk away."

"Maybe, and maybe not. But like I said, either way it was a long time ago."

"I'd like to…try…at least."

"If you're sure."

Syd gave her a ragged laugh and pushed a hand through her hair. For an instant, Emmett saw her as she'd been a few hours before, open and eager and hungry for her. Just as she had been for Syd. Just as they'd been years before. The distance now was so painful she could barely breathe. But that was then and this was now.

"Whatever you want to tell me, then," Emmett said.

"I'm not even sure where to start." Syd's expression grew distant. "I've tried and tried to find the moment it all started to go wrong."

"How about why you disappeared?"

"That's more the end than the beginning, but it's the one I can answer easily." Syd laughed again, the sound like splinters of glass. "I found out I was pregnant."

CHAPTER TWENTY-FOUR

E mmett blinked.
What? Wait. How could she not know this? When? How did the two of them end up in bed if…

A million questions lined up in Emmett's brain like cars on a rush-hour freeway, inching along with no space to move or maneuver. The congestion prevented her from processing much of anything.

Wait. She'd interviewed a thousand patients. She knew how to ask questions about sensitive issues. All she had to do was take herself out of the picture. Emmett almost laughed. Syd already did that, about five years ago, and she was just now catching on. She mentally stepped back, imagined the two of them enclosed behind a curtain in the ER. Intimate and totally disconnected. "You found out after we met? You didn't know before?"

Syd laced her fingers together. "No."

Emmett shook her head, trying to make a picture out of puzzle pieces that didn't fit. "I guess you weren't planning it, then."

"Hardly. I must have used half a dozen strips before I finally believed it. I hadn't been with…well, I didn't suspect." She sighed. "You know how it is. The internship year especially is so insane…you never sleep, sometimes you're too stressed to think about eating, and the next minute you're eating everything in sight. Your whole life is chaos. If I missed a period, I never thought anything of it."

"I came up with a lot of scenarios as to what might have happened," Emmett said wryly, "but not this one. I'm not sure what to say."

"No, I imagine you don't. If it bothers you, I don't have to—"

"No. I'm not bothered. I'm surprised," Emmett said quickly, "but most of all I want to know about you. I've always wanted to know you, not just what happened to us then, but about *you*. Everything about you—what you want, what you dream, what you need. I want to know about this, but I don't want to ask something that's not appropriate. I—"

"Why don't I just tell you about me," Syd said, "and maybe some of it at least will make sense."

"Yes." Emmett worried she'd take a wrong step and say the wrong thing or push too hard, but Syd smiled just a little, and Emmett felt as if she'd just been awarded the Nobel Prize. "Yes, that would be great. That would be perfect."

Nodding, as if telling herself she could do this, Syd said, "So, my parents are pretty good people—both of them are Navy veterans. Both served in the first Iraq war when my sister and I were toddlers. My mother was a pilot and my dad was a field doc." She stopped. "Maybe there's no point in making you listen to—"

"There is. Start wherever you want—hell, start when your parents first met—"

Syd laughed, and looked surprised at the sound. "Uh, no, I don't think we need to go back that far."

"Tell me anything, Syd," Emmett said gently. "I really need to hear this. Whatever you want to tell."

"You're really very special, you know," Syd murmured.

Emmett wasn't so sure about that. Maybe if she'd been paying more attention, she would have noticed Syd wasn't quite as swept away as she had been. Maybe if she'd just *looked* a little harder instead of leading with her hormones, Syd would have talked to her.

"Whatever you're thinking, stop," Syd said. "You couldn't have guessed. I had no idea."

"Mind reading now?" Emmett asked lightly.

"You're an easy read." Syd's smile was soft. "So no blaming yourself." She straightened her shoulders. "The parents. Being really good people doesn't always mean being flexible or understanding or very accepting of difference. I have an older sister who is kind of the poster child for conservatism. She got it from my parents."

Emmett nodded, an uncomfortable premonition as to where the story was leading already blossoming in her mind. Syd's gaze passed over her, but Emmett could tell Syd was focused somewhere else. In the past. A long way in the past.

"They were delighted when I expressed an interest in medicine in high school," Syd said. "They were even happier that the son of their best friends, another ex-military couple, was interested in me. Aaron was—is—everything they would've wanted in a son. Intelligent, handsome, humorous, ambitious, born to success. Everyone—our families, our friends, our teachers—expected us to become a couple. Of course, we did. From our junior year in high school through college and med school." Syd snorted. "Always the couple voted most likely to succeed—at everything."

"Wow," Emmett said. "A lot of expectations."

Syd laughed sharply. "Yes, expectations without much room for straying from the plan. After all, the course was clear. I can't really blame my parents completely. The picture made sense to me too, at first. I had my mother and father, Aaron's parents, and most of the families of my friends as an example of what life should be. Aaron and I fit the mold perfectly. We'd be the perfect couple with the perfect life." Syd's mouth thinned. "Except for one little thing."

Emmett said, "Except something happened that wasn't in the plan."

"Oh yes, something happened. When I was a sophomore in college, I fell crazy in love with one of my best friends. I think she probably felt the same about me, but nowhere was something like that in the picture of our future, not for either one of us."

"Did you sleep together?"

"No," Syd said, "nothing physical happened beyond a few furtive kisses, but the passion was unforgettable. After eight or nine months of being constantly together, she retreated, refocused on her boyfriend, and got engaged. They were married before they graduated. Aaron and I—"

Syd looked at Emmett. "Are you sure you're okay with this?"

"I'm fine. I might be a teeny bit jealous of the first girl, but hey—I'm here now."

"Somehow you always make me laugh when I can't imagine being able to," Syd muttered.

"I'm not trying to diminish what you went through," Emmett said softly.

"I know." Syd relaxed a fraction. "I know. Besides, I love it when you make me laugh, especially at myself."

Emmett's heart stumbled over the L-word for a second. But they had a lot more to get through, and right now, that's what mattered. "So did you and Aaron…?"

"Get married?" Syd grimaced. "No. We both wanted to wait. We both wanted medicine, and there wasn't much room for anything except studying while we were in college. We needed to have outstanding academic records so we'd have our pick of the schools. Of course we intended to train together."

"Right."

"It was easy not to think about anything else—we were both so focused on academics in college, and then medical school, and then getting our internships. I could just ignore what I felt, or didn't feel."

"And were there other girls who made you wonder? After college?" Emmett asked.

"There were feelings, but nothing I ever pursued. It was easy to ignore them too." Syd met Emmett's gaze, and now her eyes were clear and sharp and intent. "Until there was you. I couldn't ignore you. I couldn't do anything except touch you."

Emmett's heart beat in her throat, threatening to choke her. "You're saying before me you hadn't—"

Syd shook her head. "No, you were the first woman." She smiled. "My first who mattered."

"Well." Emmett ran her hand through her hair. "Crap. I wish I'd known."

Syd laughed, this time a free, nearly happy sound. "Why? Would you have done anything differently?"

"I don't know," Emmett said, "maybe. I might have focused a little more on what the hell I was doing. I was pretty much not thinking at all."

"No, neither was I. I'm sorry—" Syd stopped, frowned. "No, I'm not sorry. Not about sleeping with you."

Emmett wanted to cheer. If Syd regretted them being together, really regretted it, she was going to hurt for a long time. "I'm glad."

"So am I," Syd said. "I wanted you every bit as much as you wanted me, and I'm not sorry about any of it except what happened when I...when I found out."

"Come on, Syd. Anyone would have been thrown by that."

"No. Most people wouldn't have sleepwalked through half their lives and ended up in someone else's story." Syd took a long breath and shivered as if she was cold.

"Are you okay?" Emmett asked. "Can I get you a sweatshirt or a drink or something?"

"I'm okay. I...I haven't ever really talked about all of it."

"If we're going too fast, if you want to slow—"

"No, I want to finish. I have to."

Emmett wanted to hold her hand, something, anything to take

some of her pain, to hold some of it for her. She couldn't do that for Syd any more than she could do it for her patients. All she could do for the injured was give them her skill and her caring and her promise to do her best. Syd had asked that she listen, and she would.

"Whatever you want to say, whenever you want to say it," Emmett said.

"I've never wanted to tell anyone before," Syd said quietly.

"Thank you," Emmett said, "for letting it be me."

Syd paused, gathering herself or her thoughts. "When I told Aaron, I could tell he was angry, although he never said so. We were barely even halfway through our first year, and he was competing for one of the combined general-plastic surgery slots along with five other interns. He couldn't afford any distractions."

Emmett clamped her teeth together so she didn't say anything at all. She was trying not to dislike the guy. But what an asshole.

"But to give him credit," Syd continued, "he wanted to get married, and why wouldn't he? That was the plan, after all, and had been for ten years. Our families, of course, supported the idea when he told them, and my sister was instantly ready to start wedding planning."

"Can I ask," Emmett said hoarsely, "why you didn't tell me?"

"Aaron and I hadn't been intimate for months." Syd grimaced. "Of course the last time had to be the time for the less than one percent failure rate to happen. I'd known, somewhere I wasn't quite ready to say out loud, that I wasn't going to marry Aaron. As soon as I told him about the pregnancy I told him that too, and he...he actually laughed. Said of course I was, why wouldn't I?"

Emmett winced. "You told him why?"

"Oh yes, and everyone else too." Syd reached for her hand. "Everything pretty much blew up at that point."

Emmett clasped Syd's hand loosely, worried she'd transmit her own anger and helplessness through her grip if she wasn't careful. None of this was about her—she had been collateral damage in a battle Syd had fought alone. She wished she could have been there, ached to have been able to offer Syd some support, but she could offer her some of that now. "And you were still working. I can't imagine handling all of that and the internship too."

"I was trying to at first," Syd said, "but when both families got involved, I was afraid if I tried to work, I was going to make a mistake. I took my vacation early so I could try to deal with our parents and him and everything else."

"That's why I couldn't reach you when I tried," Emmett said almost to herself. "When I didn't hear from you for a week, I tried paging you. After two weeks, I called the hospital but they said you were unavailable. You weren't there then, were you?"

"No." Syd covered her eyes for a second. She'd lost color, and her hands were shaking.

Emmett reached for Syd's other hand and when Syd gripped hers tightly, some of the knots in Emmett's middle loosened. "You don't have to tell me the rest of it now."

"I'm okay. It's just when I think about it, I feel like I made so many mistakes." Syd's eyes filled with sorrow. "Years of them, Emmett. Years of lying to myself and to Aaron. I hurt people I should never hurt. I hurt you."

"No," Emmett said firmly. "I cared for you right away, and it hurt to lose the chance to have more with you, but that wasn't your fault. This was too big, Syd, too much was going on. You'd just met me, and even if you'd told me—the timing was all wrong."

"We slept together," Syd said softly. "Enough times to know we meant something to each other."

Emmett couldn't deny it. She knew exactly how many times they'd slept together, but the number could have been one or a thousand. The power of their connection had been unforgettable from the beginning, and she wouldn't pretend to Syd it was anything less. "Ninety-nine people out of a hundred would have crumbled under everything you had to handle. I don't blame you for not reaching out to me."

"If it makes a difference," Syd said, "I never went back to the surgery program."

Emmett stifled a gasp. She'd guessed, but the knowledge was like a blow. "What were you planning to do?"

"Well," Syd said, "my parents eventually disowned me when they finally truly believed I wasn't going to marry Aaron. Aaron vowed there would be a custody fight over the baby, and it's very possible he would've won that. There was no way I could continue the residency with him there, and I asked for a leave."

"You were going to go back to the residency after your baby was born," Emmett said.

"That was the plan. I was lucky—our residency director understood the situation. She told me she would help me, and she did, eventually. I think she would've found a way to keep me at University if I'd wanted, but I couldn't...I couldn't work with Aaron there."

"So Franklin."

"Yes. I got lucky with that." Syd smiled sadly. "But it didn't feel that way for quite a while."

Emmett gently rubbed her thumbs over the top of her knuckles. "What happened?"

"What happens to a lot of women in situations like that—huge stress, emotional and psychological trauma." Syd's fingers tightened on Emmett's. "I had an abruption at twenty weeks, too early for the fetus to be viable."

"Syd, that's terrible. I'm so, so sorry." Emmett felt sick. Abruption was a disastrous complication, and the incidence of maternal death was high. Just thinking about Syd in that situation made her crazy. "Your parents didn't come around?"

"No. But I got through it after a couple of months. Franklin accepted me on short notice, but I had to repeat the internship year."

Emmett shook her head. "Any one of those things would've put most people down, but you, you made it."

Syd gently disengaged her hands. "Maybe I did, but I'm not sure all the broken parts were ever fixed. I've kept it all locked away because I've had to make it through my training."

"And I've brought it all up again, haven't I."

"Yes," Syd said softly. "And I'm not sure I how I feel about that."

"I wish I didn't understand," Emmett said, "but I do."

Syd sighed. "I'd ask for time to sort things through, but that's hardly fair. I've had plenty of time up until now. I need to get through the next year and so do you."

"So what are you saying?" Emmett already knew the answer, but maybe hearing the words would make her accept it.

"I can't get involved right now. I'm sorry." Syd rose and moved out of Emmett's reach. "And I can't sleep with you and not be involved."

Emmett had been wrong. Nothing was going to make watching Syd walk away easier.

Chapter Twenty-five

"Sorry I'm late," Syd said in a rush as she pulled out a chair at their usual round table in the cafeteria.

"It's six thirty-one." Emmett smiled. "You're not that late."

Syd opened her tablet and pulled up the patient list. Technically she was late, since she made it a point to be ready for rounds before any of the junior residents, and today she was the last to arrive. Emmett didn't count. She rarely beat Emmett anywhere. Somehow Emmett always managed to be everywhere she was needed before anyone else. Easy to see why she had been the main contender for chief resident, and why none of the other residents, even the ones in her year, seemed to mind. Emmett wasn't just good, she was fair and worked harder than anyone else. If Syd hadn't been thrown into competition with her, she'd have given Emmett her vote without a second thought. "Sorry, I need to ask—Kos stopped me on the way down and asked me if I was free to scrub with him on a cranial reconstruction this morning. I was wondering if—"

"Sure," Emmett said.

"Thanks." Syd texted Kos to say she'd be there for the case and focused on her tablet as Hank started his rundown of the floor patients. Morning rounds were so much a part of her daily routine and she knew all the patients so well, she listened and absorbed the information on autopilot.

When Morty finished up with report on the ICU patients, Emmett made the OR and floor assignments and everyone got up to leave. Syd lingered until Hank and Morty were out of earshot.

"Got a second?" Syd asked.

"What's up?" Emmett slid her mini-tablet into the pocket of her lab coat and regarded Syd with a friendly but remote expression.

Syd was getting used to the distance. She hadn't known what to expect after telling Emmett about Aaron and why she'd disappeared—anger, recrimination, disappointment all seemed reasonable, and she'd prepared herself for the hurt of seeing those things in Emmett's eyes. None of that had happened. Emmett hadn't brought up their weekend conversation and she treated Syd the same as she did all the other residents—friendly and professional. But there'd been no more offers to share a quick meal between cases or grab a beer after work or finish off the previous night's leftovers sitting on the porch at home. Syd accepted that since she'd been the one to put restrictions on their relationship, she didn't have any right to miss those moments, but she did.

"I—" Syd took a deep breath, let it out slowly. Emmett hadn't once crossed the boundary she'd set when she'd made intimacy off-limits. Emmett wouldn't. Emmett had been nothing but respectful of her limits and, perhaps, if not forgiving, at least understanding. "Nothing. Wait. No, there is something. I just wanted to say thanks."

"Okay." Emmett regarded her steadily, clearly expecting something more.

Syd couldn't blame her. There should be more, but she just couldn't see her way clear to what that might be. Emmett had been the one to resurrect their past. She'd been the one to push Syd to confront what haunted her. Now the ghost was laid to rest, and Syd was still reeling from the change. So many things she'd worked hard to forget were at once raw and visible. Maybe a little less potent, but the memories still stung. The humiliation and self-recriminations still echoed in the recess of her mind, but faintly now, less sharply. She imagined a healing wound, slowly closing, new flesh filling the gaps. Would the scars be stronger for having shared the pain?

"I just wanted to say how much I appreciated…you."

Emmett's mouth quirked. "Thank you."

"You're not going to make this easy, are you?"

"I'm not trying to make it harder, but I've pretty much been clear, I think," Emmett said, no anger in her voice. "I told you how I felt. I haven't changed my mind. I'm not looking for a best friend, not with you. I'm not sure where that leaves us. I guess we'll find out."

Despite Emmett's calm tone, Syd flinched and hoped Emmett didn't notice. The rebuke was gentle but clear. And what could she expect, really. She'd drawn the line between them, after all. "Right. I understand."

"Okay then." Emmett turned to go. "I need to grab some films before the first case. I'll talk to you later."

"Right," Syd repeated inanely. Emmett went on ahead and Syd followed, wondering why she felt so damn hollow inside when she'd gotten exactly what she wanted. She ought to feel better, and she probably would. One day. She'd at least confessed her past, even if she couldn't make reparations. And she was glad Emmett knew.

And now she had a case to do, and even if her personal life was a mess, that came first. With relief, she hurried toward the OR. For a while, at least, she'd be able to avoid asking herself where her life was headed from here.

❖

"Hey," Zoey said, catching Emmett as she was heading upstairs from X-ray. "Anything good on your schedule?"

"Garrity is doing a partial liver resection for a subdiaphragmatic abscess that's involving the right lobe."

"Sweet," Zoey said. "Are you going through the chest?"

"Gonna start there. How about you?"

"Fitzpatrick is closing an abdominal wall hernia on a preemie."

"That ought to be a challenge."

"Yeah." Zoey frowned. "Dani's being really decent. I'm taking that one, and she's doing a couple of the smaller cases."

Emmett whistled. "That is generous. Don't know if I'd give that case away."

Zoey grinned. "Must be my winning ways."

"Oh, I'm sure."

"Or maybe she just wants to make nice with the neighbors."

The neighbors. Emmett instantly thought of Syd. Lying in bed and thinking about Syd so close she could be naked with her in five minutes was agony, considering Syd made it clear naked was off the table. Even the idea of sitting out back with a beer was sweet torture. If Syd was near, she'd want to touch her. Just like always. Silently, Emmett held the stairwell door open for Zoey.

"By the way," Zoey said as she passed, "how is your relationship going with the neighbor?"

Emmett's shoulders tightened. "Just fine."

"Seems a bit chilly from what I can see."

"It's fine," Emmett said, hoping that would put things to rest. She should have known better though.

Zoey leaned against the wall, half blocking Emmett's access to the rest of the stairs.

"Hey," Emmett said. "I gotta get upstairs to start my case."

"I know what time it is. They won't even have the patient over from the ICU yet." Zoey aimed a finger at the center of Emmett's chest. "And you are avoiding talking about Syd."

"Nothing to avoid," Emmett said.

"Really? So what was the heavy discussion about, then?"

Emmett shook her head. "Just clearing up some miscommunication."

Zoey tilted her head back and laughed. "You are so full of crap. Ever since then, both of you look like someone killed your dog."

"It's complicated." Emmett leaned against the wall next to Zoey and stared up the barren stairwell. Zoey wasn't going to let it go, and it wasn't as if she hadn't already told Zoey most of it. "I'm in over my head, and Syd's not in the same place."

"As in you're totally hooked, and she's looking for something less?"

"She's not looking for anything at all."

"So maybe it's time for you to move on."

"I can't," Emmett whispered.

"You're really serious, aren't you," Zoey said, a strange and rare gentleness in her tone.

"I wish I wasn't sometimes, but yeah. I have been, probably always."

"I'm glad I never fell for you." Zoey snorted. "I would've hated to spend years as the other woman."

Emmett stared. "You know it was never like that."

"I know, and I was serious when I said I was okay with the way things were. But I hate that you're not okay."

"Thanks."

"Any chance things will change?"

Emmett let out a long breath. "That's the hell of it. I have no idea, and there's not a damn thing I can do about it."

"Bullshit," Zoey said. "There's always something you can do."

"Not this time."

"Well, there won't be if you quit. And you don't." Zoey thumped her on the shoulder. "So come on, let's go be superstars upstairs."

"Yeah," Emmett said, wishing she had as much confidence as Zoey. "Let's do that."

❖

Syd finished writing post-op notes on the neuro patient and walked down the hall to Quinn Maguire's office. Quinn's secretary was on the phone and Syd waited outside the cubicle for her to finish.

Quinn's office door was open, and she called, "Hey, Stevens. Need something?"

"Um..." Syd glanced at the secretary, who was typing and talking at the same time, and then stepped up to Quinn's door. "I was going to make an appointment."

"I got a minute," Quinn said. "If this is a good time for you."

Syd slid her hands into her lab coat pockets and took a second to make sure she knew what she wanted to say. The decision had been there all along, and she just hadn't been able to see it. Sometimes the right thing disappeared in the tunnel of plans and expectations, but she knew now. Not just what she should do, but for the first time in a very long time, what she *wanted* to do.

"Okay, yes. Now would be great." She walked in and firmly closed the door behind her.

CHAPTER TWENTY-SIX

Emmett tossed her OR cap into the trash and walked beside Hank as he guided the stretcher toward the TICU. She'd been hoping the case would take another hour or two so she'd have a legitimate reason to skip the residents' reception downtown. She was much more the backyard barbecue with a little volleyball and cold beer type than a canapés and stand-around-talking type. Unfortunately, Quinn was her attending, and she'd know the case was finished. When Quinn staffed a case, she never left the building until the patient was out of the OR, even if she didn't scrub in. Emmett considered using the excuse of being on call, but Quinn had arranged for attendings to cover the floors and trauma admitting until nine, so she'd probably be missed if she didn't show. She pretty much had to go. At least she'd see Syd, who hadn't been around all day.

Pretending to be cool with the new no-touch, no personal-stuff rules Syd had imposed was a chore, but seeing her was better than wondering where she was. And sooner or later, Syd was going to let down her guard. She had to. Emmett couldn't believe she was the only one who felt the electricity between them. She kept telling herself that, and maybe one day soon she'd believe it. Or one day not-so-soon she'd be ready to move on. That idea was harder to accept than the waiting, but she just might have to. Going to bed alone and waking up wanting was readily fixable, if she decided to go back to her old remedy for loneliness. She just wasn't sure she could when Syd was a flesh-and-blood woman she saw every day and not just a memory.

"You going to the thing?" Hank asked.

"Yeah. Stay with the patient until they get him settled," Emmett said.

"Sure," Hank said. "You want the usual post-op labs?"

"Already ordered them," Emmett said. "But make sure you check them and call me if anything changes."

"Got it. Have a good time," Hank said with a little smirk.

"Hey," Emmett said, "you'll get yours in a few weeks."

"At least mine will be at Quinn's, right? And I can wear shorts and have a brew and a burger." Hank grinned.

"Just remember you'll be official then. Don't embarrass me."

Hank saluted. "Yes, Captain."

Emmett laughed. Nothing could deflate his good mood, at least for the next couple of weeks. Once his internship started, he wouldn't think everything was so fabulous. But she figured he deserved to enjoy it while he could. He'd worked hard, and he'd be working a whole lot harder soon. "I'll be back as soon as I can get out of this thing. You can go home as soon as you round on everybody."

"I'll hang around till you get back."

Emmett shook her head. "Get out of here while you still can. You won't be able to much longer."

"Good luck tonight," Hank said with unusual seriousness.

"Thanks," Emmett said quietly. They never talked about their personal lives, but she thought Hank knew he could if he needed to. He would have to be comatose not to know something was going on between her and Syd. "Appreciate it."

Hank shrugged, a little embarrassed, and disappeared around the corner pushing the stretcher. Emmett had just enough time to get changed and look around for someone who could give her a ride downtown. Hopefully she wasn't the last one here.

She'd just finished changing into loafers, dark pants, and a pale blue striped shirt when her trauma beeper went off. So much for the attendings covering. She should've known they couldn't manage without residents, even for a few hours. When she checked the number, she frowned. Quinn's office. Weird.

"McCabe," she said when Quinn answered herself.

"You need a ride down? Everybody else has left."

Emmett laughed. She wasn't surprised Quinn knew she was still there. Quinn knew where everyone was, all the time, it seemed. "I do. My backup plan was calling an Uber."

"I'm leaving in a few minutes, but I want to talk to you first. Can you drop by the office?"

"Sure. Be right over." Emmett stuffed her wallet into her back pocket, slid her phone into her front pocket, and clipped the trauma beeper to her pants—because hey, she didn't trust the attendings to survive without her—and headed toward Maguire's office.

Quinn's secretary was gone. Emmett paused in the open doorway to Quinn's office. Quinn was in street clothes similar to Emmett's. "You wanted to see me, Chief?"

"Yes, come on in and close the door." Quinn tapped a few keys on her laptop and pushed it aside. "Patient okay?"

"Yes. His gallbladder was hot but the common duct was fine. Easy to see." Emmett settled into the chair across from Quinn's desk, more curious than anything else. She'd been in Quinn's office plenty of times over the last four years, mostly discussing resident scheduling and, on rare occasions, problems. She wasn't worried.

"Pancreas involved?" Quinn asked.

"Nope, but I left a drain in just in case."

"Good." Quinn leaned back in her leather swivel chair. "We've only got two weeks before the new interns arrive, and I want the waters to be calm before they get here. The Franklins have settled in well for the most part, but we need to finalize next year's rotations and announce the status of the fifth years well before the new guys arrive."

Emmett's pulse kicked up. She had been expecting this, just not tonight. Although she should have known it was coming soon. Chief resident and fifth year assignments were usually announced by now. Everything going on personally with Syd had pushed what should have been the most important news of her life into the background.

"I agree," Emmett said, concentrating on the now, "especially since we have so many fifth years to fit into rotations."

"I'm going to make the announcement tonight," Quinn said, "since everyone will be there. But I wanted to give you a heads-up before I did."

Emmett's stomach clenched. Maybe she should've been more worried. This didn't sound like good news. And why wasn't Syd here? They'd be splitting the year somehow, right?

"You've earned it, and it's yours," Quinn said, fast and simple.

Emmett felt weirdly numb. Two months ago, if she'd heard these words, she wouldn't have been surprised. But everything was different now. Not just in terms of her residency, but her whole life, it seemed. She hadn't realized how different until just this moment. She swallowed. "What about Syd?"

Quinn studied her, and the longer the silence went on, the faster

Emmett's heart beat. Why did everything suddenly seem like the world had tilted just a little bit?

"I can't discuss other residents and their decisions," Quinn said.

"What does that mean?" Emmett said quietly.

Quinn shook her head, the look in her eyes close to sympathy. "I'm sure Stevens will tell people what she wants them to know when she wants to." Quinn paused. "But there's no problem, just so you know."

Emmett jerked. "How can that be? Syd's just about killed herself to get this far. You have no idea—"

"Whoa," Quinn said, holding up a hand. "Before you get too worked up, ask Stevens when you see her. And we need to get going. I promised Honor I wouldn't be late."

Emmett bit back her protest. The discussion was over. Quinn had said all she was going to say, but Syd would tell her what was happening. Wouldn't she?

❖

Rush-hour traffic along River Drive prolonged the normally twenty-minute ride to the College of Physicians in Center City to the point Emmett's skin started to itch with impatience. Her head spun with a jumble of questions, and she vacillated between anger and confusion. What the fuck had Syd said to Quinn? What had she done? Was she leaving the program? Going to disappear again? The idea made her want to hurl.

"McCabe," Quinn said quietly.

Emmett jumped. "Yes?"

"You need to relax. There's not a problem."

"Yeah, I think there is."

"Stevens is fine."

"Right."

Quinn glanced over at her. "Are you?"

"Of course." Emmett stared straight ahead. The churning in her middle got worse. "Maybe not so much."

"Like that, is it?"

"Yeah."

"Talking's a good place to start," Quinn said. "It usually helps to know what you're dealing with before you conjure up disaster scenarios."

"Been trying that."

"Patience works too."

"I pretty much suck at that," Emmett said.

"Most surgeons do." Quinn laughed quietly. "Waiting for someone to say the words you need to hear is a lot like trying to breathe underwater. Believe me, I know. I've been where you are."

Emmett cut her a look. "Really?"

"Really. And it was worth every second it took to get there." She looked at Emmett for a moment before turning back to the traffic. "When it's right, it always is."

"Okay." Emmett didn't say she'd already been waiting for years. She could wait—no. No, she couldn't. She'd already done that. And whatever crazy decision Syd had made, she wasn't going to let her get away again.

"Go ahead inside," Quinn said, pulling up in front of the impressive two-hundred-year-old stone edifice behind the wrought-iron fence. "I'll look for a parking place. If Honor asks, tell her I'll be there soon."

"Thanks," Emmett said, jumping out. Once inside, she scanned the crowd for Syd. Everyone had heeded the unspoken edict that all the residents attend, and quite a few of the surgery attendings who hadn't been tapped to cover emergencies were present too. She finally found Syd, standing with Sadie, Dani, Jerry, Morty, and Zoey. Their whole house-plus was there, except Hank and her. Syd looked across the crowd and saw her. That was all it took for Emmett to be sure. She was done waiting.

CHAPTER TWENTY-SEVEN

S yd listened with half an ear to the chatter of her friends while tracking Emmett's path across the room toward her. The set expression on Emmett's face made it pretty clear she was on a mission, and Syd suspected she knew why. Quinn wouldn't have told her any details, Syd was sure of that, but nothing stayed private very long at the hospital. Their lives and careers were too intertwined for anyone's decision not to affect others. She hadn't expected word to come out quite so soon, not until everything was official, but she ought to know by now her plans did not always go as she thought. Emmett knew something and she wasn't happy.

"Syd," Emmett said the instant she was close enough to speak without being overheard, "what the fuck did you—"

"Attention, everyone," Quinn said. Despite the fact she hadn't raised her voice, the entire room instantly quieted, and every face turned in her direction.

Syd appreciated the reprieve. This wasn't the place to have a discussion with Emmett, and thankfully, now wasn't the time, either.

"While I've got you all here, first, welcome," Quinn said.

She said a few more words, the usual introductory kind of thing, which Syd tuned out, sensing the tension in Emmett's body without even touching her. She was practically quivering.

"Will you relax, please," she murmured.

"I am relaxed," Emmett said through gritted teeth.

Syd snorted. "There's no reason to—"

Emmett's head snapped around, her eyes flashing. "Really, Syd? Then maybe you can explain—"

Zoey leaned in. "You two might want to keep it down."

Emmett clamped her jaws closed.

Quinn looked over the room. "In two weeks, the first years won't be first years anymore. Expectations will change. You'll find yourself responsible for new first year residents, who will be inexperienced and prone to making mistakes." Quinn raised a brow. "Not that any of you were ever like that."

Laughter filled the room. Some of the first years started to look nervous, as if it just occurred to them they wouldn't be protected any longer by their seniors. They'd be the ones offering guidance. Syd remembered the feeling well—part panic, part pride.

She brushed Emmett's hand. "I'll explain."

"When?" Emmett growled.

Quinn turned their way and Syd fell silent. Could the timing be any worse? But then, with her and Emmett it always had been.

Quinn said, "Our fifth years will be leaving for advanced training or to enter practice. Great job, everyone, and congratulations on finishing." When the applause died down, she went on, "Our new fifth years will step into their place, and one will assume the position of chief resident."

Emmett's shoulders squared as she took a deep breath.

"No," Syd whispered fiercely. "Don't say anything."

Emmett cut her a look, her gaze furious. "It's not right."

"It is." Syd grabbed her hand, not caring that Zoey could surely see. "Trust me."

She held her breath, unsure if Emmett would. She hadn't done a lot, at least in the past, to earn that trust. She hoped things had changed. For the longest moment, Emmett searched her face, and she tried to let Emmett see how much she needed Emmett to give her this chance. A chance she might not deserve but one she desperately wanted. "Please."

Quinn's voice cut through the interminable limbo.

"…Emmett McCabe."

Hoots and hollers and more applause followed. Syd shifted her palm to the center of Emmett's back. "Congratulations. Now say something chief-resident-y."

Emmett finally looked away, glanced toward Quinn, and shifted to take in the rest of the room. She ran a hand through her hair and grinned. "You might want to hold your applause for a while until you see how I do."

People laughed. Emmett relaxed.

"I've got tough shoes to fill." Emmett nodded to the present outgoing chief resident, who Syd understood everyone at PMC considered to be chief in name only, but that was Emmett. Always fair.

"But," Emmett said, turning toward Honor and Quinn, "I've got great examples to follow too. I'll do my best. If you've got a problem or complaints…talk to your seniors." More laughter. "Or I'll be around. Anytime."

When Emmett fell silent, Quinn said, "All right, everyone, enjoy the next hour or so, and then let's all get back to work."

Emmett instantly spun toward Syd. "You want to tell me what the hell is going on?"

"Yes, but not here. We need to talk in private."

"You know, Syd," Emmett said, "I'm getting tired of waiting."

"I know." Syd brushed her fingers down Emmett's arm. Emmett didn't pull away, and the relief was a gift. "Tonight. I promise."

"I'm on call tonight."

Syd smiled. "So?"

❖

Embarrassed by the congratulations she still wasn't sure she deserved, Emmett managed to extract herself from the reception after less than an hour. She hadn't had a chance to press Syd for any further details, too many people around and too many well-wishers. She'd sensed Quinn watching her, and she tried not to let her uneasiness show. She trusted Quinn, even though she didn't quite understand the decision. Syd said they'd talk, but she still wondered when and what difference it might make.

As soon as she escaped, she headed for Chestnut Street to hunt down a cab. The trip back to the medical center in Germantown took half the time the ride in had taken, and she arrived still unsettled by the whole night. Nothing had turned out the way she'd expected. Not when she'd first met Syd and foolishly imagined a future together, not when Syd suddenly reappeared and, once again, she got caught up by her relentless attraction to her, and not until tonight, when she'd pictured the two of them as partners during their fifth year, working together. A team. And—yes, she admitted—lovers.

Always getting ahead of herself.

She paid the cabbie and jogged up to the main entrance, went straight to the locker room, and changed into fresh scrubs.

"Meet me in the cafeteria for dry rounds," she said when she paged Hank. "I'm starving."

By the time Hank arrived, Emmett had a burger and fries and was starting to feel a little more like herself. She was back on her home turf, and that helped.

"So it's quiet," Hank finally said, after he ran down the list of patients on the trauma service. "Oh, hey, congratulations, Chief."

Emmett snorted. "How did you hear that?"

"Angie Michelson called to tell me."

"Angie, huh? I didn't know you two were tight."

"Recent development."

"You know she's gonna be your immediate senior in a couple of weeks."

"Yeah." Hank grinned. "Not a problem. I can handle bossy women. I grew up with you, after all."

Emmett rolled her eyes. "Watch it. Half your senior residents are going to be women."

"Like I said, I'm good with it."

She smiled. Hank had never needed to prove himself by undermining others. He just did the job better than most. "Get outta here. Enjoy yourself before you actually have to work a little."

"Right, that's why it's nine o'clock on Friday night, and I'm still here covering for you."

She pointed toward the door. "Go, before something comes in, and I make you stay."

"Yes, Chief."

Emmett shrugged. "Clock's ticking."

Hank disappeared in a flash. Once Emmett finished her belated dinner, she started on a quick tour through the ER and the trauma unit just to make sure nothing was pending that needed her attention. She ran into Honor in the ER, doing the same thing.

"Anything for trauma?" Emmett asked.

"Not so far. Nothing surgical down here at all."

Emmett frowned. "I don't like it."

Honor nodded. "I agree. Too quiet."

"Maybe word got out attendings were covering," Emmett said.

Honor laughed. "Possibly. Congratulations, by the way."

"Thanks." Emmett flushed.

Honor tilted her head. "You okay?"

"Yeah. Sure."

Honor smiled. "Good. You'll do a great job."

The quiet confidence in Honor's voice eased a lot of her uncertainty. Now if she could just figure out how things had turned out this way, she'd be mostly happy. She checked her phone. Nothing from Syd.

By ten, with everything quiet, Emmett headed to the trauma on-call room. She flipped the lock automatically and reached for the light switch.

"You might want to leave that off," a voice said from the darkness.

Emmett's heart leapt into her throat. "Syd?"

"You were expecting someone else?"

"No," Emmett said quickly. "I just…how long you been waiting?"

"Not long."

Emmett's eyes adjusted to the half-light coming through the transom window that opened onto the ER parking lot. Syd was partially shadowed where she sat on the lower bunk, but her profile was etched in silver. Emmett's breath came a little faster. She was so damn beautiful.

Syd patted the bunk beside her. "Come sit down."

Emmett's legs were oddly rubbery as she made her way across the room. She sat a few inches away from Syd, and Syd put her hand on her thigh. That light touch was enough to set every nerve ending on fire. Afraid Syd might have second thoughts and move her hand, Emmett curled her fingers lightly around Syd's.

"You promised you'd tell me," Emmett said.

"First of all, my decision had nothing to do with all of this. You deserve—"

"Don't go there," Emmett said. "You know as well as I do we're on equal footing there."

"I don't want to argue," Syd said, "and there isn't any reason to. But just remember what I said. You earned it."

"Okay," Emmett said, drawing out the word. "So what happened? Quinn wouldn't tell me anything, but all of a sudden us being co-chiefs didn't even come up."

"That's because I left the program."

Emmett jumped up. The room spun, or her head did. "What? Are you crazy?"

"Maybe you could sit down and listen for five seconds," Syd said evenly.

Emmett paced in a circle. "No. Absolutely not. What are you

doing? Are you leaving? No, you can't do that. You said you wouldn't—God damn it, Syd. You can't—"

"Emmett," Syd said sharply. "I'm not leaving."

Emmett stopped in her tracks. "You're not?"

"No. Will you sit?"

Emmett forced herself back to the bed, but even after she sat, her legs wouldn't stop jumping. "You're not leaving?"

"No," Syd said, stroking the length of Emmett's thigh. "I'm not."

"Then what?"

"Do you remember the patient with the spinal cord injury and the resident who didn't answer her page?"

"What? Yeah." Emmett frowned. "What does she have to do with it?"

"A lot. Kos fired her."

"Whoa. That must not have been the first episode."

"I guess not. I don't know any of the details, and they don't matter now." Syd drew an audible breath. "Kos offered me her slot. I'm switching from general to a neuro residency."

A few seconds passed before Emmett absorbed the words. "You're switching. Now? When you're almost done?"

"Yeah," Syd said, her tone light and unmistakably happy. "I am. I have to take an extra year, but that's okay. I have some catching up to do."

"Wait, you'll be a fourth year neuro resident next year?"

"Yes," Syd said. "Luckily, Kos thinks I had enough experience early on at Franklin that I don't have to move any further back. So I'll be a senior neuro resident when you're a trauma fellow. Lucky you. I ought to be able to keep you out of trouble by then."

Emmett laughed. She could see the two of them working together, just not the way she'd always imagined. Only she didn't quite trust happy endings. "This doesn't have anything to do with us being up for chief resident at the same time, does it?"

"Do you really think I would tank my own career to make things easy for you?"

"No," Emmett said, "I just need you to know I wouldn't want you to."

Syd sighed and rested her hand in the center of Emmett's back. Their shoulders touched. "Of course I know that. You're the fairest, most honorable person I know."

"I don't know about that," Emmett said. "I just know I…" She held back the words she wasn't sure Syd wanted to hear. "If it's what you want, I'm all for it."

"I'm glad things worked out this way," Syd said, "but if they hadn't, I still would've given you my vote. And I would've told Quinn that."

"But—"

Syd's kiss silenced her, and Emmett completely forgot what she meant to say. When Syd drew back, Emmett's mind was blank.

Syd laughed quietly. "Sometimes, you're clueless. I love that about you."

"You do?"

Syd brushed her fingers through Emmett's hair, the touch as gentle and as exciting as anything Emmett had ever experienced.

"I do. There's something else I have to tell you too," Syd whispered. "I love you."

The silence went on so long, Syd wondered if she'd actually spoken aloud. From Emmett's sudden frozen posture, she was pretty sure she had. Her throat was suddenly dry. Had she miscalculated? Was she too late? *Years* too late?

"I, um…" Syd said.

"No, wait," Emmett whispered. "It's good. We're good. It's all good." She swiveled, faced Syd, grasped her shoulders. "But would you mind, just one more time."

Laughing, Syd clasped Emmett's waist and leaned close. "I love you." The words felt so good, stirred up a sensation so exhilarating, she said them again. "I love you. I totally do."

Emmett let out a long breath and rested her forehead against Syd's. "Nothing has ever made me feel so good. Everything I've worked for, dreamed about—they all matter. But none of those things fill me up the way you do."

"Oh, Emmett." Syd rested her cheek on Emmett's shoulder. "I'm so sorry it took me so long—"

"No. Not too long. It took until it was right. That's what matters. All that matters."

Emmett tilted her head and kissed her, long and slow and with a new possessiveness that sent chills down Syd's spine. She gripped Emmett more tightly, opened for the kiss, invited her deeper.

Moments passed, possibly hours, time having lost all meaning. Emmett was all she could feel. Syd's heart filled with wonder and desire and a bubbly sensation that could only be joy. When she couldn't breathe for the need to be closer, she pulled away. "I really want you right now."

Emmett's breath came hard and fast. "Me too. So bad."

"You're on call."

"I'm a quick dresser."

Syd laughed. "Then get your clothes off."

In seconds, they were naked, tangled together on the narrow bunk. "Did you lock—"

"Yes," Emmett mumbled, her mouth on Syd's breast, her hand stroking down. "I want you. Please, Syd."

Syd found her hand, pressed it between her thighs. She was ready, waiting. "Yes. Yes."

Emmett groaned, closed her eyes, pressed her cheek between Syd's breasts. She filled her, stroked slow and deep, felt Syd close around her, drawing her deeper.

Syd's fingers dug into her shoulders, urged her on, wordlessly setting the tempo. Emmett followed, reading her body, every sense attuned to the heat and tension and rhythm of her heartbeat. So different now, so much more than ever before.

"I love you," Emmett whispered and Syd arched beneath her, her cry of release the only answer Emmett needed.

When Syd whispered, "You," Emmett rolled onto her back and pulled Syd on top of her. She wrapped one leg around Syd's and clasped her hips, guiding her to the rhythm she needed. She came hard, a lash of coiled tension whipping through her. She fell back, boneless, and heard Syd laugh. She managed to smile. She liked the way Syd sounded when she claimed her.

"Please don't let my beeper go off now," Emmett muttered.

"You're tough. You will manage." Syd rested her cheek into the curve of Emmett's shoulder.

Emmett held her. Syd fit perfectly, just the way she always knew she would. "I love you. Did I remember to say that?"

Syd kissed her throat. "Several times, in a number of excellent ways."

"Oh. Good."

"We should probably get dressed," Syd said reluctantly. "Just in case."

"I know. Just as soon as I reassemble all my body parts."

"I expected you to have a lot more stamina," Syd said with utter seriousness. She leaned on an elbow, traced her finger down the center of Emmett's body, making her twitch and instantly come alive everywhere.

Emmett jolted upright. "I'm ready."

Syd laughed that wild, ecstatic laugh again. "I knew you would be. So now you can get dressed."

With a sigh, Emmett swung her legs over the side of the bed. "You're right. But I'm not done."

"Oh, believe me, you are definitely not done." Syd found the pants and top she'd worn to the reception and pulled them on. "I'm just giving you a break."

"Don't need a break," Emmett said, her voice muffled by the scrub shirt she tugged over her head. "I've got a lot stored up for you."

"Mmm. Me too." Syd kissed her. "I'm just being cautious. I don't want to wear you out the first week."

"Ha," Emmett said, tucking in her shirt. She caught Syd around the waist and pulled her close. "I am never going to stop wanting you."

Syd laced her arms around Emmett's neck. "I hope not. I can't imagine ever not wanting you. I love you. I always did, I just couldn't let myself have you."

"Well, you do now."

"I'm glad," Syd said, "because I'm yours."

Emmett's heart swelled and she wondered if she could possibly contain any more wonder in her life. "I've always seen us together. Always."

Syd nodded, the moonlight not nearly as bright as the love shining in her eyes. "We'll have that. The two of us."

"I know." Emmett kissed her. "We were meant for each other."

Emmett's beeper went off before Syd could answer.

"Well, that's good timing at least."

"That's our life," Syd whispered.

"You're right. It is." Emmett scooped up her beeper. Nothing could lessen her happiness now, not when she had Syd. "It's trauma admitting. Hold on."

"Not going anywhere."

Emmett punched in the extension. "McCabe…Yup. Okay. On my way." She disconnected and slid the phone into her back pocket. "That was Honor. Multiple calls coming in. Looks like it's going to be a busy night."

"I'll change and meet you there," Syd said.

"Hey, you don't have to. You're not on call."

"No," Syd said as they headed for the door. "But you've got me on trauma for two more weeks. Might as well take advantage."

Emmett caught her just as she pushed the door open into the hall. She kissed her quickly. "I've got you for a lot longer than that."

Syd smiled. "Yes, you do. You've got me for always."

EPILOGUE

Mt. Airy,
July 1, 4:30 a.m.

Emmett's phone alarm beeped, and Syd's eyes shot open. Her bedroom windows were open. The predawn air was hot and heavy already. Spring had fled, and the first of July carried the dead heat of mid-August. Beside her, Emmett stirred. Sometime in the night they'd kicked off the thin sheet on her bed, both of them naked. Despite the sultry weather, they'd slept tangled up, the way they usually did. Even when the idea of wearing clothes made her sweat, she welcomed Emmett's touch. Anywhere, always.

Emmett's phone buzzed again and Emmett found it with one hand, turned on her back with a sigh, and swiped it into silence. Her voice still thick with sleep, she murmured, "Morning."

"Why are we getting to the hospital at five a.m.?" Syd kissed the tip of Emmett's shoulder.

"First day," Emmett muttered. "Time to make sure the house is shipshape."

"You're not going to do this every day, are you, Chief?"

Emmett laughed. "Probably for a little while."

"Well, it'll be good for me being the new guy—again—to show up early." Syd teased about the early hour, but she didn't really mind. The new first years arrived today, and all the residents started on new rotations. She was as anxious as the new chief resident to get started. The sooner she started, the sooner she'd get over the early hurdles. She hoped.

Emmett slid an arm around Syd's shoulders, settling into the pillows as if she had all day. "Are you nervous?"

Syd kissed her. "I'm okay. Come on, we should get up. I know you're anxious to get there."

"No hurry." Emmett tightened her grip. Some things were more important than the job, at least when she could let them be. Now was one of those times. "How are you feeling?"

"Me? I'll survive. Been here before, you know."

"Syd," Emmett said softly. "What you're doing, it's tough. I don't think I could do it."

"It's not hard." Syd sighed. "Okay. Not *that* hard. Being the new guy again, when I'm also going to be a senior resident, when I should probably know a lot more than I do and I won't know what I *don't* know until I'm in the middle of it, that part's hard. But I want to do this. I couldn't open myself up to anything after what happened, not for years. Not to what I really wanted for myself, for my career, or with you. But it's right now. I have you. I have us. And I'm ready for the rest of it."

"Kos wouldn't have put you where he did," Emmett said, "if he didn't think you were ready."

"I sort of know that, and I try to remind myself of it when I get the flutters. Don't worry about me. You've got your own stuff today."

"Nothing all that challenging," Emmett said. "Lots of administrative stuff."

"Lots of stuff that you're the best person to handle. Along with cases of your own to do." Syd kissed her. "Come on, coffee at least, before we leave."

"I'll hunt some down while you get ready." Emmett grabbed the jeans and shirt she'd left on the chest at the end of Syd's bed. She had about as much of her stuff in Syd's room now as she did in her own. In fact, the two halves of the house were slowly merging into one as whoever happened to be around congregated in one place.

"All right." Syd jumped up and kissed her. "I love you. I'll meet you in the kitchens."

"Right." Emmett pulled on her clothes and went down to check the coffee status in Syd's kitchen. Dani sat on the counter, legs crossed, a box of Cap'n Crunch cradled between her bare thighs. Emmett didn't look too closely since she wore only boxers and a tank top, and Dani might not be shy, but she sort of was. "Coffee?"

"Not yet," Dani mumbled around a handful of Crunch.

"Any more of that?"

Dani clutched the box to her chest.

Emmett shrugged. "Guess not. Tell Syd I'm putting coffee on next door. You're welcome to it."

"We got milk." Dani frowned. "I think."

"Don't know if we do."

"Somebody needs to shop."

"We need a wife," Emmett said.

Dani grinned. "I'll start the search."

"Good, make it fast." Emmett waved going out the back door, hopped the railing between the adjoining porches, and went in through the door to her kitchen. Zoey was up, dressed in a pale yellow sleeveless top and cropped sage pants. Coffee dripped into the pot.

"Thank God," Emmett muttered.

"Hey," Zoey said.

Emmett grinned. "You look…summery."

Zoey snorted. "I only get to wear real clothes going to or from the hospital, so I figure I might as well wear something nice for five whole minutes."

"Maybe you need more of a social life."

"Uh-huh. In about six months. I've got the transplant service starting today, remember? With a new intern and a first year resident." Zoey rolled her eyes. "I'm just hoping they don't kill anybody right away."

Emmett laughed. "Where's Hank?"

"I think he might've left already."

"The new interns aren't set to meet with Maguire until six."

Zoey shrugged. "You know Hank. Early bird."

"He gets that from me," Emmett said.

Syd came through the door. "Who gets what from you?"

"Hank. My smarts and good looks," Emmett said.

Zoey groaned. Syd smiled.

The door banged again and Dani bounced in. The Cap'n had kicked in. "Anybody seen Jerry?"

"No-show around here last night," Zoey said.

"Not next door either." Dani frowned. "Maybe he's at Sadie's, but I could've sworn he said he was coming home. We finished rounds late last night, and he said it was too late to wake her up."

Syd said, "Why don't you call—"

Emmett's trauma beeper went off and everyone groaned. "Wouldn't you know it. In two hours, I'd be handing this off to you, Dani."

"I'll take the call if you want," Dani said.

"I got it."

Emmett called in, listened for a few seconds, and said, "No problem. Be there in five." She shoved her phone in her pocket and looked at the expectant faces of her lover and friends.

"That was Honor. All hands on deck. Sounds like something big."

"Let's go," Syd said.

In an instant, everyone headed out into the morning. A new year had begun.

About the Author

Radclyffe has written over fifty romance and romantic intrigue novels, dozens of short stories, and, writing as L.L. Raand, has authored a paranormal romance series, The Midnight Hunters.

She is an eight-time Lambda Literary Award finalist in romance, mystery, and erotica—winning in both romance (*Distant Shores, Silent Thunder*) and erotica (*Erotic Interludes 2: Stolen Moments* edited with Stacia Seaman and *In Deep Waters 2: Cruising the Strip* written with Karin Kallmaker). A member of the Saints and Sinners Literary Hall of Fame, she is also an RWA/FF&P Prism Award winner for *Secrets in the Stone*, an RWA FTHRW Lories and RWA HODRW winner for *Firestorm*, an RWA Bean Pot winner for *Crossroads*, an RWA Laurel Wreath winner for *Blood Hunt*, and the 2016 Book Buyers Best award winner for *Price of Honor*. In 2014 she was awarded the Dr. James Duggins Outstanding Mid-Career Novelist Award by the Lambda Literary Foundation. She is a featured author in the 2015 documentary film *Love Between the Covers*, from Blueberry Hill Productions.

She is also the president of Bold Strokes Books, one of the world's largest independent LGBTQ publishing companies.

Find her at facebook.com/Radclyffe.BSB, follow her on Twitter @RadclyffeBSB, and visit her website at Radfic.com.

Books Available From Bold Strokes Books

A Fighting Chance by T. L. Hayes. Will Lou be able to come to terms with her past to give love a fighting chance? (978-1-163555-257-7)

Chosen by Brey Willows. When the choice is adapt or die, can love save us all? (978-1-163555-110-5)

Gnarled Hollow by Charlotte Greene. After they are invited to study a secluded nineteenth-century estate, a former English professor and a group of historians discover that they will have to fight against the unknown if they have any hope of staying alive. (978-1-163555-235-5)

Jacob's Grace by C.P. Rowlands. Captain Tag Becket wants to keep her head down and her past behind her, but her feelings for AJ's second-in-command, Grace Fields, makes keeping secrets next to impossible. (978-1-163555-187-7)

On the Fly by PJ Trebelhorn. Hockey player Courtney Abbott is content with her solitary life until visiting concert violinist Lana Caruso makes her second-guess everything she always thought she wanted. (978-1-163555-255-3)

Passionate Rivals by Radclyffe. Professional rivalry and long-simmering passions create a combustible combination when Emmet McCabe and Sydney Stevens are forced to work together, especially when past attractions won't stay buried. (978-1-63555-231-7)

Proxima Five by Missouri Vaun. When geologist Leah Warren crash-lands on a preindustrial planet and is claimed by its tyrant, Tiago, will clan warrior Keegan's love for Leah give her the strength to defeat him? (978-1-163555-122-8)

Racing Hearts by Dena Blake. When you cross a hot-tempered race car mechanic with a reckless cop, the result can only be spontaneous combustion. (978-1-163555-251-5)

Shadowboxer by Jessica L. Webb. Jordan McAddie is prepared to keep her street kids safe from a dangerous underground protest group, but she isn't prepared for her first love to walk back into her life. (978-1-163555-267-6)

The Tattered Lands by Barbara Ann Wright. As Vandra and Lilani strive to make peace, they slowly fall in love. With mistrust and murder surrounding them, only their faith in each other can keep their plan to save the world from falling apart. (978-1-163555-108-2)

Captive by Donna K. Ford. To escape a human trafficking ring, Greyson Cooper and Olivia Danner become players in a game of deceit and violence. Will their love stand a chance? (978-1-63555-215-7)

Crossing the Line by CF Frizzell. The Mob discovers a nemesis within its ranks, and in the ultimate retaliation, draws Stick McLaughlin from anonymity by threatening everything she holds dear. (978-1-63555-161-7)

Love's Verdict by Carsen Taite. Attorneys Landon Holt and Carly Pachett want the exact same thing: the only open partnership spot at their prestigious criminal defense firm. But will they compromise their careers for love? (978-1-63555-042-9)

Precipice of Doubt by Mardi Alexander & Laurie Eichler. Can Cole Jameson resist her attraction to her boss, veterinarian Jodi Bowman, or will she risk a workplace romance and her heart? (978-1-63555-128-0)

Savage Horizons by CJ Birch. Captain Jordan Kellow's feelings for Lt. Ali Ash have her past and future colliding, setting in motion a series of events that strands her crew in an unknown galaxy thousands of light years from home. (978-1-63555-250-8)

Secrets of the Last Castle by A. Rose Mathieu. When Elizabeth Campbell represents a young man accused of murdering an elderly woman, her investigation leads to an abandoned plantation that reveals many dark Southern secrets. (978-1-63555-240-9)

Take Your Time by VK Powell. A neurotic parrot brings police officer Grace Booker and temporary veterinarian Dr. Dani Wingate together in the tiny town of Pine Cone, but their unexpected attraction keeps the sparks flying. (978-1-63555-130-3)

The Last Seduction by Ronica Black. When you allow true love to elude you once and you desperately regret it, are you brave enough to grab it when it comes around again? (978-1-63555-211-9)

The Shape of You by Georgia Beers. Rebecca McCall doesn't play it safe, but when sexy Spencer Thompson joins her workout class, their nonstop sparring forces her to face her ultimate challenge—a chance at love. (978-1-63555-217-1)

Exposed by MJ Williamz. The closet is no place to live if you want to find true love. (978-1-62639-989-1)

Force of Fire: Toujours a Vous by Ali Vali. Immortals Kendal and Piper welcome their new child and celebrate the defeat of an old enemy, but another ancient evil is about to awaken deep in the jungles of Costa Rica. (978-1-63555-047-4)

Landing Zone by Erin Dutton. Can a career veteran finally discover a love stronger than even her pride? (978-1-63555-199-0)

Love at Last Call by M. Ullrich. Is balancing business, friendship, and love more than any willing woman can handle? (978-1-63555-197-6)

Pleasure Cruise by Yolanda Wallace. Spencer Collins and Amy Donovan have few things in common, but a Caribbean cruise offers both women an unexpected chance to face one of their greatest fears: falling in love. (978-1-63555-219-5)

Running Off Radar by MB Austin. Maji's plans to win Rose back are interrupted when work intrudes, and duty calls her to help a SEAL team stop a Russian mobster from harvesting gold from the bottom of Sitka Sound. (978-1-63555-152-5)

Shadow of the Phoenix by Rebecca Harwell. In the final battle for the fate of Storm's Quarry, even Nadya's and Shay's powers may not be enough. (978-1-63555-181-5)

Take a Chance by D. Jackson Leigh. There's hardly a woman within fifty miles of Pine Cone that veterinarian Trip Beaumont can't charm, except for the irritating new cop, Jamie Grant, who keeps leaving parking tickets on her truck. (978-1-63555-118-1)

Death in Time by Robyn Nyx. Working in the past is hell on your future. (978-1-63555-053-5)

The Outcasts by Alexa Black. Spacebus driver Sue Jones is running from her past. When she crash-lands on a faraway world, the Outcast Kara might be her chance for redemption. (978-1-63555-242-3)

Alias by Cari Hunter. A car crash leaves a woman with no memory and no identity. Together with Detective Bronwen Pryce, she fights to uncover a truth that might just kill them both. (978-1-63555-221-8)

Hers to Protect by Nicole Disney. Ex–high school sweethearts Kaia and Adrienne will have to see past their differences and survive the vengeance of a brutal gang if they want to be together. (978-1-63555-229-4)

Perfect Little Worlds by Clifford Mae Henderson. Lucy can't hold the secret any longer. Twenty-six years ago, her sister did the unthinkable. (978-1-63555-164-8)

Room Service by Fiona Riley. Interior designer Olivia likes stability, but when work brings footloose Savannah into her world and into a new city every month, Olivia must decide if what makes her comfortable is what makes her happy. (978-1-63555-120-4)

Sparks Like Ours by Melissa Brayden. Professional surfers Gia Malone and Elle Britton can't deny their chemistry on and off the beach. But only one can win... (978-1-63555-016-0)

Take My Hand by Missouri Vaun. River Hemsworth arrives in Georgia intent on escaping quickly, but when she crashes her Mercedes into the Clip 'n Curl, sexy Clay Cahill ends up rescuing more than her car. (978-1-63555-104-4)

The Last Time I Saw Her by Kathleen Knowles. Lane Hudson only has twelve days to win back Alison's heart. That is, if she can gather the courage to try. (978-1-63555-067-2)

Wayworn Lovers by Gun Brooke. Will agoraphobic composer Giselle Bonnaire and Tierney Edwards, a wandering soul who can't remain in one place for long, trust in the passionate love destiny hands them? (978-1-62639-995-2)